HERE'S AN APPLE, SWEET ADAM

Cindy Jean Wilson

WESTBOW
PRESS
A DIVISION OF THOMAS NELSON

WestBow Press books may be ordered through booksellers or by contacting:

WestBow Press
A Division of Thomas Nelson
1663 Liberty Drive
Bloomington, IN 47403
www.westbowpress.com
1-(866) 928-1240

This is a work of fiction. Names, characters, places, and incidents are products of the author's imagination or are used fictitiously.

ISBN: 978-1-4497-5040-4 (sc)
ISBN: 978-1-4497-5039-8 (hc)
ISBN: 978-1-4497-5041-1 (e)

Library of Congress Control Number: 2012907901

Printed in the United States of America

WestBow Press rev. date: 5/14/2012

When an ambitious California athlete discovers gold in Colorado, idealistic dreams follow. Majestic views entice these sweethearts—until disillusionment, hostility, and emptiness bring them face-to-face with the Creator. Can a once-storybook romance be redeemed and passion rekindled?

Acknowledgments

To my wonderful husband who glimpsed a peek into my soul and believed in my ability to capture a story on paper,

To cherished friends and family who interceded on my behalf as I began painting with words,

To treasured houseguests Steve Kotal, Sr. and Dutene & Maxia Joseph for detailed insight I would have missed without your wise input,

To several delightful authors who encouraged me to continue writing when everything inside me shouted, "Quit!"

To Alice Fredericks, Barb Davenport, and Julie Webb Kelley who offered words of support as I raced toward the finish line,

Thank you from the bottom of my heart!

Chapter 1

Idealism

HOLLY CLARK STARED AT the gauze-covered figure, unable to recognize one familiar feature. Ugly tubes protruded from the nose, mouth, arm, and groin; contraptions pulled the extremities into contorted positions. The body lay motionless except for an occasional rising of his chest. Was there some mistake? Could this possibly be her husband?

She brushed a strand of her golden hair back.

Her lips were parched, her throat ached, and sweaty hands trembled. Fluid oozing from his head caught her eye. *Aaugh!* An offensive smell gripped her nostrils as waves of nausea overcame her senses. IV's, blood, anesthesia—it didn't matter. She clasped her hand firmly over her mouth, pivoted, and rushed from the room. Just in time.

Reaching a chair in the waiting room, her knees buckled. Was this the end of their lifeless relationship? She struggled to maintain control but memories flooded her mind.

Adam had been a tower of strength. He was so energetic; no one could beat him physically. After the ski accident in college, he hiked with his leg in a cast before the week ended. *Oh, for one more laugh together.*

Her loneliness escalated as the clock ticked.

Suddenly the starkness of the situation gripped her. *She* was the one without hope! Nothing she attempted had meaning—it was all in vain.

"Oh God, I need somebody to help me!" she cried. "Where have I gone wrong?"

Eighteen years earlier, circumstances were entirely different.

A handsome jock who catered to her whims entered Holly Elizabeth Armstrong's world. *Was it a dream? Where should they begin? What would bring the most happiness?* The deep blue sky, with fluffy clouds that looked like little white sheep, kept drawing her attention upward.

Adam Clark blinked on arrival in Steamboat Springs, Colorado with college friends for his Christmas vacation. "Hey! That sun's bright," he said, putting on sunglasses. He stretched his lanky legs.

The airport was smaller than he expected.

"This might be my ticket to the big league," Roger said, puffing his chest. "Hurry guys, I can't wait to race down the slopes and smell fresh mountain air."

"I'm ready to ski with the pros," Danny said, attempting to hide his fear of skiing among world-class athletes who frequented this particular location. Travelers jockeyed for position as they exited. Someone bumped Danny.

"Excuse me," a man with an obvious ego said.

Adam glanced around for a shuttle to the ski lodge.

"We need luggage first. Can't go anywhere without ski pants and gloves," Joe Wallace said, motioning to a loaded conveyor belt in the baggage claim area. The four friends huddled together retrieving their bags.

With gear in hand, they headed toward the information booth, passing a beautiful blonde leaning against the wall deep in thought. A glint of sunshine on her hair caught Adam's eye and he gazed intently. She had the loveliest tresses he had ever seen. Their eyes met briefly— before an announcement for an incoming flight caused her to rush away.

To his surprise, the same magnificent hair appeared the next morning whizzing down a mountain. Just as Adam maneuvered a turn at the juncture of two runs, the streak of shimmering gold raced past obviously experienced at skiing these slopes.

What luck! If only he could catch her.

Astonished, then exhilarated, Adam lost his balance and sprawled on the fresh snow. Danny and Roger struggled to maintain control but tumbled over him. Skis and poles littered the landscape. Adam winced. Not knowing the extent of his injuries, he managed to stand up. With adrenalin surging—bolstered by pride—he ignored the increasing discomfort and continued to ski to the bottom, hobbling to the first aid station where ski patrol determined medical care was necessary.

"Sorry, guys. I'll be back soon," he said as medics prepared to take him to the hospital.

"Let us know your status," Roger said.

"We'll enjoy the snow for you," Joe and Danny said in unison.

Leaving the ski slope was difficult. Physical pain gripped his body as emotional aspirations turned to anguish. *The beautiful butterfly got away!*

Adam had scheduled this vacation to escape his stress-filled academic life. Skiing would exercise his body and invigorate his spirit, as well as put him in the company of fascinating females. One year had passed since his breakup with Karen.

It appeared he wouldn't enjoy any part of this holiday.

Dr. Ted Armstrong, a local physician, set his fractured leg before expressing concern about Adam being unable to ski for the remainder of his vacation. "What a bummer—you with a cast and your friends having fun. Have you talked to family yet? You're from California, right?" To make the unfortunate situation tolerable, he invited Adam to recuperate at the Armstrong home. "You'll need special assistance until you can move about, even with crutches. Why don't you stay at our house until you mend a bit? My wife, Susan, won't mind. She's cared for other patients after ski accidents."

Considering his options, this seemed an acceptable arrangement. "I guess," he said—though spending his vacation with a doctor was the last thing he envisioned doing. He pictured his friends racing down the slopes and remembered the girl he had seen on the snow.

I wonder who the gorgeous blonde was. Now I won't get a chance to find out ...

Adam was in complete shock when she entered the guest room. His jaw dropped. He stared. He blinked. Was he dreaming? Maybe he was hallucinating from pain meds. Before his eyes appeared the reason for such a bizarre twist in events and he gawked in disbelief.

"Enjoying the mountain air?" the pretty girl said. "I understand you took a spill and ended up meeting my dad."

"Uh, uh …" Adam fumbled for words but could think of nothing to say. He became oblivious to pain in his leg for a moment.

"Don't be discouraged," she said. "Looking at the peaks from this window can be almost as pleasurable as skiing down. There is always next year. Some people come back every winter."

Her voice captivated him, further.

He racked his brain for something to say but she was gone before he could think of an intelligent response.

As he convalesced, Adam became acquainted with this delightful creature named Holly. He liked spending time together and the enjoyable discussions they shared were almost as invigorating as skiing. Adam could hardly sleep at night, kept awake by the suspense of what morning would bring.

"No Christmas break has ever been this exciting!" he said to Joe on the phone.

With pent up energy, Adam jumped at Holly's suggestion to hobble down a riverbank path that twisted around the base of the mountains on his final Saturday. While there, he became aware how sensuous her lithe body looked jumping over rocks. She stood barely to his shoulders but her powerful charisma commanded his attention. With sparkling brown eyes, she relished sharing tales from her past.

"This stream goes all the way down to the Colorado River, merging into a massive waterfall before taking a final plunge," she said.

"I'd love to see it."

They enjoyed precious time together for one magnificent day.

Their relationship continued when Adam returned home to Oceanside College in California. Numerous e-mails were followed by late night phone calls and their romance began to blossom. The ski trip turned out to be an exceptionally lucky break.

"OSC is having a Valentine Extravaganza I'd like to attend with you," Adam said. "I can't wait to see you again."

She eagerly accepted.

Crimson, rose, and delicate pink décor flooded the newly remodeled building as love songs radiated from the gym. "Could I have this dance for the rest of my life … would you be my partner every night … when we're together it feels so right …" he sang. Holly hummed along. Hearts and butterflies hung from streamers. Dimmed lighting reflected shadowy participants having a good time. Desire flourished as couples danced in intimate embraces.

"I'm glad you're here," he said, proud to have such a beauty in his arms.

During an upbeat tune, she switched into lively gyrating causing a temporary pause as other students watched—an interesting contrast to her sometimes-intense introspection. Adam joined in, thrilled for another privilege to connect.

As the evening progressed, she revealed other surprises.

Holly's hair gleamed in the candlelight as they sipped cranberry cocktails and nibbled cherry filled brownies. Her charm was contagious. Others tried to join the couple but she pulled Adam away, trying to carve out more privacy.

"What are your goals for the future besides becoming a banker?" she asked.

"To stay in shape." He didn't have much else to offer. His mind was preoccupied with her.

"My dreams include having a wonderful relationship with someone like you," she confided. "Do you sense the strong connection between us—as much as I do?"

A passionate kiss said it all.

"I love the way you look at me … with your smile that glows …," he sang. "If it could last forever … only heaven knows."

Her Anjali perfume lingered in his nostrils after she returned to Colorado. A photograph provided memories of her scarlet gown with dainty hearts cut along the neckline. Etched in his mind were sensations of her body, pressed against his, as they danced in the moonlight later on the beach.

Caught in a whirlwind courtship, they became captivated with each other's strengths. They focused on the premise this was a perfect relationship, oblivious to any flaws.

His heart longed for love—camaraderie.

Her soul ached to feel needed—wanted.

Holly brought joy to Adam and her charm consumed him. A brilliant mind inside her gorgeous head had opinions on every topic and he appreciated her intelligence. Attractive, fun, and a superb conversationalist, her constant self-criticism was unfounded.

"I'm going to stay up late tonight to figure how to improve my performance—I should have done better," she said, while preparing for a play at her college.

"You'll do great," Adam insisted.

"What if they replace me? I forgot important lines," she explained after opening night jitters left her pondering the ability to continue successfully.

The play ended with rave reviews.

Adam admired Holly's participation in tennis, swimming, golf, bowling, and jogging. Enthusiastic and optimistic, her seductive torso evoked jealousy from females and drew raves from men. If only he could see her more often.

"Can you come another weekend?" he begged. "I miss you so much."

It was never long enough.

The way she looked in his eyes when he touched her face and shoulders before gently sliding his fingers down her torso, enticed Holly further. Any hesitancy was always fleeting; her hand pulled him closer. Just like a woman to attract and then resist.

Their chemistry set off fireworks.

Her desire for validation—his approval—made him feel important. Unable to verbalize in a way he felt comfortable, he found giving material objects a better method to demonstrate love. Showering his fair maiden with impressive presents became a recurrent exercise.

"Oh Adam," Holly said after receiving another small box. "Where did you find this incredible bracelet? I'm the luckiest girl in the world."

"Couldn't help it when I walked past a store window," he said. "The precious gems sparkled and made me think of you. Sapphire, amethyst, ruby, and topaz, emerald— I thought you would enjoy them side by side."

He slipped it on her slender wrist ...

Each gift was an expression of Adam's affection and she became increasingly convinced of her growing significance. Most of the people she dated exhibited selfish traits—like Anthony Venturi and Brad Phillips—but Adam was different. Everything revolved around her and she seemed to be the sole object of his desire.

Only her parents cared that much.

Holly felt safe with him, like her worries would disappear in bright sunshine if she remained in his presence. Her beau appeared secure and *always*-in control. When he suggested she transfer to his college so they could spend extra time together, she quickly accepted.

Concentrating on schoolwork was becoming an increasingly significant dilemma. A transfer was essential—to finish her own education. The change regardless of the complications seemed worth it. It would be difficult separating from her family but that was inevitable, being away from the man she adored.

The important thing was being close to Adam.

"You decide how to accomplish a task and then pursue it passionately," her father said. "We're going to miss you. By the way, I've appreciated your help in my office, Cupcake. You have lots of good ideas."

Adam Nathaniel Clark was the oldest son of a college professor and elementary school teacher from the mid-sized college town of Oceanview, California. His parents were practical, spending time with three sons after completing chores. Academia was important but needed balance. Scott and Becky Clark relished physical exercise if it involved being together as a family. A screened porch stretched across the back of the house. Their yard surrounded a pool, accompanied by a spacious deck. The temperate climate enabled them to socialize *al fresco* during the school year.

Ocean surfing dominated weekends.

"Why hang around indoors when there's so much to do outside?" his father said. "When you're sick, stay in bed. If not, get active."

Adam was a mysterious and respected older sibling who intrigued much younger brothers Josh and David, who enjoyed a special bond because of the closeness of their ages. They were proud of Adam—and he was protective of them—but apart from sports, they knew little about each other. A fierce competitor, Adam overpowered them when they worked out. His teasing verbal taunts pressured them to cultivate skills most males admire. He challenged them to become better than they were, so Josh and David trained with friends to improve.

"Someday we'll retaliate," Josh promised.

"Go for it! You won't be a threat until I'm an old man." He tousled their dark heads and the fire inside burned brighter.

Known for his athletic excellence in high school football and track, Adam lacked skills to compete on a professional level. Earning a living became his priority but he intended to work out the rest of his life.

Math concepts were easy for Adam whose career plans centered on banking. He scrutinized the stock market as it sought new highs and rewarded wise investors—taking pride in his own promising ability since investing birthday money at sixteen.

With his father's tenure, college expenses were minimal.

When Holly arrived in Oceanview, Adam portrayed a knight in shining armor. With a gallant smile, he introduced her to family, close friends, and acquaintances. Over the weeks, he familiarized her with what to do and where to go in town. She became his prized possession, one worth protecting. Spending time getting to know his family seemed unimportant.

"We can do whatever you want tonight," Adam said one night after dinner. "Do you want to hear the concert on campus? Or, would you rather … go down by the lake and talk while we feed ducks?"

His free-spirited girlfriend had her own mindset.

Time passed quickly with pleasant meals and enjoyable outings scattered among romantic study dates. Outside of classes, they spent most waking hours together with few exceptions—except when participation in sporting events superseded.

Spring was in the air and hormones raged.

Holly jumped on Adam's back as they ran through the park. "I'm glad you have broad shoulders to hold onto," she said. Zigzagging across the grass, he tried to shake her loose and she giggled.

"I'm not carrying you the whole way."

"But you're the one who wants to jog. I came to be with you," she said. "I'll sit on this bench and wait until you're done."

He continued to carry her home.

With graduation looming, moving elsewhere without Holly was unimaginable. She provided security and stability. Always looking awesome—and willing to do what he wanted—she was an asset. Never would he take her for granted. In addition, spending her life with Adam was the wisest decision she could make. *How could anyone resist such a wonderfully talented and caring man?*

He escorted Holly to the Cascades Restaurant, with a scenic glass tower overlooking a series of waterfalls. While dining, they chatted about fascinating buildings and people. After entrées of steak and shrimp, Adam began his speech.

"The entire Armstrong family is unique. Your father is a talented physician. Your mother's hospitality and kindness are unequalled. And no other female compares with you. You dazzle with your sparkle—an exceptional diamond if I've ever seen one."

Adam gathered courage, took a deep breath, and continued.

"Of all the women in the world, there's only one I want for my wife. Will you marry me Holly?" He opened the velvet box with an extraordinary princess cut gem to display on her finger.

"I will. I will," she said with eyes glistening and a smile from ear to ear.

He leaned to kiss her. On cue, a waiter brought two glasses of champagne and a raspberry torte drizzled with chocolate to seal the agreement.

The future looked bright as they made plans to entwine their lives.

Holly assumed it wouldn't be difficult to continue the comfort level she was accustomed. "Adam is wonderful and my life can only get better," she said to everyone within earshot.

"Your ring is beautiful!" best friend Carissa James said.

"I can't stop looking down," Holly said. The carat gem was of highest quality and twinkled even when it was dirty.

In spite of the storybook relationship, her frustration in courtship was a secret. Adam avoided subjects that resulted in disagreement. "With a permanent commitment to each other, those issues can be worked out over time," he said repeatedly.

It was meant to be.

Bridal magazines, wedding books filled with tips, and catalogs of invitations replaced textbooks. Summer was near. "Weddings are a once in a lifetime experience and I deserve the best," Holly told friends. Her wide-eyed enthusiasm enchanted those around her.

"This will be the best production ever," Carissa said.

"I can't wait to see pictures!" her bridesmaid Jill Hetherington added.

Friends gave ideas but Holly set out to acquire exactly what she desired. She visited specialty shops catering to couples planning nuptials. Storekeepers encouraged a sense of opulence and extravagance while attempting to cultivate expensive choices—with this bride-to-be a captive audience. The high school valedictorian who secretly yearned to be a prom queen was more than receptive.

Holly and her mother attended a bridal extravaganza in Denver that offered a wide assortment of gowns and accessories. They were overwhelmed with the extensive selection, guaranteeing a fairy-tale day. She brought brochures home to show attendants Carissa, Lori, and Jill.

"The sapphire dresses are amazing! Wait till you see the rest of my choices!"

Weeks passed quickly.

It was a joyful time confirming final details, enjoying bridal showers, and celebrating pre-nuptial activities. After a whirlwind courtship, one essential ingredient was lacking.

When Adam secured a coveted position at Desert State Bank in Albuquerque, New Mexico, the couple met a realtor and viewed potential houses. After looking at property on Brookshire Lane, the enthusiastic banker reached for Holly's hand.

"There are significant choices we need to decide but being with the girl I cherish more than anything in the world *is* most important right now."

Playfully she pulled away and dashed down the sidewalk.

Adam sprinted after his golden haired fiancée and caught her in a warm embrace. "I didn't become star quarterback in high school without ambitious goals. You do want to live with me, don't you?" He kissed Holly passionately. Her brown eyes melted like chocolate in the sun. *He was a good catch.* A young girl watched from her bedroom window unnoticed.

"Let's go to Cappuccino Paradise and talk," Adam said.

"Great idea! I'm thirsty and tired."

Holly had little interest in purchasing a home but relished spending time with her sweetheart. They could figure out future housing over coffee. "All I want is a fantastic place to live, with a wonderful garden," she said.

Life was a bit more serious for Adam. Black and white made perfect sense but Holly's fondness for color fascinated him.

An only child, Holly delighted attentive parents. With no siblings for competition, she consumed much of their time. Her antics as a youngster hinged on frivolity yet provided mental stimulus and emotional closeness that she relished.

Ted and Susan Armstrong lived near Steamboat Springs, Colorado nestled in the Rocky Mountains. The environment provided a tranquil setting for a sensitive child intrigued with creation. Wherever she gazed, the sky, water, and earth radiated beauty. Scenic views were spectacular either looking up at the mesmerizing elevations or down from picturesque lookout points.

"Wow! Look over there!" Holly heard repeatedly.

"Mom, can we stay longer?" she would ask—watching a chipmunk or fuzzy brown caterpillar crawling up a branch. Curiosity was a familiar companion as Holly pursued whatever caught her attention. Brighter than most children, a sense of not fitting in formed her identity.

She enjoyed socializing but treasured solitude.

Hunting for treasures wherever she could find them, Holly looked for unusual, unique, and colorful—anything she could add to her stock of memorable finds. Collections included butterflies, wildflowers, and seashells. Each item was carefully labeled and stored.

Dr. Ted Armstrong was a respected physician with a schedule that required flexibility for emergencies. Everyone expected him to come and go, if necessary.

"I'm sorry to miss your play tonight, Cupcake. I know you'll do great!" he said, backstage in the school auditorium shortly after arriving. "Mom will take pictures for me to see later."

"But Daddy, I can perform my part when you get home tonight." Holly explained—resourceful when she needed to be.

Susan Armstrong found pleasure in entertaining. Picnics, parties, and celebrations at the Armstrong home were common occurrences.

The carefully tended garden provided extra gratification for a daughter who savored colors of the rainbow in flowers, vegetables, and fruit. Holly gathered armfuls of green, red, and yellow produce for guests to enjoy. Arranging beautiful centerpieces became her specialty.

Holly and her mom visited relatives who lived close when they weren't providing hospitality. Cousins Shari and Lori were older but participation in their activities was expected—usually as a spectator.

Granny Armstrong relished her position as the family's center of attention. She was a lively individual, warm and loving, who added great joy. Her storytelling ability intrigued and her zest for living refreshed.

On early morning walks in the woods, Holly learned mountain bluebirds sing lovely songs and the crest is a tuft of feathers on a bird's head. "The same muscles that help birds fly, also help them breathe," Granny explained. "As a bird beats its wings, it fills and empties its lungs. That's why it can go long distances without getting tired." When hikes ended, her grandma always looked up and said, "Thank you."

Holly was puzzled—but assumed Granny enjoyed her company.

At Christmas, Granny strung popcorn and cranberries on trees out back. She also hung chunks of fruit and nuts. "We can't forget the birds and squirrels. It's a holiday for everyone," she said. Sometimes Holly and her cousins helped thread the treats. Birds seemed to notice the love and flocked to Granny's yard.

These acts of kindness made Holly feel valuable.

Family relationships and fond childhood memories would always be significant but soon she would move to a different locale and forge a stronger bond with Adam, the handsome California jock devoted to her happiness.

Life would surely become everything she imagined.

An extraordinary weekend at the majestic Rocky Mountain Lodge was the perfect launch to paradise. Creation would surely show its splendor in a grand finale before their wedding festivities were finished.

Following a delicious rehearsal dinner and breathtaking sunset, the romantic duo spent time with family on a terrace—watching a surprise late evening view of the Aurora Borealis.

July sixteenth began with lots of sunshine and flowers.

Wedding consultant Shari Agave produced intricate details exactly as Holly requested.

Transformed into a botanical garden, the massive ballroom focused on a central area for the ceremony. Mini-cascading waterfalls gave a natural concert as scents from massive blooms filled the air. Around the perimeter, tables were surrounded by floor-to-ceiling windows with views of the mountains.

Groomsmen Joe, Danny, and Roger—dressed in tuxedos with sapphire vests—escorted Carissa, Lori, and Jill down a petal-strewn pathway. Bouquets of tangerine, lemon, scarlet, rose, and violet flowers complemented the bridesmaids sapphire gowns. The attendants waited under a rose covered canopy with the officiate presiding over the ceremony … while a string ensemble from the local college played Chamber music.

Holly arrived with her father by horse-drawn carriage at the entrance of the lodge, where the five o'clock celebration preceded a formal dinner and reception. The bride looked radiant on her father's arm, wearing a gorgeous ivory gown with Cluny lace. Her hair sparkled in the sunlight.

So did the diamond necklace Adam gave her the evening before.

The charming blonde looked into his twinkling blue eyes as they said vows, making promises she intended to keep. Her sweetheart beamed. He traced a heart on his chest. Holly hoped it would guarantee eternal love, though maybe it was a reminder of her newest acquisition with more surprises to come.

She liked the feel of two sparkling rings on one finger.

Clinking champagne glasses brought an extra gleam to her eyes accompanied by kisses from the groom. No matter what life brought, nothing could steal these precious moments. Ecstasy would be hers from now on.

Cutting the four-tiered cake coincided precisely with the setting of the sun, while the horizon filled with topaz, tangerine, and crimson glory. Luscious almond cake left a sweet taste in Holly's mouth as the newlyweds swirled around the reception floor smiling, greeting guests—yet in their own private world.

He pulled her closer.

"This magic moment—so different and so new … I know that you feel it too … by the look in your eyes … together forever—until the end of time …" Adam sang in his rich baritone voice as they danced.

Family and friends were elated to be part of the festivities. They enthusiastically offered words of encouragement and expressed wishes for the couple's success.

"Congratulations to the dream team!" Carissa said.

"Of all people, you two have the best probability to accomplish your goals," Joe Wallace said beaming.

"We have confidence you'll have a successful marriage," Susan Armstrong said.

"July 16th will long be remembered," a chorus of voices promised.

Everything was in place for the best foundation anyone could hope on the road to happiness. Adam picked his bride up, ready to carry her through the ballroom doorway as photographers clicked final pictures. Holly kissed his cheek.

Rainbow confetti descended as they left.

Chapter 2
Perfection

THE BEAUTIFULLY LANDSCAPED YARD was picture perfect with a gazebo behind the spacious home. Most evenings, Adam and Holly Clark relaxed outside watching stars emerge from their daytime sleep. He barely recognized major constellations but she knew them all. Each group fascinated her and she told interesting stories about their legends. "The Pleiades are my favorite! The six visible stars are make-believe sisters."

"Look Holly. You're surrounded by hundreds of sparkling friends," he teased.

"You're envious but I think my talents separate me from others."

"You certainly light up the room when you walk in," Adam answered. "I bet you could illuminate a house—we'll see if our electricity ever goes out."

"Do you see Orion?" she asked.

"Yeah … over there." He pointed. "You told me the first time I visited Colorado. He's a hunter but I can't see his gun."

"Seriously, did you know our ability to see in the dark improves as minutes pass? Our eyes adapt. You can see the bow after a while. Keep looking. Betelgeuse is easy to spot because it's red," she said.

Adam leaned back.

"Sorry. I was distracted by a PowerPoint presentation I'm giving tomorrow," he said after a few minutes of silence.

After pondering the sky Holly said, "Watching the stars reminds me of my childhood in Colorado where I spent hours wondering about the universe. How does each star group mysteriously appear in such precise order every night?"

"Good question," Adam said. "But we need to call it a night, my love. You discuss theories that have no answers—however, morning requires I function at the top of my game. We can talk more this weekend."

Occasionally after a weekend of pruning, they would start a fire with branches—then roast marshmallows. It was amazing how resourceful Holly could be when she needed to. Adam was surprised at her plans to entertain him.

"Here you go, Your Highness. Is this marshmallow to your liking?"

She giggled.

"Who lives better than this?" he asked.

"I never dreamed life could be so great. The best part is that we have the rest of our lives to enjoy each other. As long as you're here, I'm going to be okay," she said.

Adam agreed.

Time together discussing dreams intoxicated the duo. He stroked Holly's hair as they laughed and talked into the night. The gleam of firelight enlivened her senses. They avoided negative issues—"We'll discuss that when it becomes a significant factor in our lives," Adam said—chatting about interests, instead. Their personalities meshed well, with both focused on goals. Each determined to tackle any task that presented itself.

What more did they need?

She cuddled, longing for more, but the embers finally flickered out.

Self-absorbed and oblivious to the world around them, Adam and Holly chatted briefly with new neighbors. Perhaps their lack of interest was obscured by their enthusiasm.

"Morning Fred," Adam said rushing to his car. "Looks like rain."

"Good morning, neighbor."

Fred Anderson waved. Three adolescents followed him to his Sequoia and they sped off. A stone wall surrounded the Anderson's property protecting an elaborate pool. Fred and Nancy were significantly older and appeared to have an advantage over most middle aged. Intrigued with Fred's success, Adam observed him with interest. Although friendly, the Andersons darted here and there with energetic children and had little time to bond.

Neighbors to the south were reserved. Pete and Mary Stewart liked privacy and kept to themselves most of the time. Their young children Jason and Lisa played outdoors alone most days.

Occasionally, Holly saw Lisa peeking through the fence.

The Stewarts had fashioned an exquisite flower garden in their back yard. Living near the oasis was a blessing—birds of every color and description enjoyed the delightful surroundings. Cheerful songs filled the air. The shy warbler perched on her nest while a flash of red in a nearby tree signaled a cardinal. A screeching blue jay warned that the birdbath belonged to him and a friendly robin with vivid vest hurried across the grass trying to satisfy her enormous appetite with a juicy worm.

Holly was impressed.

She remembered walks enjoying nature while contemplating life as a child. How did birds find enough food? How could a hummingbird fly backward? Why did sailors navigate across oceans and pilots fly to their destinations through space using the stars as a guide? Her questions raised more.

Creation soothed her spirit.

At school, they taught about the big bang. *How could it have just happened?*

Eager to return with his bride to the bustling college town of Oceanview, Adam agreed to make a presentation in California. Holly was apprehensive being apart for two days but her husband assured her it would be fun staying with his family. "You can swim all day, or read on the deck. My mother won't attack you. If she does, my brothers will protect you," he said.

"But people from Germany are living with your parents. Can I just come with you to Los Angeles and shop?" she asked.

"People from a variety of backgrounds stay at our home. Visiting professors live there for months while teaching at OSC. Hans and Halle Kirchner from Heidelberg, Germany will make an endearing impression during this six-month stay. Don't worry. You'll like them, Holly. Their worldviews and lively conversation are captivating. Who knows, we may even visit them some day."

His words proved true. Holly loved every minute except for one confrontation with Adam's mother.

"Do you have concern for anyone but yourself?" Becky Clark asked the final morning. "After being waited on for breakfast and lunch, you sit by the pool all afternoon secluded from the world—with one goal, pampering yourself!"

"I didn't know you needed my help," Holly said.

"Exactly my point!"

She bit her lip. Obviously, Becky felt intimidated by her presence knowing she was now second fiddle to Adam. Holly cleaned the bathroom and took her dirty linens to the laundry before she left. She had much to prove to this unappreciative woman.

For Holly's birthday, a shiny candy-apple red Grand Cherokee Jeep was parked in the driveway. "Let's go out for breakfast," Adam said. "I'll wait in the car." Within seconds, he honked.

Holly was delighted. "It's perfect—and the leather smells incredible."

She enjoyed long drives to see breathtaking views from the nearby mountains. Luscious greens in the foreground—blending with vivid blues of the sky—was a picture-perfect background for exhilarating bursts of color in nature. Streaks of crimson rustling through branches, a flurry of gold, wildlife scavenging, and cascading waterfalls provided a way to escape the barrenness of a dry summer in a lonely desert.

With her husband intent on becoming a highly valued bank employee, little time remained for frivolity with her. She would change that.

Washing the Jeep, Holly splashed water on Adam. He chased her with the hose. "Come on my little chickadee. Now it's your turn for a bath." Her wet shirt enticed him further. They frolicked in the yard until neighbors arrived home.

As the months advanced, their expectations ripened. Adam's career soared and confidence in his abilities increased. Holly believed her dreams would be fulfilled eventually.

They just needed a bit more tweaking.

It was a great time to be alive, a good country to be living in—and the future was bright as sunlight streaming through cut glass windowpanes. As individuals, they were capable of much. Together, who knew? Their palette began to take shape and the colors were vibrant.

Holly was overjoyed to see tender shoots of green pushing through the earth. Glorious blooms appeared overnight—as if they were magic. Wisteria exuded a wonderful fragrance that permeated the entire yard. Delicate roses with ruffled edges surrounded a dense center where a beautiful butterfly perched.

Birds chirped and chimes tinkled in the breeze.

Getting on the ground, she pulled weeds around hearty plants. She loved gardening and the best part came when produce could actually be consumed. Her mind wandered to futile tasks and people who engage in worthless issues. Religion was one. "Why did unknown deities intrigue so many?" Clinging to forms of the supernatural for support showed signs of weakness. This foolishness prevented achieving important goals. Why inhibit your independence?

She picked dirt from under her nails—waiting for Adam to come home. He was late again. What could he possibly be doing that couldn't be accomplished during a normal banking day?

Soaking in bubbles loosened grime and energized her spirits. The scintillating vanilla aroma provided incentive for baking cinnamon rolls. She scrubbed her back and legs with a loofah, while gently exfoliating and envisioning smooth skin for cuddling with Adam later in the evening.

He was late again.

The cinnamon rolls, hardened on a plate, still waited in the middle of the counter by morning.

"Hooray for the holidays!" Holly said glancing at the calendar. Buying Easter candy and favorite food to make for dinner, she prepared a special weekend alone with her husband. Visions of quality time together permeated her thoughts.

Adam ended up playing tennis with a co-worker on Saturday.

After a lazy Sunday breakfast, they read the newspaper. Holly lounged in a negligée giving her husband time to regroup from his endless responsibilities at work. Adam bit off a chocolate rabbit's ear and headed to the garage.

"It's Easter … The least you could do is spend the day with me," she said loudly, as the door shut. "I have plans today."

He didn't seem to care.

"Do you have any idea what I put up with?" she said following him out.

"Chill out, Holly. It's a nothing day for a change. Do you expect me to work 24/7 and never stop to relax?"

"I expect you to pay attention to me for a change. I'm entitled to happiness."

"Yes you are and I'm doing everything in my power to make that happen. Thanks for your support," Adam said with a grin. He reached to find something on the top shelf over his workbench.

She changed into jeans and a purple shirt.

Getting watercolors out to paint, Holly fumed. Painting pastel bunnies in a basket—while munching on jellybeans—was followed by a picture of wildflowers in a meadow. The afternoon was uneventful and quiet.

Adam tried to tempt Holly to golf with him and she tried to lure him into a deep discussion about ethics. They ended up grilling steaks and watching a movie about a shipwreck after dinner.

Leftover Cadbury cream eggs and marshmallow peeps ended in the garbage.

Time became a source of frustration for Holly. Introspection consumed her days but the more she thought, the less sure she was of accomplishing her dreams. What would truly satisfy was one-step away and her attempts seemed to come up short.

Contemplating life wasn't quite as enjoyable anymore.

A visit home to Colorado brought increased feelings of insecurity. Her father spent cozy evenings around the fireplace in spite of being busy.

Dr. Ted Armstrong was a caring man inviting strangers to his house. Somehow, they became good friends—as Adam had experienced—respecting and appreciating him.

"Why did you invite Adam to stay here after his accident?" Holly asked.

"His plans for the week were shattered; his family was far away; mountain air would do him good; and I relish arriving home to find good company."

"So you liked Adam?"

"You bet! He was intelligent, responsible, appreciative, energetic, and I thought he would make a great son-in-law. Why do you think I sent you in to greet him?"

"Oh Daddy," Holly said, remembering the moment.

"Sometimes an idea pops into my mind—just like my daughter's. Where do you think you got your good genes?"

"I was impressed too," Susan said.

Holly twirled her hair while gazing at the Rocky Mountains. Reflections of the setting sun through elongated windows warmed her spirit. Just being in Colorado had a calming effect. A lavender mist settled in and she turned on the lamp.

Ted and Susan Armstrong appeared content and at peace with life. Neither worried about the future or regretted the past. Holly wondered about their reasons for their satisfaction and watched closely.

Maybe I'll discover the answer someday.

The moon was shining when she pulled into the driveway back at home. Adam came out to meet her—apparently watching for headlights coming down the street. His embrace felt better than ever. They lingered for a minute.

"There's going to be an eclipse of the moon tonight," he said. "Let's sit outside and watch." He put her suitcase inside the door. "How are your parents?"

"Fine. Daddy told me he picked you and brought you home—the best present he could ever give me," she said smiling.

"That's a nice compliment," Adam said. "So did you have a good time?"

"It was all right, I guess—but something inside me kept trying to understand serenity and how peace is obtained in life's chaos." She tried to persuade Adam to respond but he refused.

"That's too profound for me," he said.

When the earth's shadow began to eclipse the moon, the yard became eerily silent. They watched the moon slowly transform into a coppery ball. "Why does it take so long?" Adam asked after several minutes.

"Lunar eclipses sometimes continue for an hour, unlike solar eclipses," Holly explained. "I like sitting out here with you."

"Let's call it a night. I have an important meeting tomorrow."

Adam, who had exhibited carefree ways during courtship—splashing Holly while rowing a boat, spinning yoyo tricks, and jumping under the falls fully dressed—grew more intense. He was pleasant, enthused about what he did, but his passion for achieving involved functions at the bank.

"You're turning into a serious workaholic," she said.

"I'm providing luxuries for you to enjoy while proving my dependability," Adam answered.

"Well I miss the fun-loving hunk you used to be."

"What happened to accomplishing goals and conquering the unknown? This is my career," he said.

Banking was an interesting field for someone adept at numbers and Adam propelled himself to loftier objectives. He challenged his closest colleagues. Spending hours studying new ventures and developing innovative options was like eating candy. The days flew by and he longed for more productivity.

"Your father wants you to call," Holly said when he got home. "He's concerned you rarely take time to connect with your brothers anymore."

After Adam hung up, she asked about the conversation.

"When I was a boy, I wanted to be a leader; have others look up to me," he explained. "As a first-born son, it was my right and privilege to be in charge. I was a realist and took what opportunities came my way. I was also a dependable son—who kept the peace and guided my brothers. I wanted my father to believe I'm responsible, practical, and sensible."

"So he doesn't think you're doing what you should?" Holly said.

"People are individuals and I appreciate our differences. Maybe he has a point. In high school, I earned my position as quarterback of the football team because I knew how to play the game. There's no reason to back away from my goals now—but I'll try to contact Josh and David more often. There's still plenty of time."

Chapter 3
Dream Vacation

ADAM AND HOLLY SCAMPERED like kittens in a basket of yarn planning their first vacation overseas. The mailbox overflowed with travel brochures. Stacks of informative pamphlets crowded food on the counter.

"I finally have a chance to visit friends in their native countries," Adam said. "With only three weeks, we need to choose carefully. Would you like to see anything special?"

"I'm happy with whatever you decide," Holly said.

Her mind filled with images she had only seen in books, places she imagined—famous places, exotic places, unfamiliar places. However, she knew Adam waited years for this opportunity. Staying at a resort on the Italian Riviera she enjoyed in a movie might be fun.

She spent weeks daydreaming while doing chores, contemplated options before sleeping, and brainstormed around the kitchen table. Working with an atlas and maps, Adam calculated time and distance. Holly's personal choices became a scavenger hunt as they narrowed destinations.

"My cousin Lori told me about incredible sites to see in Scotland," she said, opening one of the books she checked out from the library. "Look at this! We might even see a bagpiper in the highlands." Favorite countries, cities, landmarks, and scenery were plentiful and—from her point of view—each person appropriately described why this stop was imperative. Adam patiently listened as he took notes.

"My mother said … If we miss the Eiffel Tower, we'll regret it."

"The Emerald Isle is Granny's favorite place," she added.

"Thank them for their advice," he said, hurrying to play tennis with his co-worker Bill.

"Will you be back before dinner?" Holly called. The door shut before she could hear his reply. Her urge was to run after him but she remained silent and finished painting her nails cranberry.

She blew on them for a few seconds—in lieu of expressing her opinion.

Adam contacted his friends to finalize the itinerary. "They're excited! Pack your bags." With tickets in hand, there was nothing to do but wait.

Holly bustled around town selecting gifts for hosts. A local craft shop offered an assortment of easily transportable items. Among her selections, she found chiseled oak picture frames in which photographs— taken later with their friends—could be inserted. "What great parting gifts!" These mementos would ensure friendships continue long into the future.

She researched travel tips and chose clothing and accessories to pack. Extra ideas came to mind as she finished. An inexperienced traveler, Holly had no idea she needed to cut the pile in half. Eliminating items followed—because large suitcases hold only a certain amount of necessities.

"What if I need those things?" she asked Adam.

"We already have a bigger problem getting this stuff in here," he said, jamming the contents in and closing her luggage.

As the airliner soared toward Europe, Holly leaned against his arm and smiled. How she loved this man who gently stroked her hair. She nuzzled closer. Savory stuffed chicken breasts with a raspberry-pineapple salad was served somewhere over the Atlantic around midnight. Puffed cheese tarts followed.

"Adam, what made you like me in the first place?" Holly asked when they finished eating. "Why did you want to marry me?"

Their private chatter—none too loud or deep because other passengers were within earshot—filled the hours. Sleep eluded them on the long flight, except for brief naps flying non-stop to Paris.

The darkness that consumed them suddenly turned into bursts of colorful sunrise off the wings of the plane—pinks, golds, oranges, reds, magenta. The warmth of the light permeated their inner beings. Enjoying the moment together, while having a chance to visit places they dreamed of, brought a new kind of euphoria.

The Goyets warmly greeted Adam and Holly at the Charles De Gaulle Airport—known as Paris Roissy. "Bonjour, mes amis. Bienvenue." Madame Goyet brushed their checks warmly with a kiss on each side.

Holly enjoyed the European custom immensely.

Sitting at an outdoor café eating lunch, they chatted about Parisians, the language, French cuisine, sightseeing, and incredible museums—the Louvre, Centre Pompidou, the Musée d'Orsay. Accordion music played softly in the background. The melodic language overwhelmed Holly's ability to focus on their conversation.

Bicycles, loaves of bread, and fresh flowers were abundant. A variety of sounds and fragrances mingled in an overload on their senses. A gendarme waving his arms at the corner enhanced the interesting atmosphere.

With little sleep and a bit of jet lag, they spent the rest of the day relaxing in the French countryside.

A crowing rooster and kitten purring outside the guest room door aroused the travelers from their dreams. Aroma from coffee drifted across their noses, almost unnoticeable at first—then growing more robust. "Bonjour, ma belle. Je t'aime!" Adam kissed Holly on the check.

Holly rubbed her eyes, yawned, and pulled the duvet back.

"Get dressed so we can enjoy the croissants Madame Goyet made," he said.

She rummaged for a change of clothes—too tired to care. Fumbling with makeup she asked, "Do I look okay?"

Adam nodded, moving toward the door with his camera.

The streets were crowded when they arrived back in Paris and headed toward Montmartre. Holly looked forward to the charming artsy shops in this district. They wandered through back streets and a local vineyard, stopping in boutiques, observing Parisians.

The view from Basilique du Sacre-Coeur was magnificent. Lavishly decorated, the basicilica's exquisite turquoise, red, and yellow mosaic and enamel work sparkled in the sun. Holly longed to design a project using tiles at home, although much simpler.

Arriving at La Bourse, the French Stock Exchange, Adam stood captivated in the domed hall where he watched the busy commodities market.

"Fortunately, tourists are only welcome from 11-12 each morning," Holly said.

Adam's thoughts drifted to his investment with Joe Wallace in college. Smart enough to keep his parents in the dark about activities they disapproved, he avoided talk about using savings to speculate. He knew it was a risk but felt the gamble would be worth it eventually. *If only Holly was curious about financial matters.* How can I explain my motivation and interest her in investing? All she cares about is wealth that results from my hard work.

He wouldn't dare mention it.

Holly was preoccupied, pouring over travel books and gleaning vital information about the Louvre. Sometimes her informative facts were useful—most of the time they were boring.

"Arts flourished in France during the 17th and 18th Century, and Paris was the best place to experience it," she said. "I'm glad we're here."

"The Mona Lisa is a lot smaller than I imagined," Adam said. He used his best French to explain the works of art privately to his wife and the two ended giggling so loud they had to cut their tour short.

With barely enough time to stop at the Cathédrale de Notre-Dame, before browsing bookstalls along the banks of the Seine, they waited for the dinner cruise to begin. "For you, my darling—a visit to Paris would be incomplete without a boat ride down the river."

The twinkling lights were spectacular, food delicious, and guide knowledgeable as he described the history of Paris in broken English, pointing to landmarks. Holly struggled to stay awake as they meandered down the charming river. She snuggled against Adam.

He had romantic ideas planned for later in the evening.

Quietly walking to the hotel, both stumbled into bed. They would rejoin the city soon but sleep was overcoming them. Their heads sank into pillows as dreams of the City of Lovers filled their minds. Nothing could keep them awake tonight. Sounds of dishes breaking on the street below their window, in the Latin Quarter, jolted them briefly.

Morning was peaceful in contrast.

Holly kissed Adam. "Please … let's get a chocolate crêpe or pain au chocolat. I'm starving!" she whispered.

He consented and pulled on a shirt. "Are you sure you don't want to eat downstairs?"

They sat with pastries and coffee on a bench in the square, watching the city wake up. Street sweepers finished rounds and shopkeepers rearranged wares. Birds feasted on leftover pieces of baguette.

The morning schedule included a tour of Musée d'Orsay before watching a Christian Dior fashion show. Shopping in nearby boutiques Holly found silk scarves, perfume, and crystal that she adored.

Adam gave money to a vender with a monkey who played organ grinder music for them. The furry critter hopped on Holly's shoulder sniffing her neck. "He likes you," he teased. "Give him a kiss."

She refused.

At the Aquarium du Trocadéro, delightful fragrances surrounded them with one particular scent lingering in the air as they left. "Gardenia—don't you just love it?" Holly said.

"C'est magnifique!" he said. "Reminds me of you."

Seeing the world from the Eiffel Tower made Holly's heart skip a beat. Adam pointed to landmarks they visited. "We're going to stop at L'Arc de Triomphe and walk down Avenue Des Champs Élysées after we leave here."

This enchanting city exceeded preconceived expectations, from picture-perfect images in magazines to raving reviews from friends. Its allure griped their minds and they absorbed every sensation possible from the vibrant Parisian life.

Watching people enjoy the nightlife ended a perfect day. "We used to be like that couple," she said, motioning to a young female being courted by a handsome male who was caressing her, oblivious to others in the darkness.

Adam pulled Holly closer and pressed his lips to hers.

His hand on her left shoulder moved slowly down her back—pausing as a car passed on the bridge. Flickers of light cast shadows. He continued to accept the challenge as his fingers searched for places she never intended in public. She sighed, as he breathed heavier. Moments of frustration between them disappeared as their passion reignited, drawing their bodies together in a dance of desire.

She was headstrong and wanted her way. He was passionate about his interests. The only way to solve the problem was to rustle in the bushes beside the River Seine, daring and courageous—to give her excitement and the contentment she longed for.

Stopping at a patisserie on the way to Fontainebleau, Adam and Holly bought scrumptious pastries and steaming coffee.

They met the Goyets for a final day together in front of the Palais, a grandiose chateau built in the 12th century. "Here in the Red Room Napoleon Bonaparte signed abdication papers," Holly said. "Marie Antoinette had her own apartment."

Walking through the building gave Holly goose bumps. "It seems unreal to jump back in time and picture life as it was then," she said. She was in awe of the natural beauty of palace, fountains, and gardens—taking mental notes so she could make improvements to her own yard.

Always a nature lover, she inspired to even loftier goals.

Monsieur Goyet showed them his famous village with its strikingly elegant parks and forest. Adam appreciated being with his friends. After eating fondue for dinner, Adam and Holly laughed as the Goyets' lively grandson entertained them with hilarious antics. They took photographs so they could remember.

"Excusez-moi. Pardon," he begged, "You like to see more?"

"Oui … Absolutely!" Adam answered.

The show continued until Madame Goyet insisted he say, "Au revoir, à demain." It was bedtime.

Holly couldn't help thinking, "Someday I'll have my own sweet son. I can't wait!"

Traveling south through the magnificent Loire Valley, Adam headed toward the city of Moulins. The French countryside was enthralling with fairytale castles scattered around the hills. "That is beautiful! What a sight!" Holly said early in the day.

"I wonder how they could build a structure like that," Adam said, rounding a picturesque bend.

"How much time do we have to see castles today?" Holly asked. "Each one we come to is more fascinating than the last."

There were many, and it was hard to choose, but the clock kept moving. Arriving at the MediHallel Moulins, they went through the 15th century Cathedral with its remarkable stained-glass windows.

"I'm doing that someday," Holly promised herself. *My friends will be dazzled by my creativity.*

She reached for Adam's hand but he had already moved ahead.

The clock tower, with its animated figures, fascinated both of them. "Amazing, isn't it?" Adam said. They laughed as the figurines moved around a column. "Ready to go?" he asked. "How much longer are you going to be?"

"Just a few more minutes," Holly said.

"I'm hungry. Let's get some food," he said, pulling her toward him. "Come on my little cupcake or I'll have to eat you instead."

The hotel window presented a view of streetlights under the moon—illuminating a bridge over the river. Reflections cast on the water were mesmerizing. Adam wrapped his arm around Holly as they took in the sight.

"Some moments are filled with peace no matter what the circumstances," she said. Minor troubles encountered by couples are like those ripples—maybe annoying but sure to be gone by daybreak," she thought.

In the morning, a sunrise over the river was exceptional. The gorgeous pink and orange sky layering with tangerine, peach, and coral, required numerous photos before they could leave.

"Just one more," she pleaded.

Stopping at another patisserie for lunch, they ate jambon and a baguette while overlooking a placid stream. It was hard to imagine a more tranquil existence. "Do you wonder what our lives will be like in ten years?" Holly asked.

"No idea."

"We need to figure out what our vision for the future will be, how to make our relationship more satisfying as we grow older," she said.

"Why?"

The bread was dry, hard to swallow—and the lump in her throat began to hurt—so she paused. *What was he really thinking? Why did he struggle with giving his opinions about deep issues? Did he honestly not care what happened?*

"Don't be so serious and spoil the day," Adam said. "We only have a short drive." He picked up the trash and reached out his hand. They walked to the car silently.

Driving into a health resort on the shore of Lake Annecy, Holly was ready for pampering. They enjoyed a leisurely massage for couples before walking around the downtown quarter with its quaint houses and winding canals. Ducks swam over for pieces of leftover baguette.

"Those red roofs are what I imagine it's like in Italy," she said.

"We're right on the border. Someday I'll take you there, I promise— and I've heard gondola rides in Venice are inspiring."

He squeezed Holly's hand.

They dined on a terrace, watching lights flicker on around the hillside. The wine was superb following a feast from the Greek Isles. Holly was quieter than usual so Adam tried to engage her in conversation.

She glanced away.

"I worked hard for this trip. The least you can do is make it enjoyable for me," he said.

Misty eyes flickered in the candlelight.

Her words began like a jammed waterfall before it crescendoed down a steep mountainside as he sipped wine. "You're passionate about your career, Adam, but you refuse to connect with me emotionally. Maybe you mean well, but the little you give me *is not* enough. I'm growing desperately lonely—waiting for you to really care."

"It's the same ole dance!" he said, setting his glass down abruptly. "You keep coming back to you. Are you filled with anything besides selfish interests, Holly?"

He motioned for the waiter.

Adam stood and turned toward the hotel. Her crying made him angrier and he walked away brusquely, not stopping until he reached the hotel lobby. *Is it too much for Holly to respect me and appreciate my sacrifices for her?*

Switching direction abruptly, he scurried into the lounge before she could follow. A booth in the back was empty so he settled in. Thank God, for dim lights that precluded being seen by someone intent on stealing his joy; but not from the cute server who was intent on making him feel special.

After a couple of drinks, an attractive and friendly masseuse joined him. Her blouse plunged at the neckline and sexy voice begged for more interaction—but talking to her provided the release he needed, to get control of his emotions. She seemed to understand his plight.

By the time he returned to his room, Holly was asleep so he crawled into bed and slept like a baby until morning.

Going through the mountains to Switzerland, Adam stopped to take pictures.

Holly gasped at fog lightly covering the mountainside—with the Alps sticking out from the top. "I've never seen such beauty. It looks like a marshmallow on top of whipped cream." The details sharply etched into her mind. It was imperative she paint this scene when she returned home. *The starkness of the mountains was somehow mellowed by the mist, yet they remained strong and stable* just like a relationship she envisioned with her husband.

Finding the Roulet home in Fontaines became easy once Adam got on the right highway. They lived in a village at the foot of the mountains. Jean Paul and Cristelle were genuine European artists. Viewing their artwork and discovering what motivated them, provided an interesting evening even for Adam.

"Enchantée," Holly said as she helped clean up.

With French flowing through their minds, Adam and Holly fell asleep long after midnight. *We may have problems communicating in English but there are other ways to connect*—was the last thing Holly remembered.

After a delicious breakfast of trésse, yogurt, and coffee, the Roulets took their guests sightseeing. Cobblestone streets were difficult to walk on after the rain. Holly gripped Adam's arm cautiously.

"I've never shopped in an outdoor marketplace. This is so much fun!" she said before slipping on the pavement.

She jumped up embarrassed.

"Can we tempt you with delicious Swiss chocolate?" the Roulets asked. "Have you tried Lindt & Sprüngli truffles?"

Adam joined in the conversation. "A few souvenirs will help Holly feel trés jolie." The shopping bag was so heavy, Adam needed to carry it—but her countenance brightened considerably.

For lunch, they went to an outdoor café in Le Locle where they glimpsed La Vue-des-Alpes and then a Clockwork Museum. The proprietor gave them a private viewing of his unique music boxes—which were even more incredible in action. Adam took videos of the animated figurines spinning and swirling.

Dancers spun with abandon.

Butterflies fluttered above a cottage while a singing bird sat on the window box.

Five o'clock bells played the most beautiful music ever heard when Adam and Holly left. It sounded like angels.

Quaint chalets, surrounded by gorgeous wildflowers, were impressive as they descended. Each picturesque village held its own charm with assorted scenes elaborately painted on exterior walls of some homes. An old woman surveyed the activity from her porch. A goat herder frolicked on the mountainside with his capricious herd, the joyful bleating audible even from a distance.

"What's the chance we could live here someday?" Holly asked.

"And what do we live on?"

"My art creations. You could be my promoter and travel the world showcasing them, if you want a little variety."

He laughed. "I'll stick with banking."

Conversations with locals found them cordial and interesting folks. Most worked in shops making and selling crafts. Some raised goats and provided villagers with dairy products. A sample of goat cheese was a delightful snack. Some offered services for tourists who visited throughout the year.

Enroute to Germany, Adam tried to locate the Gasthof Krone in Northwestern Switzerland. Unable to find Gempen—in a remote area on a mountain—he stopped to ask directions. "Vie gehts herron," he began. Accustomed to speaking French the previous week, switching to German while tired was more difficult.

Through gestures, he determined the correct route. Following curves to the top of the mountain, they encountered fog halfway. Holly was almost asleep but sat up alert when the car swerved.

"What in the world have we gotten ourselves into?" she said. "Should we turn around?"

"You need to learn to trust me," Adam answered.

The midnight bell from a church steeple rang as they arrived.

The proprietor leaned against a counter, urging them up the stairs with a key to room #14. "Vie talk in morning. Ja?" His endearing smile, hidden beneath a thick gray mustache and beard, reminded Holly of Father Christmas.

Snuggled under a cozy duvet, they almost slept through breakfast.

"Hallo. Guten Morgen," Father Christmas said cheerfully when they descended the steps into a homey room below—serving as lobby, dining room, and kitchenette. He motioned to a table.

An elderly woman polishing a platter smiled. "Ja, hier ist …" She pointed to a buffet on the side wall where trays of breakfast rested. Not much was left. Crumbs and tiny pieces of assorted foods indicated more had been offered earlier.

"Danke," Adam said.

They helped themselves to yogurt, dark bread, thinly sliced ham, and fruit compote.

Strong coffee followed with rich cream.

A gentleman read a newspaper in the corner and a woman sat in a rocker by the front window.

Mist still surrounded the quiet town as Adam and Holly meandered over the mountainside before heading back the same road they traveled up the evening before. Thick foliage—now in view—hugged the road.

No other car was in sight the entire ride down.

"What do the guests do up there anyway?" Holly asked. "Doesn't look like a thriving metropolis."

"We're in between their high seasons," Adam said. "They have skiing in the winter and hiking in the summer."

"Maybe if we'd been able to see anything but shadowy figures twenty feet away, it might have seemed a more appealing place to visit—that was a long drive to see a hotel," Holly said pensively.

"I was thinking about buying the place for you," Adam joked.

They snacked on sausage, cheese, and rolls driving through the Black Forest. Spectacular scenery, dotted with manicured houses and farms, required occasional photo stops. Animals scampered among the foliage. Trees formed an umbrella over the road in one section—almost like a cathedral.

Adam sang as he drove. His spirits were at an all-time high and he wondered why it had taken so long to travel here. "What will it take to accomplish the rest of my goals? Have I missed valuable opportunities that seem unimportant but in reality are essential?" he thought.

Holly looked out the window quietly.

They stopped at a bank to exchange money but a sign read, "Closed for lunch hour." Eventually Adam found a gas station that offered euros for US dollars.

Arriving in Heidelberg, they stayed with Hans and Halle Kirchner who lived near the Schloss Castle in an interesting two-floor bungalow.

"Europeans have different tastes in furnishings but I like your style," Holly said to their hostess in English. Halle smiled.

For dinner, they ate in an Italian restaurant, listening to German patrons speak, while three Oriental singers dressed in full costume entertained. It provided quite a picture of ethnic diversity. Afterward, they walked along the bank of the Neckar and saw a romantic view of the town.

In the morning, Frau Kirchner served a delicious breakfast of cheese and meats, yogurt with raspberries, pastries, granola, and coffee. Adam accompanied Herr Kirchner to the University where he taught economics and stayed to attend one of his classes.

Holly spent the afternoon shopping with Frau Kirchner at the Galleria Horton and several perfumeries. She felt a close kinship with Halle—their names being similar, though opposite in personality. Halle was a robust woman with a love for life but tranquil spirit. Her words were unintelligible for Holly but her tone conveyed warmth and caring, more than was heard in most conversations.

The look of surprise in her eyes when Holly complained about Adam's actions caused a moment of silence. She wasn't supposed to know any English.

Both of the Kirchners had a mystical quality unknown to the Clarks. When Holly mentioned it in bed, Adam said, "I noticed the same thing." Fascinated, Holly determined to find out more.

"What is most important to you?" she asked Halle the next morning.

"I love zie outdoors vit God's creation. He talks vit me in garden."

Holly beamed.

"My childhood was spent hiking in the mountains and becoming one with nature. I used to feel energized collecting flowers or jumping over streams. My favorite moments were dreaming under the stars. The constellations intrigue me. I wonder how stars fall into such orderly patterns—accidentally."

Halle tried to answer but was unable. Her limited knowledge of English prevented sharing religious thoughts in a language other than her own. She ran to find a Bible while Hans explained the basics of their beliefs in German.

Their eyes glistened.

Halle Ehrmann Kirchner was apparently from a small town in northeastern Germany; her grandfather was a judge. Obviously, she was intelligent. With ample resources, sharing what she had was important. Mentoring students from the university community was her priority. The Kirchner home was a retreat for young people needing rest or kindness. Tuesdays involved a special fellowship time.

Neighbors appeared often.

One brought a warm strudel; another came with a pot of stew to show her thanks—Danke! Danke!—kissing both cheeks multiple times during brief visits. Halle always said something meaningful because her eyes misted and big smiles emerged.

"Make husband feel most valued guest in home," Halle told Holly in a private conversation. "Watch his eyes; listen his heart. No one more important." It was obvious she did what she suggested.

If Holly's husband was like Hans that would be easy.

Perhaps when Adam matured and valued her more highly, things might become idyllic for both of them.

Saying goodbye, Halle pressed a broche in Holly's hand. "Heirloom from my grandmotter. Gift from my heart to you!" Holly beamed.

Multiple kisses back and forth on checks kept their heads shaking in an emotional farewell.

Hans offered a prayer in German.

Adam and Holly hugged the Kirchners and reluctantly parted.

"What delightful people," Adam said. "I don't remember them being that wonderful."

"Being here brought joy to my heart," Holly whispered through tears. "We agreed to correspond by letter but I hope we meet in person soon."

Adam's friends Frederik and Anne-Lise Nowatny met them at the train station in Salzburg. Finding the Nowatny's home was tricky. They pulled up beside a 500-year-old house with a creek running along one side and a waterfall on the other.

"Our property was bombed during World War II," Frederik said as they took a brief tour. "My family hid in a cave under the waterfall to survive."

"We remodeled recently," Anne-Lise added. "It took five years to complete."

The first floor looked old with one-foot wide rock walls but a modern kitchen gleamed. On the third floor, where guest rooms were located, beautiful oak paneling lined walls and skylights opened the ceiling to the sky. The most incredible bathroom Holly had seen—with six jets on the showerhead and a Jacuzzi—waited to be used.

"Wow!" Adam exclaimed.

"I'm first," Holly said.

Salzburg captivates tourists day and at night so their schedule was packed. To begin Adam and Holly took a cable railway to Hohensalzburg Fortress. Situated on a hilltop, it protected the city during the 11th century and offered a wonderful view.

Touring the DOM Cathedral and St. Peter's Cemetery—when a monk in a flowing black garment passed—Holly stared as Adam snapped a picture. "I wonder why religion is so important to these people," he said.

"I think it's a true struggle for significance," she answered. "People latch on to the spiritual looking for meaning in their lives."

"They're missing so much that they could be doing."

"Like having a female in their arms for starters?"

Adam chuckled.

The Clarks sat on the banks of the Salzach River listening to waltzes by Strauss while drinking whipped-cream coffee. Holly savored it slowly. "I want the taste to stay in my mouth and this music to remain in my mind forever," she said.

Adam smacked his lips and made a mustache with the cream. "How 'bout if I keep this forever?"

Holly laughed, almost choking on her drink.

She stopped to take a picture.

A performance by a native folk group followed with brightly decorated costumes and lively dances. Group members, accompanied by a zither and accordion, sang from their hearts. A little boy yodeling caused the crowd to forget where they were. For a moment, they visualized being on a mountain and watching a goatherd.

Applause brought everyone back to reality.

In the evening, Adam took Holly on a romantic horse drawn carriage ride. Columns of colored lights reflected on water below the dazzling fortress; while the stately buildings illuminated against a darkening cobalt sky appeared grandiose. Golden alleyways with shimmering highlights were radiant. He sang songs from *Sound Of Music* as they clopped around the city.

A little chilly, they snuggled closer.

"I've always wondered about week-long European weddings," Holly said. "Who plans it and what is involved?" She regretted not adding more warmth to her own ceremony. Frederik Nowatny played a video of their daughter's recent wedding. Anne-Lise shared personal details. Holly learned a lot—listening to broken English for hours. Adam fell asleep before they finished.

Returning to Germany from Austria, they stopped in Berchtesgaden known for its talented woodcarvers. A restaurant nearby offered a tasty lunch and apple strudel with whipped cream for dessert.

"Look, Adam, each side of Lake Konigsee—one of the most popular Bavarian Alpine Lakes—has jagged cliffs that rise into mountains and resemble a family silhouetted against the sky."

"Reminds me of us."

Holly read aloud from the travel book as they continued. "Bavaria is spectacular with rugged, snow-capped mountain peaks and deep blue lakes. There are beautiful villages with lovely homes scattered between. Fussen, Germany is on the Austrian border. Neuschwanstein, a palace that served as the model for castles at Disneyland and Disney World, is located there. King Ludwig II—who died before he finished building most of it—inspired the castle."

"Oh please, can we ..."

"We're going to stop," Adam interrupted. "I knew you would enjoy this." To get to the entrance they rode in a carriage pulled by horses.

Holly's aching muscles struggled to climb the stairs. "Maybe we should have skipped the hike yesterday," she said. Inside however, the decor was stunning and castle atmosphere absorbed all her discomfort. Impressive rooms caused her imagination to soar and she barely noticed the walk down.

The drive across Germany was thought provoking.

"I wonder what caused barbarians to pursue victory so passionately," Adam said.

"Germans appear strong yet were weak among their neighbors," she read from the travel guide. "The fighting tribes created a turbulent past—yet each left a rich legacy, in spite of the tyranny they caused." Maybe that insight would help them find satisfaction in the future.

Flying home, they reminisced about their travels.

A young French girl—traveling to Massachusetts to visit her grandmother—sat on the other side of Holly. Nicole lived in Boston before her father died in an airplane accident over the ocean. She sang, "Oh What a Beautiful Morning" most of the trip. Holly practiced speaking French with her.

Someday I want to have a happy child just like her.

Chapter 4

Greed

HUNGRY FOR A NEW thrill Holly rushed under the apple tree ... but not to dream this time. With her palette full of oil paint, a new work of art began to unfold. Streaks of aqua and sapphire at the top, sage and spruce green for trees, mocha strokes for a roof—one detail after another was methodically added. She expected a masterpiece and set out to accomplish her goal.

Birds sang sweetly watching Holly reproduce a scene from the banks of the Seine River. Her exceptional talents separated her from others—set her apart, or so she believed.

Nope! Wrong shade. She changed her mind and mixed the gray again.

Much better.

Memories of the trip were still vivid and she considered different views.

Laughing with the Goyets; peering at the monk dressed in black; Adam saluting a French police officer when a carriage driver sneezed startling his horses, were just a few vivid recollections. The details would fill many picture frames as she recalled sights and sounds of Europe—visualizing the highlights in watercolor and oil.

Another cup of coffee would be nice.

She painted benches, lampposts, pigeons, bookstalls, venders with their carts, an array of tourists … a café on the corner. Bright images of people stood in sharp contrast to a pale city. "Perfect!"

Amused by light patterns on her canvas, she glanced at the sun. The morning began mild but the temperature felt like 90° and was rising. Sweat trickled down her shirt. Her hands perspired.

Holly put away her art supplies and went inside to find something to eat. Packed with food, the refrigerator held nothing appetizing. She fingered several possibilities and settled on a bagel with peanut butter and glass of milk.

Shopping would be more fun.

Squeezing into what seemed the last parking spot, Holly hurried to her favorite store, Athena's Gold. *Great timing!* She forgot they were having a sale and hoped to find bargains. Adam would be home late so there was time to browse. Confusing wants for needs, her stack of purchases grew. Preoccupied, she almost missed her mobile phone ringing.

"Hi Julie … What did the doctor say? … You what? … Congratulations."

Holly looked at clothes while her friend Julie Welch babbled about carrying twins.

Mixed emotions kept her from empathizing. She desired to have a child someday but the responsibilities seemed foreboding. "Six months is a long way off … We can talk about babies later … Bye Julie."

As the afternoon progressed, Holly sauntered into a bookstore to buy magazines but found an irresistible novel, *The Enchanted Meadow*. The landscape on the cover indicated the story took place in Ireland; and the lovers seemed to have the relationship Holly hoped to achieve. After paying for her purchase, the aroma of chocolate lured her into the Sweet Treat Shoppe nearby.

Plunking a quarter into a trivet on the counter, she consumed a sample of the day's specialty before temptation took over.

Lingering was an expensive process as time equaled additional sales. Her taste buds jockeyed for position as she breathed whiffs of the pungent scents. *How can one choose from such delectable delicacies?* Her mouthwatering urges resulted in Holly selecting Italian Meltaways, Triple Chocolate Delights, and Forever Pleasurable Peppermints.

She threw in a box of European truffles at the last minute.

"I'll order Chinese take-out for Adam," she decided in the car. The surprise visit would do them both good. He planned to work late until his meeting at 7:00 pm.

Humming, she drove to the bank.

Adam was getting out of his car with an attractive brunette as she pulled in. They paused in the parking lot when Holly stepped out of her Jeep.

"This is my new assistant, Shanna," Adam said hurriedly. "We needed to run an errand before tonight's presentation."

He fumbled with his tie.

Shanna clutched an envelope tighter. "Nice to meet you," she said, clearing her throat. "I've got lots to do before the meeting. Dinner took longer than we thought." She ran into the bank.

"I didn't expect to see you tonight. What's up?" Adam asked when they were alone. "What a nice surprise."

"My days are lonely with you gone so much," Holly said. "Looks like you have better things to do than spend your time with me, though."

"It's not what you think."

"Your actions speak the truth. Do you need a lie detector test?" she asked. "Maybe I should have asked Shanna more questions before she raced off."

"We were both hungry. End of sin. End of conversation." He retreated into the bank for his meeting as she returned home for solace.

Adam made reservations at *The Mountain View Bed & Breakfast* for the following weekend so they could spend more time together. "There's also a new movie coming out; and an Italian restaurant nearby sounds appealing."

"Are you serious?" Holly said. "I won't know what to do with all the attention. Incidentally, I look forward to intimate talks with you."

She gathered her belongings in an overnight bag. *Anything else I'm gonna need?*

"You look wonderful in that sweater," Adam said as she climbed into the Jeep.

"Perhaps you've forgotten that being around me means a good time ... with a little spice thrown in."

"Voila! Why didn't I think of that sooner," he replied.

They drove off with Adam singing, "You're nobody till somebody loves you ..."

Results were better than expected. The movie was more interesting than Adam's friends described. Dinner was charming, with free aperitifs as an incentive to dine. The owner, Gianni dal Sasso sat with them— sharing reasons for starting this restaurant and moving from Italy. They exchanged contact information.

Accommodations at the Bed & Breakfast were superb with a comfortable king bed and eight fluffy pillows. Linens were pulled back and chocolate truffles rested on two pillows when they returned.

Sitting on the balcony, Adam tried being affectionate but Holly preferred conversing.

"Tell me your opinion about the couple in the movie," she said.

"What do you want to know?"

"Come on Adam, I want to know if you think they'll make it?"

"No idea."

"How can we have a close relationship unless you learn to say more than the obvious?" Holly crossed her legs under her. She pursued trying to reach a deeper level of conversation.

"I have more important things to do tonight," he said stroking her hair. "Make yourself comfortable and snuggle with me."

"You exasperate me," Holly said—yielding to his warm embrace. He sent shivers down her spine as his fingers danced with temptation over meadows of joy, in fields of passion. Her breath quickened and heart pulsated with desire.

Fortunately, the bedroom walls were sound proof.

The hostess provided a delicious *"Breakfast from the Heart"* in a luxurious garden courtyard. Holly savored her husband's attention. Extra time for relaxation benefited Adam as well.

The relationship usually brought joy in spite of difficulties.

Holly took pride in being able to accomplish what others were unable—thankful the stresses married friends experienced did not apply to them. "If only my life continues to be so good," she said to Carissa on the phone.

"It's not my fault I picked a loser," Carissa answered, struggling with an imminent divorce. "I knew before we said our vows that it wouldn't work but he led me on, promising major changes after we got hitched."

They reminisced about Colorado and happier days for Carissa.

"Remember those trips up the river kayaking, picnics in the woods, checking out the latest gossip while shopping, watching ski jumpers ... like Henri Burundi from France," Holly said.

"Ooh la la!" Carissa said. "Do I ever!"

"You need to come visit me," Holly suggested—eager for company.

"As soon as I get this legal stuff straightened out."

With autumn leaves changing color, Holly pursued her love of painting. She set up an easel and brushed a rainbow of hues across the white background as often as she could. Pictures of scenic Europe and panoramic views of the Rockies were most common.

Attempting to paint watercolor using a new technique observed in Switzerland, she studied fervently to perfect her skills. With no major responsibilities, Holly could use time as she pleased. Reading a best seller or gossiping with friends over coffee brought enjoyment—but being able to express creatively, energized her spirit and relieved tension.

"How'd it go today?" Adam asked.

"Not bad," Holly said. "My education never ends."

"Are we going to get money for these pieces someday?"

"Yes ... how much are you willing to pay to keep them?"

Holly looked through picture albums, re-living the dream vacation she and Adam shared in Europe. Deciding on a favorite moment was impossible with various highlights and shared recollections. The cuckoo clock ticking in the foyer was a constant reminder of her unfinished ambition—projects still undone. *Someday when I'm older, I may need a challenge.*

With music playing in the background and the comforts of home readily available, Holly entertained herself. She looked forward to

Adam's occasional call reminding her of his love. Waiting for him to finish at the bank in the evening, she dozed reading books.

Though she enjoyed being around her husband, she understood his reasons for working overtime. Her father arrived home late—and frequently returned to the hospital—so Holly was accustomed to his absence. It made being alone without Adam bearable … sometimes!

"Sweetheart, there's a hot bun in the oven for dinner," Holly said from the bedroom when he arrived home one evening. "Be careful, the bottom might be sticky."

"Are you feeling okay?" Adam asked.

"Now that you mention it—No! I feel like throwing up."

Adam bolted around the corner.

"Can you help me with this?" she said, folding a diaper. She laughed watching his face change—from concern—to confusion—to delight! He rushed to hug her. "Careful daddy, don't squish the little one."

Life was exciting with Thanksgiving and Christmas approaching— and new life springing up in their home. Conversations were upbeat and frequent. Doctor's visits were enjoyable shared experiences.

"I should be done by 7:30 pm," Adam said on the phone one evening. It took longer than expected and Holly was asleep when he unlocked the door. She didn't notice him slipping into bed and stroking her hair in the moonlight.

"Good morning sleeping beauty," he said in the morning. "You were deep into your dreams and kept murmuring about how wonderful life was with me."

"Are you kidding?" she asked, laughing.

Feeling more tired than usual; she cleaned and prepared for the holidays. With chores finished each morning, she baked and decorated. Both sets of parents were coming for dinner on Saturday because Adam had an announcement to make.

"Hi Daddy … Hi Mom … come on in," Holly said.

They kissed and hugged. She received emotional comfort being with her parents. It was nice seeing them again.

The house spilled over with laughter and good will when the Scott Clark family arrived. Accustomed to having family and friends around for special times, both families were more talkative than usual. Adam and Holly were quieter than usual.

After dinner, Adam stood and said, "We're making plans to welcome a newborn into our home this summer. The baby probably will look like one of you … and I know Holly will make a great mother."

"Congratulations!" the future grandparents said in unison.

"How are you feeling, Sweetie?" Susan Armstrong asked.

"I'm eager to hold my first grandchild," Becky Clark said.

"When is the due date?" Dr. Armstrong inquired.

Everyone was overjoyed to hear the news. They couldn't wait to see this precious infant and asked question after question. In his most father-like tone, Adam shared all he knew.

Holly reflected quietly. It would be a big change—one she spent much time contemplating.

Invigorated with enthusiasm from the prospective grandparents, she poured over magazines looking for ideas. Her past glances at friends' nurseries with little interest changed into intense curiosity. Depending on the findings at the next doctor's visit, they would learn whether it was a boy or girl …

Immediately after hearing the report, Adam planned a tree house. He scoured books, scrutinized magazines, and got pamphlets from the hardware store. When blueprints arrived with the ordered kit, he began building.

"Can you hold these pieces of wood?" he asked Holly.

"I assure you, Adam—our child won't be climbing a tree for several years. We need to look for infant furniture instead."

So the future father became involved in physical preparations instead. Hours of painting and decorating followed shopping for supplies. Week by week, the French-blue nursery improved—looking like a comfortable place for a child to reside.

They bought accessories to match.

Surely, their son would enjoy the wide assortment of animals cleverly displayed. Monkeys, elephants, kangaroo, lion, bear, and rabbits took a nap while they waited to meet Jake. With each change, the upcoming birth became more positive.

Warmer days increased her discomfort as the pregnancy progressed. Holly's attention span shortened and nothing kept her busy for long. Starting projects, she gave up and listened to music instead. In the evening, she sat under the apple tree and watched neighbors return home. Soon she would have more in common.

"My friends are planning a baby shower," Holly told Adam.

"What do we need?" he said.

"Lots of things—clothes, toys, infant equipment, bathing supplies, diapers." Her thoughts were seldom on anything else.

She glowed in the middle of supportive friends. Having her mother attend the celebration was a bonus. Finding space to store the gifts was a challenge—but storing things in the right place was Holly's passion.

Happy with the nursery, at ease after parenting classes, and ready to become parents, Adam and Holly waited for the special day. Making jokes about her weight, Adam pretended to pick her up. "Oh my, can someone help me," he called to pretend listeners. Then he shrugged his shoulders.

"I'm saving the stinky diapers for you to change," Holly promised.

The opportunity came sooner than she expected.

Jacob Theodore Clark arrived on Sunday, June 7th weighing barely seven pounds, 20 3/4 inches long, with fuzzy blonde hair. His blue eyes were like his father's. He was a handsome little guy—no doubt smart. His father watched him sleep.

"I can't wait to play football with him," Adam said.

"How soon do you suppose he'll walk?"

Jake's vocal cords changed quickly when he woke and wailed for food. Adam watched in amazement as Holly fed him, uncertain which was more beautiful—his wife or precious son.

The new father brought roses, chocolates, and magazines while Holly was in the hospital. "Having a baby is the best thing that's happened for quite a long time," she told her mother on the phone.

"It's not so bad. Everything's going to be fine," she said to friends.

Susan Armstrong arrived, ready to help, with a big smile on her face. Holly allowed her mother to pamper all of them—rising early to make breakfast, cleaning bathrooms and changing diapers, providing childcare so Holly could get her hair cut, serving tasty dinners, and getting up in the middle of the night to rock little Jake.

Nanna Armstrong made grand parenting appear a joy!

Life with an infant wasn't quite as easy after she left.

In spite of being a proud new father, Adam left for work early and stayed late. Seldom did he see Jake awake—though he heard him cry at night. "Maybe you should sing in that rocker, like your mom did when she was here. I need my sleep."

"I could use your help," Holly said.

"It's not my intention to shirk duties but having a child requires more income. If you want more money, you need to give me some latitude. Perspiration is what counts. Inspiration is just frosting."

She seethed all night long, even while her newborn slept. Words were a waste. Adam didn't get it! She balanced herself close to the edge of the bed; her pillow eventually fell on the floor.

Tired of her new role with its constant demands, Holly grew frustrated. She enjoyed holding and playing with an infant—but calming his tears seemed impossible. Nothing worked. She knew enough to put him in the crib. *Guess I can't avoid the inevitable.*

"Holly, you need to come here. Jake's crying," Adam said.

"What difference does it make?"

"You're his mother."

"There's nothing more I can do right now." She finished reading Condé Nast Traveler and went to find a snack. This was her time to recharge so she could continue giving unselfishly.

Taking Jake out in public made the new mother nervous. Germs were a constant concern because people crowded around cute babies. Strangers touched his face, tried to kiss him, and leaned close—trying to babble in baby talk. Coughing, sneezing, and blowing noses were far too common. She was proud of her adorable bundle but anxious to get him home.

Whenever he felt warm, the apprehensive mother called her father. As a doctor, he knew answers to the questions and helped calm her fears. "Jake is thriving—Hang in there, Cupcake," he assured her.

Determined to succeed, Holly arranged a get-together with young mothers from her community. "Let's meet at Schiffler Park on Tuesday and Thursday mornings," she told everyone she knew with small children.

Gail Mint arrived with six month Heidi, Shelley Breeze with 2 year old Sam and four month Sarah, and Julie Welch with her one-year-old twins Tim and Tina. They congregated around the playground. Holly purchased turkey and provolone sandwiches for the moms. Children snacked on cheerios and juice. The morning included laughter from busy friends while children tried to get their mother's attention.

"You charm the socks off anybody who gets sucked into your orbit," Adam said hearing the details.

"You're gone all the time," she complained. "I'm lonely."

The outings turned out to be enjoyable breaks during months of monotony. She envisioned going on hikes, hunting butterflies, and flying kites somewhere down the road.

Regardless of efforts to mother Jake, it didn't seem enough.

Babies are supposed to laugh and coo during the day, fall asleep after dinner, and sleep through the night. Her child didn't. Bathing him, washing his tiny clothes, folding and putting them away, cleaning up the house, and pacing with a hyperactive baby—there wasn't enough time in one day.

Her spirits were buoyed when Jake's grandparents arrived. Nanna Armstrong cherished spending time with her only grandchild. Grandpa Armstrong loved watching his grandson perform heroic feats attempting to move forward.

"Do you remember when I organized your filing systems and color-coded patients' charts?" Holly asked her father.

"Of course—you were my best worker!"

Having parents close boosted her confidence. It also allowed free time to focus on herself. While they visited, she energetically cleaned closets and reorganized contents before shopping for needed replacements. The world looked brighter.

"Look what Jake can do," Susan said one evening. She sat him on the floor beside the mirror in the foyer. He inched over fascinated and tried to talk to himself.

"Ja ja," he said smiling.

"We have another great communicator in the family," Dr. Armstrong said.

"How soon do kids speak in sentences?" Holly asked.

They all laughed.

A month later, Adam's parents and brothers visited. He took a vacation from the bank that week to stay at home. Holly assumed it was to spend more time with his son but playing basketball, tennis, and going to the river were his eventual choices—leaving her alone with Jake while her husband kayaked through the river and down the rapids with his family.

"We tee-off at six-thirty in the morning so I'm going to bed early," he said leaning over to kiss her goodnight.

"Great … do you have plans for tomorrow afternoon?" Holly asked.

"Not yet," he answered.

She envied his carefree and lighthearted frivolity. Maybe life would improve when Jake was older …

Adam sensed Holly's melancholy and tried to cheer her. He winked across the table. "You bring warmth to my soul, like a full moon on a lake. Let's take a walk."

"It's cold outside," she answered.

"How about using our neighbor Stephanie Anderson to baby-sit on Saturday? She's good with babies."

"Going out to eat requires too much preparation," Holly complained.

"Let's watch a movie."

"I sleep through movies."

Nothing interested her except unfinished tasks. When Adam volunteered to help, Holly left him alone doing one task—but he usually diverted his activity to other things needing attention. Most nights, he slipped into bed late.

Before drifting off, he whispered sweet things in her ears. "You're a good mother." He touched her hair as it glimmered in the moonlight. He pulled her toward him.

She pretended to be asleep.

Somehow, he had no urge to understand her expectations. How could he miss her desires? His focus was thriving at the bank where other people took priority, while she struggled at home.

Holly shopped at Athena's Gold the following Saturday to treat herself. With an assortment of Triple Chocolate Delights from the Sweet Treat Shoppe, she headed back home to a sleeping husband and son.

"I'm organizing a birthday party for Jake and need extra money," she said.

"What are you planning?" he asked,

"I'm not talking anything lavish—just a family affair. Don't worry. I'll keep it simple."

Jake's first birthday on June 7th included a funny clown entertaining sixteen toddlers, an inflatable jungle gym for them to climb on, a delicious yellow cake with edible animals, and wonderful pictures!

Holly worked hard to provide an enjoyable weekend for family members who visited.

"You have a knack for getting things done dramatically—proving your excellent entertaining skills," Ted Armstrong said.

"This was above and beyond," her mother added. "I can't believe you organize such incredible get-togethers. The best part was sitting out in your garden last night and hearing Adam sing."

"We won't miss his next birthday … or any other," Scott and Becky promised.

"I didn't intend for it to get that elaborate," Holly said after they left. Adam reached for her in bed but she pulled away exhausted. If he'd been more helpful, things might be different.

He stroked her hair instead.

As a couple, Holly and Adam had few meaningful moments together. With their attention on someone other than themselves, that was understandable. They were conscientious parents and tried to provide stability for Jake.

She brushed her hair before smoothing lotion on her hands. "My nails look pathetic. I need a manicure."

"I thought you did that on Saturdays?" he said. "Are you talking about a professional job?"

"What do you expect from me, Adam? I'm home alone all day doing boring tasks with no time for myself. Can I be pampered once in a while?"

"I indulge you whenever time permits. How about catering to me for a change?" he asked. "Can't remember the last time you went out of your way to make me feel valued like a real man?"

He put his arm around her shoulder and leaned to kiss his wife.

She jerked out of his reach and huffed off to start laundry. "If you aren't willing to budge, neither am I."

Adam responded with unkind remarks.

If she only knew the truth about how he felt. He muttered under his breath, trying to maintain control. When he reached for his favorite shirt that she was stuffing in a wastebasket, his poise evaporated. "You stinking airhead."

She twirled and slapped his face. "Don't ever call me that again."

He let loose saying things he immediately regretted but the truth needed to come out eventually. She could no longer pretend to be a sweet, cooperative wife when everything she did revolved around herself. "Is it a surprise I bathe myself in work to escape?" he asked.

Holly knelt on the floor sorting laundry while continuing to ignore him.

Shanna understood everything he was going through. He couldn't wait until Monday.

Sure enough, the facts made Holly feel guilty and her demeanor changed within an hour. She tried to sit on his lap to apologize … sort of. "I'll try to pay more attention to you," she said.

"You'll need to prove it."

When they retreated to the bedroom, she crawled on the bed arching her back and pawed his body like an animal in heat, changing into a lioness on the prowl. He pushed her away playfully, enticing her with disinterest—but she pursued with a fierceness he'd never seen.

"I think you enjoy fighting," he said, relaxing—resigned to the inevitable.

"Maybe you like being dominated by someone superior, until you're finally under subjection," she said.

He responded like a normal red-blooded male being challenged and took control of what he mastered on their wedding night.

"Oooohh, Adam," was all she could say.

❦

Jake was a happy toddler, receptive to new activities and enjoyable around most people. Playing with friends seemed natural. His favorite toys were cars that were always in motion, or beating on a pan. "Side ... side," he would say at the door.

"Just a minute Jake, I need more coffee."

Holly was relieved. She also wanted to be outside in the sunshine. She spent a significant amount of time with her son since he was the only one available most of the time. He was the apple of her eye.

"Oh, look at the baby bird ... he fell out of his nest," she said gently, kneeling on the ground. "Don't touch!—his mother will take care of him." Together they peered at the tiny creature.

"We need a swing set and sandbox," she told Adam when he joined them. "He's active—like his father."

"We'll get one on Saturday. I knew we should have finished that tree house."

Holly laughed.

Money paid for Barnum and Bailey Circus tickets was definitely worth it. Jake learned to jump, beg like a dog, and turn summersaults like a circus performer. He entertained them for hours. They couldn't stop laughing—similar to watching the Goyet's grandson Pierre in France.

"His personality requires action and an audience," Nanna Armstrong said. "We'll be there next week to help."

Full of energy and eager to learn, Jake thrived. He loved poking puzzle pieces through the fence to see if the neighbor girl would throw them back over. Lisa watched him frolic in the yard chasing bubbles but when he tried to kiss her, she ran back into her house.

Holly used his naptime for personal creative pursuits. Decorating stationery for letters to Granny, perfecting her calligraphy, and making handcrafted presents for friends whittled the hours. Preoccupied with one particular task, she hung tiny clothes on a line across the kitchen.

Adam can take them down when he gets home.

Baby sister, Abigail Susan Clark, was born on April 16ᵗʰ weighing 6 pounds 14 ounces and was 20 inches long. A wispy haired towhead, her bright blue eyes matched her daddy's.

"Isn't Abby beautiful?" Holly said, holding her the first time. She cradled the sleeping infant, lightly stroking her face. The newborn freshness smelled better than daisies. "Do you want to hold her," she asked.

Adam was like a strong tower, protective but gentle. He kissed and rocked his daughter as he paced the room. Glancing out the window, he began to sing. "Hey, hey, hey snowflake … my pretty little snowflake …"

"Beautiful serenade," Holly said when he finished. "I bet she's going to like spending time with you."

"A famous composer wrote those words years ago, probably while dreaming about having a beautiful female in his arms. And yes, I intend to spend lots of time with my little princess. Picture her taking horsy rides on my shoulders, chasing butterflies with a net, and twirling around a dance floor with her tippy toes on my shoes."

Watching her interaction with big brother Jake was more fun.

He quickly developed leadership skills. Eager for her to stand and play, he said, "Get up baby." Putting part of his sandwich in her mouth, Holly raced over. He also tried to share juice.

One day Holly found him picking her up—so she could ride in his wagon. He couldn't understand his sister's reluctance to join in his energetic pursuits.

"No, Jake! Abby is too small to do that."

"When will she be bigger?" he asked, eager to share his life with a playmate.

Adam and Holly's second child didn't have as pleasant disposition as her brother. She fussed more and was difficult to please. Frequent ear infections woke her up and she cried many nights. Adam pulled a pillow over his ear and slept soundly.

Holly paced back and forth holding Abby.

Often she fell asleep in the rocking chair. At her wits end, she did anything to find relief—soothing lullabies for the nighttime, walks with a stroller during the day, Holly was determined to succeed in her role as mother.

Jake was cooperative, even protective of his sister. He entertained her, cajoled her, and offered special courtesies in an attempt to make her happy. Trying to make mommy and sister laugh became his aim.

"Look Abby," he said. "Clap your hands. One, two, free … can you count with me?"

His sister glanced at him inquisitively.

"Watch Benji dance!—Here's my monkey—or Jumbo needs a kiss," all quieted her for a while. Imitating Mommy, he would read *The Three Bears* or his favorite book, *Corduroy*.

Weekends with Adam at home were better. He tried to make life tolerable and less stressful—offering hugs, laughter, and exercise. His spirit of adventure was contagious, tempting Holly and the children to join in the fun.

"We need a leader for our marching band—I have a flute, horn, and drum," Adam said. He held out a pan, ruler, and banana. "Mommy can be the spectator."

"Who wants to go to the zoo with me?" he asked when they finished.

"Have you ever seen the ocean? One of these days we'll visit Gram and Gramp in California." Adam promised in the car.

Remodeling the exterior of their house instead of going on vacation, Adam paid special attention to the roof, windows, and trim. "Why not fix it exactly the way you like, as long as you have to paint anyway?"

"Not every husband is as handy as mine," Holly said admiring his work.

"Most people are lazy," Adam said, climbing the ladder with agile dexterity. He chiseled an intricate design in the cupola, matching the pattern around the soffits. Posing as a Greek Olympian when his wife brought a tall glass of lemonade, he asked, "Do I look like a responsible member of our community?"

Holly threw kisses and promised to appreciate him more in the coming years. "Changing things around here every once in a while will keep us from getting bored," she added.

He worked tediously—committed to hours of renovating and maintaining an already well kept home. The time-honored tradition of perfection fit right in. Adam believed doing things well, commanded respect. "It's important to preserve your home territory," he said. "Someday I'll be the bank president."

"So you need to paint that better," Holly said.

"Better? How could you possibly say that?"

"I'm joking … come on. Let's take a break."

"Work is good. Play must be earned," Adam whispered.

Holly wrinkled her nose.

Adam and Holly convinced themselves the house should look nice for neighbors. Not ready to shirk their duty, they continued scraping, sanding, trimming, and painting. Their efforts resulted in success but Holly made the experience worthwhile in her zany, high-spirited way.

"You're a genius, sweetheart. That ecru trim with tan makes our house stand out. It looks better than any other house on the street," she said as they cleaned up.

"Of course, what did you expect?" Adam winked.

Holly knew she should be satisfied but lack of contentment increased instead. She was distressed to discover that what she envisioned as a child wasn't possible. If it was attainable—it wasn't fulfilling.

Her idealistic daydreams became a source of discouragement. Living in a splendid home, surrounded by a well-manicured yard—with a handsome husband and two adorable children didn't give Holly the emotional wholeness she assumed would follow. "Something is missing!" she whispered when no one could hear.

What is it and how soon will I find it?

She was certain with a few changes her goals could be reached. The fragrance of the apple tree aroused her senses even more.

Chapter 5
Boredom

A RINGING TELEPHONE PIERCED the air as Holly raced to answer—bored with her daily routine. Chatting with someone would be a nice break. Toilets could wait and cookies would satisfy fussy children for a while. Life was so tedious.

"Hello … Oh, Hi Granny … It's nice to hear your voice. I miss you so much." Grandma Armstrong had a calming effect—or energized, depending on her needs. Holly pictured the snowy-haired pixie sitting on a bench near her magnificent garden with a bucket of freshly picked veggies and big smile on her face.

"How's my precious granddaughter?" Granny asked.

"Eager for some fun," Holly said.

"I wish you could see my garden. The onions and lettuce are plentiful, cucumbers are plump, and beanpoles are loaded with produce. A raccoon carried one of my tomatoes to the corner of the fence while I watched from my porch steps. And I chase frisky rabbits away from the carrots hourly," Granny said laughing.

"Sounds like a busy summer."

Holly's thoughts drifted back to her childhood in Colorado when days were filled with activities that broadened, stretched, and enriched her mind. Learning new things made her feel happy. Figuring things out—interesting stuff that intrigued—gave a feeling of accomplishment. Outdoor adventures were regular occurrences.

"What are you up to these days, Sweet Pea?"

"Not much, Granny. I'm busy doing nothing."

"I remember when NOTHING was boring for you," Granny reminded her. "You always found reading a dictionary interesting."

Holly wiped a tear from her eye. "I need to visit you, Granny."

"Come whenever you can manage to get away. Your children will be a joy to see again."

"I'll talk to Adam about driving up to Colorado. It's been six months since I tasted your berry pies and hiked through the countryside."

"I hope it works out. Bye, sweetie. I love you."

After hanging up, Holly quietly reflected. Gone were fun experiences when the world stood still while she made wonderful discoveries.

Sometimes Holly ran as fast as she could across the grass, hoping the wind would lift her colorful kite so it could soar into the azure sky. With little level ground around the mountains, that feat required endurance and determination. Successful, she would sit back and watch it make lazy patterns below the clouds as she dreamed what lay beyond the rugged horizon.

How a butterfly develops its wings, forcing its way out of a cocoon, fascinated her one summer. She and Granny spent a week keeping track of the progress.

"I'm bored to death," Holly said to Adam that evening. "People were designed to stretch themselves and learn more."

"Okay. Why don't you figure out how to flip that switch on from over here?" he joked. He busied himself with paperwork that needed attention.

"Do you know why sand is white, pink, or black on different beaches? Or why seashells are unique shapes and what animal lives in each one?" she asked.

"Too many questions—too much detail for me," Adam said. "Why do you care?"

"I wish you'd seen my kitten Topaz chasing a ball of string around in circles until he became dizzy. It was hilarious watching him expend energy—in such a frivolous way."

"So you want a cat?"

"If you'd just listen!" She continued, "You never express what's going on deep down in your head. Surely you're curious about something other than your career."

"In my head … hummmm. Sounds like psychology to me."

"Are you afraid I'm smarter than you?"

"Apparently that's the way it is."

Adam stood and stretched. He reached to touch the ceiling three times, missing every one—then headed out of the room before she could say more.

"So you don't want to hear about me hiking up Blind Man's Bluff with my father and how it brought a feeling of personal success when I reached the top? The panoramic view looking over the mountainside was spectacular. The majesty of nature combined with intricate patterns and colors of the landscape all merged to give me a feeling of euphoria."

"Wow! Can we go to bed now?"

"I thought you'd be impressed."

Holly lay in bed thinking.

She knew her parents compensated because she was their only child. They provided outlets for her to embrace life whole-heartedly and discover its most interesting facets. The crystal hanging in her bedroom was a reminder of the intriguing *unknown*.

She overheard more than one conversation about her abilities. "Holly needs opportunities to experiment—find out how things work," her mother told her father.

"I know what you mean," he said. "She asks questions and demands to know answers. We need to nurture her thirst for knowledge."

As a teenager, Dr. Armstrong requested her help in his medical office greeting clients, answering phones, and doing extra work that needed catching up. "Although she's young, her skills exceed most of the staff in my office," he told friends. "As much as she relishes fun, Holly doesn't evade work," he announced at a picnic for employees.

"I appreciate her assistance with gardening chores," Susan said.

Holly loved watering and caring for various plants as they grew but her favorite task was gathering the assorted vegetables and flowers each time they entertained. The fragrances and bright colors came alive on the table as she deftly arranged them in a most appealing show of nature's finest.

Now a stay-at-home-mom, she repeated uninteresting jobs that required no brains, little imagination, and continual drudgery. Even baking was a chore—with more time spent cleaning than creating—unless friends came over to appreciate her efforts. Restlessness began to emerge and Holly felt it intensely.

"How are things going?" Carissa asked on the phone.

"Boring … even with two kids."

"I always assumed you'd do interesting things your whole life."

"So did I. Playing baseball for a cheering crowd provides a thrill for Adam. Diving off a 10 meter board, making a hole-in-one golfing, and acing tennis balls across the court are things he enjoys doing," Holly said. "My personal strengths are quite different but I'm not able to use them right now."

"Guess I'm fortunate to have my freedom," Carissa said. "However that might not last long. I hooked up with the cutest guy last month who spends his evenings with me."

Sneaking away from the radio station with a new beau to hunt for antiques, invigorating weekend trips together, and secluded fishing jaunts that fully satisfied their appetites with much more than trout sounded appealing to Holly.

"I'm jealous. If Adam doesn't start paying more attention maybe I need to look around for greener pastures."

"You'll never guess what Granny sent … *When Did Wild Poodles Roam the Earth?* by David Feldman," she said to Adam on the phone. "Do you know why babies blink less often than adults?"

"I'll be home around seven. We can talk about it then."

After arriving home, he explained his boss was in his office when she called. "You can't ask me silly questions when I'm at the bank. Bottom line is—I have business to finish."

"Well I work too, but it's very boring."

"I'm getting sick of your dull existence. The problem is you, Holly. You need to grow up and get a life. Life is sweet for everybody else. Find something significant to do and learn to be content. The answer isn't in a book." He stormed out after burying her under an avalanche of hostile words.

She glanced at a new bestseller resting on the table. Through books, Holly satisfied her curiosity—gained insight into complex issues. Learning was a process and she intended to continue. Adam believed education was a tool towards his career. "Once you finish a goal, move on."

He was wrong!

Newscasts about a local drought crisis affecting the entire southwest caught her attention. Somebody needed to come up with a workable plan. Holly determined to make a difference.

She went to the bookshelf and looked through encyclopedias. She researched aquifer levels and water restrictions. Aware of environmental issues and wildlife standards, her concern for flowers and animals flourished.

"Are you going to another City Council meeting?" Adam asked. "This project supersedes your attention for Jake and Abby."

"The kids enjoy staying with a sitter," she answered.

"So what does water conservation have to do with our family?"

"Are you questioning my concern for our children?" she asked. "Where did that idea come from?"

"You need to open your eyes, as well as your ears. There's a lot you appear to be missing." He cranked the volume of his basketball game louder staring straight forward, ignoring her voice rising.

She stepped closer, leaning in his face.

"If I had realized what a jerk you really are, I would have left years ago." Adding choice words, she refused to back away. Her brown eyes blazed. She picked up the remote and threw it at the wall.

"You're a spoiled brat!" he insisted. "Go ahead and try to survive on your own. The world doesn't revolve around you. You're unimportant in the scheme of things. No one wants to be around you. Go hug a tree. Smell the daisies. Play fishy, fishy, in the brook and watch the water splash." He stopped to take a breath.

Protecting her goals would never stop. There was too much at stake. She thought a minute before brushing her hair back. Her instincts took over. Buried under his rubble of intimidating words, she stormed out.

Trying to add quality to their days, she decided to take the kids on educational outings. "The zoo recently remodeled adding exotic animal exhibits," the receptionist said. Holly's legs ached when they climbed back in the Jeep after an eventful day. They returned home laughing and happy.

"We saw monkeys eating bananas," Abby reported to her father.

"I ran from hungry alligators," Jake said.

"… and squealed as tigers wrestled each other." Holly laughed, remembering his hysterics.

"Wish I had gone," Adam said, listening more intently than usual.

"Feeding dolphins and watching panda cubs climb trees were highlights for them," Holly added.

Energized, she gathered additional information about classes at the Art Center, demonstrations at the Science Center, and performances at the Theater-in-the-Round.

Holly was more enthusiastic than her children were.

The calendar filled up quickly.

Five weeks of *Muffins, Muppets, and Mother Goose* proved to be Jake's favorite. "Please Mommy, can we do it again. It's so fun!" he said. "Abby likes it too." Making up plays and interacting brought out his heightened love of performing. He begged to continue in the *Peanut Gallery* with stories, songs, and dance.

Scheduling swimming lessons at the Aquatic Center; with fitness activities at the Gymnastic Corner thrilled Adam most. "I wholeheartedly believe in physical exercise," he said. "Perhaps the kids will be talented in sports someday like me."

"Good job, Holly!" he said.

"No one ever complimented me for my mothering skills before," she said quietly.

"Why don't you purchase a membership for yourself at the Athletic Club," he suggested. "We could spend more time together."

She agreed.

Taking time to condition her body might improve her spirit as well.

They exercised as a pair for a short time—but separated before long. Different conditioning agendas took priority. Having Adam baby-sit while she worked out proved even more beneficial.

Bronzed muscles rippling from the trainer's t-shirt motivated her to ask questions. When Max leaned closer to show different options, her heart beat faster. On occasion, he touched her body as she transitioned from one position to the next. Goose bumps erupted and endorphins overwhelmed. She hoped he would take more liberties without her consent. He obliged.

He stayed beside Holly to guide her progress and answer concerns, sensing what she needed; he offered verbal, tactile, and emotional incentives. The bond strengthened with each visit.

She coaxed him on with arousal and receptivity.

Hellos started to include affectionate greetings—increasingly overt, depending on the amount of scrutiny around them. Others were usually preoccupied with their own interests.

Occasional visits to his office for strategic planning proved to be the best place to confide. His eyes focused on her intensely. "My husband is a workaholic; his assistant provides more than an emotional connection," she said. "His lack of attention when he comes home late proves it's true; but until I find my own place of stability, I'm unable to confront him and move on."

Max did what he could to lessen her stress.

"Do you want to stop by my condo for a few minutes before you head home?" he whispered, eager to take their relationship a step deeper. "I have plans you'll enjoy." He nibbled her ear until she giggled.

"Not right now—but who knows what the future might hold."

He brushed her chest with his forearm while adjusting weights; reaching past her thigh, he grasped a lever below the bench. "What can it hurt when you're so unhappy? We might discover utopia."

Holly's face flushed. He tried other ideas but she stopped short of abandoning her marital vows.

"You're a big tease," Max repeated.

Before the holidays, her figure was shapely again.

Fit and looking great, Holly turned her attention to a fresh wardrobe. It felt good to try trendy outfits on as she twirled in front of mirrors.

She blushed at the compliments but glowed inside when friends were envious.

"Adam is gonna love that red dress!" Gail Mint drawled.

"You could model for us," a clerk at Athena's Gold said. "You look incredible!"

She had devoted herself to babies for four years so it felt good to feel extraordinary again.

The bank Christmas Party offered a special opportunity to come alongside her husband. With his new position, Holly provided glamor and poise—exuding the charm she was known for. Newfound confidence allowed her to shine.

During the evening, she spotted Adam in his office with Shanna. Their private conversation ended abruptly when Holly approached. "We were just going over plans for Monday morning," he said defensively.

"Oh, don't let me stop you."

She could tell they did not intend to continue with her around. It was only a matter of time!

Accustomed to hospitality in her childhood home, Holly expected to continue the tradition after she married. Having children interrupted the plan temporarily. Now she was ready to pursue entertaining with gusto.

Much to her dismay, inviting others to their home occurred only when Adam could squeeze it into his hectic schedule. He spent long hours establishing his career—"zeroing in on what is important and disregarding the rest," he said. Often he was too tired to socialize.

"Sorry, Holly. I've got reports to finish."

"What about me?"

"I'm on the cutting edge of the banking industry. People look to me for answers."

"Well, books were my closest friends when I was a child. I'm the one with facts at my fingertips," she said.

"Then get a good book and entertain yourself."

Holly slammed the bedroom door. Fortunately, she had a romance novel and Ghirardelli to help get in a better mood. She twisted her ring as she read. Characters leapt off pages as she quickly turned them, as fast as her mind could grasp the words. The plot thickened with amazing detail. Eager to survive an antagonizing delay waiting for the climax, she flipped to the back. "Aahhhhh!!! They tricked her."

She dropped the book on the floor.

Adam slipped in bed beside her before midnight. She pretended to be asleep. When he leaned over to kiss her, she bristled and scooted closer to the edge.

"So what was your problem last night?" he asked in the morning.

"You get your rewards from Shanna. What more do you want from me?"

"I don't know what you're talking about," he said.

"You can fool others, but you can't fool me. The way you dress for work isn't to please the men. The cologne is a giveaway; so is your big smile when you come home late with your shirt crumpled." The more Holly thought, the more animated she got. "I see the way you look at her; I'm well aware you're having an affair, Adam."

"That's not true."

"Prove me wrong. I've heard Shanna admit to late lunches with you, overheard deeply personal conversations, and a rendezvous after hours was never denied."

"You're mistaken, Holly. I admit to spending time away from the office with my assistant but we have never had physical contact. Developing an emotional bond with another female could possibly be inappropriate but I guarantee there is no affair going on. In the busyness of my days, food occasionally becomes a necessity. I won't eat with Shanna again if that's the problem."

She shrugged, not fully believing his interests were focused entirely on remaining faithful. It didn't matter at the moment. Remodeling their home was her new focus.

Adam fiddled in the garage with a bicycle tire. "In your arms ... I can still feel the way you ... and there ain't no way ... I'm letting you go now... 'Cause I'm keeping you forever and for always ...," he sang.

She shrugged pouring herself another cup of coffee.

"Our house needs some changes," Holly said. "Turquoise and lime used to invigorate me but now look out of place—and the furniture is either inappropriate for children or simply needs to be updated. What do you think?"

Adam nodded as he watched a tennis match.

"Are you paying attention?"

She decided to call someone who cared.

"Your personal identity is expressed through your home," she told Carissa on the phone. "It must be warm and comfortable, yet vibrant—then you invite others in to appreciate your tastes and talents." She dreamed of creative occasions for inviting family and friends over.

"What do you have in mind?" Carissa asked.

"I don't know but the first impression is vital."

"I can't wait to see the finished product," Carissa said.

Holly struggled to conceptualize what she desired. Piles of magazines on home decorating and remodeling were devoured—cutting, pasting, and highlighting—looking for ideas. Scrutinizing the latest styles and fads, she made notes and lists.

Believing herself a Plain Jane, Holly sought to prove she was classy.

She had a hard time narrowing choices to one style, color scheme, and plan. The myriad of colors and décor she craved eventually settled into a manageable ensemble to embellish their house. "Ooohs and aaahs" eventually heard would make her efforts seem worth the time spent.

Holly's love of nature greeted visitors in the foyer—with colorful wildflowers and shimmering gold in the elegant living room. Guests were transported into the exotic world of an African safari in the family room. The tropical retreat with palm trees, ivory, and wild animals called to put your feet up and reach for a book about faraway places. A hand-painted bombé chest, realistic lion, and miniature elephant urged people to touch them.

"Wow! I knew it would look great," Carissa said.

Solid oak furniture filled the rooms. A staircase beckoned to the second floor where lovelier rooms awaited fortunate friends and guests. "Looks like we spent a fortune, doesn't it?" Holly said.

"I'm sure you did," Carissa answered.

Out of the blue, Adam scheduled flying lessons. Fascinated with airplanes since childhood, he arranged training after meeting a flight instructor at a party.

"What is this about?" Holly asked.

"Play is a reward for hard work. My boss encouraged me to take time off and pursue my hobbies," Adam said. "Because I trek along so tirelessly—were his exact words."

"What a nice compliment!"

"Accomplishing tasks at the bank by two o'clock, I can devote full attention to aviation maneuvers in the afternoon," he said. "Time on weekends will be like frosting on the cake."

With careful attention to details, Adam took to the air like a bird. In a matter of weeks, he talked about a solo flight and getting his license. "With my eagle eye, I'm quickly picking up elements of flying. My instructor Doug Johnson wants me to get comfortable with take offs and landings before he solos me—maybe on Saturday. I need to wear old shirts until then."

At night, he flew toy planes with Jake and studied flight plans until bedtime. Using an E-6B computer was exciting.

"I can't believe you're attempting this," Holly said. "Is your life insurance in order?"

"You'll be proud of me someday, I promise."

With a ripped shirt, a 100 on his written test, and a little card certifying he could proceed, Adam rushed home elated. "Taking off gives a thrill like none other."

By summer, he was a member of a flying club. "When are you going to come with me?" he asked Holly.

"I don't know, Adam."

"Remember when we watched water cascading down the lush green mountainside over the falls? This is more fun!" he said.

Normally eager for another thrill, Holly was uneasy during her first plane ride in the Cessna 172. Adam rattled numbers to the tower as he touched controls. Pointing out the scenic beauty below, once he reached a safe altitude, the picturesque countryside intrigued for a while. Seeing the landscape from above with its foliage and varied textures was different than she expected.

She was thankful for his pursuit of excellence in everything he attempted, especially during the landing. "Aaahh, terra firma," she said stepping out.

"You could be praising me for a smooth landing."

"We're still alive. That's what counts," she said.

Adam promised a night flight over the city the next weekend. She reluctantly agreed—but fear of flying kept her enjoyment level low.

Envious of the excitement in her husband's life, Holly spent extra time with girlfriends. As a busy mother, she felt the need for personal refreshment. Monthly "Girls Night Out" events became a regular occurrence—participating in an assortment of activities without husbands or children.

"What do you do?" Adam asked.

"Eat at restaurants, attend theater and ballet, listen to concerts, and work on crafts—whatever catches our imagination. We don't have many chances to bond anymore so this brings us closer."

The friendly females enjoyed carefree camaraderie so much Holly planned a weekend getaway at a hotel. Swimming, eating pizza, watching movies, a pillow fight, and painting fingernails made them feel like teenagers again. They gossiped and complained long into the night.

"We can have a pillow fight here," Adam said after hearing about the fun.

"If you give me $50 to spend at Treasure Island tomorrow."

"You already have enough books," he answered.

Holly believed her friends shared similar interests and lifestyles; but as months passed, phone calls required she listen sympathetically to a variety of complaints she had little interest in hearing. Demands to offer encouragement, provide reciprocal childcare, and give emergency assistance required more than she was willing to give.

Peggy eventually moved out of town, Karen got a divorce, and Liz left her husband for another man.

Troubled by the discontent her friends faced, Holly sought solace for her own unhappiness. She felt alone—incomplete as a person and yet unable to find an answer. Maybe Adam still loved her but she didn't feel like the center of his life anymore. An elusive emptiness pervaded her spirit. Something was missing.

A call from Granny changed Holly's mood.

Her 75th birthday celebration couldn't be missed. "I haven't seen my precious granddaughter for over a year. Will you come?" Granny asked.

Holly meant to take Jake and Abby on previous occasions but colds or activities prevented visits to Colorado. Without checking a calendar, she accepted.

"Sure thing!"

In her haste, she forgot a special *fifties* concert with friends—but getting together with Granny far outweighed anything else. Fresh mountain air would be good for her spirit.

"That's a great idea," Adam said when he heard. "I have an important seminar in Phoenix or I would go, too. Enjoy the party!"

Great-Granny laughed with Jake and Abby mesmerized by her side, while telling intriguing stories about her past. Her incredible memory and lively imagination conjured up interesting details.

They loved seeing her eyes twinkle and hearing her chuckle.

Remembering when toddler Holly climbed on the counter to eat fresh cookies they just baked, Granny grinned. "She was supposed to be taking a nap when I found her—with frosting all over her face."

"Say it again, Gigi," Abby begged over and over.

Granny played games with her great grandchildren and proved she could still jump rope. Twirling it around her agile body, she jumped without missing. Holly watched in amazement! She had forgotten the special songs Granny sang when she jumped rope. "Handy spandy, sugary candy, French almond rock. Bread and butter for your supper are all your mothers got." *It was such fun being around her grandmother.*

"Do the Little Bear song again," Holly begged.

Granny agreed.

When Jake and Abby saw the birthday cake glowing with candles, their eyes opened wider. "Wow! It's like the 4th of July!" Jake said. The candles shot off sparks as they got hotter and hotter—and Great-Granny blew them all out.

"Gigi did it!" Abby shrieked.

Holly delighted watching her offspring with their childish enthusiasm—enjoying this old woman who gave so much joy. Their innocence reminded her of early years. What was it about Granny that appealed to the heart?

When they returned home, Adam was amused with Gigi's stories. He listened as Jake and Abby chatted about *Mommy being a little girl,* a long time ago.

"Mommy ate the cookies," Abby added.

Holly smiled. Would she be that kind of an interesting person when she got older? She determined to buy a jump rope. *I'll try harder to find amusement for my children—and myself.*

A family down the street needed homes for a litter of purring yellow kittens. Holly agreed to adopt one and selected the cutest—with Abby's help. "I like this one, Mommy. She's friendly."

The Clarks' backyard provided the perfect kingdom for Butterscotch. Scampering across soft grass, she frolicked. Jumping to catch a butterfly was her favorite pursuit.

Jake and Abby chased her.

She peered out the kitchen window, waiting for Holly to finish dishes. Birds were singing as they flitted from tree to bushes filled with berries. The kitten couldn't wait to get outside. Impatient, she paced at the door. Purring, she rubbed Holly's leg. Finally, the door opened and Butterscotch darted out.

Holly spotted a squirrel scurrying to a tree, carrying a nut. Butter saw the same thing. A race ensued with the squirrel running back to his original shelter under a bush. *Just like my life,* Holly reflected. "I go back and forth doing daily tasks and accomplish nothing. The squirrel must feel as frustrated as I do."

"Let's draw pictures on the sidewalk," Holly said handing her children pieces of colored chalk.

"People are flying in my airplane," Jake said. Eight heads were sticking out of a rectangle.

"My girl is dancing," Abby said. "Can you help me Mommy?"

Drawing animals made Holly's heart joyful but drawing people caused her to frown. She decided the *people* had no personality. Adding houses, sun or moon, flowers and trees, and animals made the stick figures look better.

After buying plastic Easter eggs to hide, Holly found baskets and called her children to the yard. "Are you ready to hunt for surprises? Look around for bits of color I've hidden."

Off they ran.

Jake spied an orange egg in the far corner. Putting it in his basket, he noticed Lisa Stewart and decided to throw it over the fence.

Abby found a purple one … then pink, yellow, and green eggs by the house. She sat on the patio eating candies inside.

"I'm a secret agent," Jake told his sister. He explored the garden for more missing eggs. "Look at this, Abby!" he shouted.

Stooping to look closer, Abby observed a broken blue egg under the tree. She tried to pick it up but the shell crumbled in her fingers and a baby bird fell out. Sobbing, she leaned on the dirt in despair.

Holly went to her rescue. "When things die, they go back into the ground and turn into dust," she explained.

"No they don't!" Abby shouted.

Questions about life and death ended the festivities abruptly and Abby ran in the house sullen—leaving her basket of candy under the tree.

"Can we make cookies?" Abby asked later that afternoon.

Making cookies together was a new activity. They measured flour, broke eggs, mixed ingredients, and talked about Gigi. Abby giggled as they worked. She had begged for this opportunity since hearing Great-Granny's stories.

Decorating them, Holly glanced at the clock. "Oops! I'm running out of time. I need to pick Jake up at Joey's." She scooted Abby out of the way so she could embellish the cookies properly.

"They don't have to be perfect, Mom!" Abby said.

However for Holly—they did. She measured success by reaching her standard of excellence. Lacking contentment, her illusive dreams were becoming tedious like chores.

Chapter 6
Offer to Help

BASKING IN THE SATISFACTION of orchestrating a fabulous Hawaiian Luau—complete with live music and entertainment—Holly cleared the last platter off the counter. The magnificent decorations, delicious food, and fantastic atmosphere delighted each guest. Adam was talkative and an observant host while she used her exquisite charms to entertain.

With over forty people in attendance, a quantity of appetizers and main course entrées accompanied the pig Adam had roasted on a spit. Holly splurged on food making scalloped pineapple, au gratin potatoes, a tropical fruit medley, shredded crab salad, élégante rice, barbequed ribs, smoked salmon, assorted rolls, and a significant quantity of delicious deserts—consequently they would eat leftovers for days.

"Next time, I'll talk to a caterer," she promised herself.

"You look ravishing!" Adam said early in the evening. Holly's honey blonde hair was pulled back with a hibiscus flower at her temple. She wore a grass skirt with bright pink hand-smocked tank top and the daintiest sandals he had ever seen.

"Darling, you look great yourself!" she said, smiling with a Cheshire cat grin.

He wore a white shirt with rainbow flowers that she insisted he wear. He scurried past with an assortment of colorful leis bought for the guests.

Decorations of exotic fish and tropical flowers were scattered around groups of multi-colored candles. Coconut lights, strung over French doors, brightened the terrace. Accent lighting around the bushes and house set the entire backyard off—as a showplace. Mounting a spotlight to each corner of the patio, Adam directed light to the stage where musicians and hula dancers performed.

Tony Pena, a co-worker of Adam's who sang with a small band, provided live music. "Welcome … to Paradise," Tony said with a big grin. The guitar started playing. "Pearly shells from the ocean … shining in the sun … covering the shore …"

They crooned Hawaiian love songs with an electric guitar and bongo, and twirled flaming torches. Dancers were college students just home from Hawaii, eager to show off new costumes and hula moves.

"I wanna go back to my little grass shack …" Tony continued.

Guests laughed and talked, in between Hawaiian games and a hula-hoop contest. Holly watched Adam act like a teenager. He grinned.

A turquoise, amethyst, and orchid sunset filled the sky as they relaxed. Iridescent white clouds turned amber and rose, suddenly flooding the horizon with coral, crimson, and tangerine. Holly caught a glimpse as she carried a tray outside, stumbling on the step. It astounded her. Where did this brilliant color originate?

"Dreams come true in Blue Hawaii … and with all this loveliness … there should be love … dreams come true … and mine can, too … this magic night of nights with you." The band threw kisses and put instruments away.

Stars twinkled in a darkened robe of space.

"Ladies and gentlemen—here is your hostess, the one and the only Holly Clark," Adam announced as friends gathered in the foyer to leave. Walking down the stairs, she paused briefly in the middle. She blushed as the guests watched. Then they clapped.

"What an evening to remember," Adam's boss Tom Mitchell said as he left.

"Thanks for some great ideas," Shelley Breeze added.

As the Clarks shut the door and began cleanup, both were pleased.

Brushing her teeth before getting in bed, Holly heard singing from the bedroom. "For every grain of sand upon the beach, I've got a kiss for you—and more leftover for each star, that twinkles in the blue."

Candles flickered on the dresser.

Adam kissed her tenderly, pulling her body closer than she could remember. His hands moved down her torso in methodical rhythm as he sang about love. He paused momentarily—removing her gown—before sweeping Holly off her feet and pulling her down on the bed beside him. His fingers playfully cajoled in a dance of passion as intensity heightened.

"I've forgotten how delightful you are," he said. Testosterone skyrocketed as feelings of love emerged from the former all-star athlete. His actions and embrace reached new heights of attentiveness.

She sighed as joy turned to ecstasy. How could an evening get any better? "Oooohh, Adam."

Lounging on the flower-strewn patio the next morning, Holly sipped Hazelnut coffee—deep in thought. Dressed in a sea green linen tunic that nestled her physique with playfulness, sandals thrown to the side of the chaise, she contemplated the previous evening.

"The party was impressive, wasn't it?" she asked.

Accumulating receipts, Adam grimaced as he tallied the bill. "Our joy of giving to others needs to stop." He gasped to find the total so high, deliberating on the next step to take.

"How much do you think the luau cost?" he said.

"No idea."

"Then I suggest we begin living within a budget."

"What do you mean?" she asked.

"Our finances are being drained. I can no longer support unlimited spending."

"I don't want to know what you're talking about," she said, reaching for her sandals.

"This problem needs immediate action—or we'll require emergency intervention soon."

"Don't be so dramatic, Adam." She leaned across to grab the paper he scribbled on to see for herself.

"Last year we brought in over $330 million at the bank. The difference between expenses and profit was enormous. This year is the opposite."

"And what is your point?"

As he presented his proposal, she appeared to listen but nothing made sense. She glanced at her empty cup pondering his words.

"I don't know, Adam … How will this affect our children? Will our friends notice the sudden change and stop socializing with us? Will our families be embarrassed or reprimand us for foolish overspending? There are lots of questions you haven't answered."

Having to limit expenditures was new—and she bristled. Strategic planning for needs now overshadowed obtaining her *wants*. It was difficult to understand why these procedures were necessary in the first place. *Surely, Adam miscalculated and things would be back to normal soon.*

"This is ridiculous," she said to Carissa. "I'm entitled to happiness."

"Do you have a time frame? Is there a deadline?"

"We both should have married for money," Holly joked. In the meantime, she needed to figure out how to turn this around.

Accustomed to making choices based on her desires, Holly determined which economical products provided quality. Amazingly resourceful when necessary, she found coupons, sales, and rebates to be worthwhile. Cutting back on personal needs was more difficult emotionally than physically, however.

She felt like a prisoner.

"Losing our social life is hard for me," she told Adam. "You have tennis matches and baseball games—but I have nothing."

"I have no intention to exclude fun times," he said. "You're intelligent Holly; find low cost activities we can enjoy. We can always spend more time in conversation—that should make you happy."

"It doesn't hurt to explore our options, I guess."

"There are ways to relax outdoors," Adam continued. As a family, we can swim, visit the zoo, or have picnics at the park. I'll even push everyone on swings."

"Could we invite friends over to play games after dinner, with a desert and drink?"

"Absolutely! And with creativity, you'll think of more ideas," he said.

Holly contemplated the situation. While there were some advantages, she couldn't envision living like this long term.

Watching her joy diminish, she pondered a different strategy. Friends boasted about money they were making at jobs. *It's imperative we regroup and get back to how things were.*

Walking around the yard, she admired their landscape—especially the garden area. Spending time outside had been beneficial. Hard work resulted in a surplus of colorful flowers and succulent vegetables that would last into winter months. The weather would be turning cooler, now that it was fall.

Holly's taste buds screamed with desire as juicy red apples ripened.

Overhearing a worker grumble about overwork and insufficient employees at the grocery store, she weighed the possibility all week. Talking to a manager, the perfect job opportunity popped in front of her.

"Hey Adam … I have a great idea." She couldn't help beaming from ear to ear.

"You have lots of them."

"Let me explain. Have you ever noticed that each path we walk down has vividly colored flowers framing the gate?"

"That sounds vaguely familiar."

"If you'd just listen. There's something I think you should know."

"Does it have anything to do with you wanting more money?"

"The floral department at Kroger needs help arranging flowers over the holidays," she began. "It would involve doing what I've loved since childhood—while making money. It's a dream come true!"

"Please, Holly …"

"I'll be working while the kids are at school. My friend is available if Jake and Abby need to stay home for any reason. And it will only be through Thanksgiving and Christmas."

Convincing Adam turned out to be harder than she envisioned. Holly deliberated on what to say next. *He was unable to provide for their needs with his income alone.* How could she persuade him to accept her help without offending him?

"I'm trying to make our financial situation easier for you," she said. "With presents to buy for Christmas, how can you resist?"

Adam cleared his throat and stared at her.

Holly persisted. "I tried to incorporate your wishes with the budget—now you're being uncooperative with my request. Why do you refuse to even consider this option? Think it over rationally, Adam. You'll always be the provider. I'm just offering to help."

"If it's money in my pocket—I may be better off," he finally said.

"Good decision. You'll see how much better your life is," she promised. "Don't be afraid. Things will work out. Instead of me asking you for money, I'll pay for my own expenses."

"I like that—now you're being practical."

Purchasing a crisp white blouse was her next assignment. She couldn't decide between a poet shirt or classic V-neck with collar—so bought both. Rare shopping trips necessitated being pro-active when she found any needed items.

More smoothly than imaginable, Holly added this 9-3 task to her daily schedule. Friends told stories about difficulties they encountered working but she determined not to let *those* become her problems.

Being around textures, fragrances, and colorful flora energized the new florist. Unloading cases of pre-cut flowers, a rose with an unusually strong scent was set aside to savor while she worked. Most roses have minimum fragrance. She hummed to herself. Soon she would arrange holiday bouquets.

Bringing home gingerbread, peppermint sticks, and frothy cocoa delighted Jake and Abby. "Surprises are exciting!" she said.

They were eager to share their daily news and spend time with her over dinner preparations. "Mommy, Brad fell at recess and cut his head," Jake said.

"Does he have a bandage?"

"I don't know. He went to the doctor."

"My pink crayon broke," Abby said sadly. "It was my favorite color."

"Maybe Jake will let you share his."

"You can have it Abby—I never use that color," he said kindly.

With a sparkle in her eye, she tried to be sweeter than ever when Adam returned home at night. Leaning on his arm, she described how much happiness the job brought. Trying to look nice for customers— and for Adam—she fixed her hair in special styles, wore Anjali perfume, and painted her nails.

Holly had a special flair for arranging holly, azaleas, English ivy, and poinsettias. Festive ribbons and bows caught customers' eyes, and sales loomed.

Hours flew by and the extra income was a sizable amount when Adam and Holly went Christmas shopping. With a feeling of accomplishment and exuberant about future possibilities, their New Year began happier than the last.

Life never seemed brighter!

Although her original job ended, the florist indicated he could use Holly for special occasions when she was available. Without hesitation, she jumped at the opportunity.

"I would love to! Thank you so much."

She rushed home to tell her husband.

Adam became accustomed to the few hours Holly spent arranging and selling flowers. "With you busy, complaints about my late hours have been significantly lessened," he said smiling.

"I knew this would be a wonderful thing for both of us," she said.

"The moonlight still makes your hair gleam," he said climbing in bed next to her.

Guarding her newfound independence Holly strove harder to be a wonderful wife and mother. She woke early, disciplined herself to finish chores quickly, and paid close attention to the needs of her family. Mentally, she prepared for the next day before getting in bed.

Things appeared fine.

Talking to Carissa on the phone, Holly said, "We talk and laugh quite often. It's as if we finally have this amazing connection. Unlike yours, ours is a unique marriage."

"Depends on which man you choose—whether it works or not," Carissa answered. "I've picked two losers."

Holly sat back smugly.

"Granny's coming to visit next week," she told her family at dinner. Excitement erupted around the table.

"Can we go to the zoo?" Jake asked.

"I want her to dance with me," Abby said.

"We'll have time to do lots of things with Granny," Adam said.

Early on Saturday, the Clarks climbed in their Jeep and rushed to the airport. Smothering their great-grandmother with hugs and kisses, Jake and Abby talked non-stop all the way home.

"Give Gigi a chance to put her things away. Then she can tell some stories," Holly said.

Granny winked.

"Okay, who wants to hear about a pirate?" she asked—sitting down in a chair. Jake and Abby cuddled close to her. "Once upon a time, a mysterious ship docked at the wharf in Harbor City with an eerie light glowing below deck ... It was twilight with dark clouds filling the orange sky ... Jake saw pirates creeping over the side. One set of dark eyes spotted him watching from his grandfather's bait shop on the shore ..."

Even Adam sat down—interested in the story Granny made up.

"Tell us another," they begged when she was done.

"It all started one dark and rainy night ... Abby read in a corner of her bedroom, over by the window ... focused on a picture of a princess dancing in a beautiful emerald green gown ... Boom! ... The lights suddenly went out ..." Granny finished telling the tale—whispering some of the time, raising her voice occasionally, and once in a while laughing.

"Time for lunch," Holly said.

"We're not hungry," Abby answered.

"Let's eat; then I'll tell another," Granny said.

Back in the chair after gulping some soup, she started telling another story. "A secret agent behind a bush looked perplexed ... and stepped into the shadows after struggling with a code for a few minutes... Looking for the treasure map was MUCH more difficult than he expected ..."

When she was almost finished, Abby interrupted. "Tell about a girl this time, Gigi."

So Granny began again. "A princess in the garden was swinging when she eyed a beautiful cake on a platter … Tempted to have a taste, Abby dragged her shoes on the ground trying to slow down … The birds watched gleefully from the branch while she brushed crumbs off her dress …"

The week passed quickly with adventures, frivolity, and wonderful memories. "Next time bring your jump rope," Jake said as she was leaving.

Everyone was energized and happy.

Holly eagerly anticipated a field trip to the Art Center as a chaperone for Jake's class. This was one obligation she looked forward to and thankful to be involved. Her enthusiasm was contagious.

Jake placed his backpack by her shoes in the foyer.

"I want to go, too," Abby whined.

"When you grow up, you can go there with Dad," Jake said, making her cry harder.

The sunny day with twenty-three excited second graders, traveling by bus, was full of fun even before they arrived. Enjoying a short movie, watching children create varied masterpieces, excited them further. Divided into groups and handed aprons, interactive play in four areas followed: weaving, working with clay, sketching a clown, and painting with acrylics.

Boxes with their works of art were souvenirs.

As the class prepared to leave, Holly discovered they were looking for an Art Educator. This full time position was precisely the career she longed for. With an intended major in Art Education, her plans included teaching—until marrying Adam changed everything.

She was waiting with a packet when he walked in for dinner.

Telling Adam the details took no time at all. "Today on the field trip, I answered questions the kids asked—that none of the Art Center employees knew," she began.

"Jake, tell your dad."

He fidgeted with a gold engraved kaleidoscope his mother bought at the Art Center Gift Shop. The amber, ruby, turquoise, and amethyst glass spun as he turned the outer wheel. Adam reached for it, wanting to try himself. Jake eagerly shared the treasure.

"As we left, a fantastic opportunity came up," she continued. "There's an opening for another educator and I would be perfect."

Skillfully, Holly wove compelling reasons to start this job and answered Adam's reservations about her increased responsibilities. She refused to stop talking about it. "The Art Center is ideal—only fifteen miles from home and minutes from the school. I can take Jake and Abby, and a neighbor will carpool in the afternoon. My interview is next Tuesday."

"You made this decision without me?" Adam asked. "Why stress myself when there's nothing I can do."

Persuading him turned easier than expected.

The interview went well and the Administrator Theresa Marshall asked for her insight, even before she started work. She chatted nonstop at dinner.

"I'm off Mondays and holidays—additional time can be arranged, if necessary. I can even work from home in the evening on occasion. When Jake and Abby have special activities, I can still attend."

Adam read the newspaper as she enthusiastically shared more details than he cared to know.

It didn't matter.

Exuberant about this wonderful opportunity, she busied herself choosing clothes. Artsy garments gathered over the years would be hits. Even the special dirndl she bought in Germany would look cute.

The first day went smoother than she envisioned.

Holly questioned whether feeling productive or having additional income was a better benefit as she drove home. This position as an Art Educator included arranging school fieldtrips, planning workshops for the community, plus scheduling and teaching enrichment classes.

Pulling files from old college classes, she plunged into her assigned tasks with abandon—oblivious to longstanding desires she had previously regarded so highly. Each day held great anticipation for the scheduled activities and she focused on doing her job well. She had never expected this particular dream to come true.

Diplomatically, she interacted with other employees who needed her skills to balance the program.

Holly's demeanor lit up as she rediscovered what fascinated her in childhood. Life was again filled with activities that broadened, stretched, and enriched. The variety appealed to her personality and required creativity.

"Raising children failed to instill a sense of satisfaction for me, or provided any appreciation for my efforts. In fact, it lowered my self-esteem. I'm grateful to move on," she told coworkers.

Rejuvenated in the evening and eager to talk, she offered interesting bits of information during dinner. Jake and Abby's blank stares helped her feel less guilty as they scooted off to their bedrooms. Quality time would improve when they got older. Adam needed to finish his reports.

With extra minutes, she could tackle the kitchen.

Dirty dishes crowded the sink so she opened the dishwasher. Deep in thought, she pictured several incidents in the Art Center break room—when Abby distracted her with a question.

"Mommy, my friend Sally doesn't like me anymore," she said leaning against her mother's leg. "Can she come home and play with me tomorrow?"

Pushing her aside to finish loading dishes Holly said, "Abby you need to put your pajamas on."

"But Mommy ..."

"Do as you're told—right now! No more talking."

As Holly finished wiping the counter, eager to take a hot bath, Adam came into the kitchen with a concerned look on his face. "Abby appears to be precocious in her grasp of language like you," he said. "She was crying in bed so I asked what was wrong. I think you need to pay more attention to her."

"I spend time with my children, Adam, and there's nothing more I need to give. What are you suggesting?"

"She has a lot on her mind."

"I do too," Holly replied.

"We all make decisions and now I have to worry how yours will affect our children," he said, turning to leave.

"Wait until they're older. You'll see the results."

"I can only imagine."

The financial bonus of Holly's career quickly became obvious—with escalating incidentals as children grow older. Most of the extra money provided enrichment classes and dance lessons. Paying for occasional haircuts, manicures and pedicures, and new shoes came from her funds, in addition to replenishing her wardrobe as the seasons changed. Holly tucked some away for personal use.

"I'll treat you to a movie," she offered her hubby.

Adam accepted.

At the ticket counter, Holly realized she had no cash and sweet-talked him into paying. "Does it make you feel good—being responsible for our expenses?" she asked as they found seats.

Rain poured down in buckets as she hurried kids to the Jeep. Despite evening preparations, the morning started terrible. Abby misplaced a shoe and refused to wear another pair. Jake spilled his lunchbox on the sidewalk. Another child might eat school lunches—but he despised cheese burritos.

Fortunately, Holly would be in her office soon, involved with more important matters.

Talking to Adam on the telephone, she made light of the morning misfortunes. "I can't wait to get together with Tom and Carol Mitchell tonight. Which restaurant did we decide on? Being a little tired tomorrow shouldn't be a problem," she said.

A late evening at the bank cancelled those plans.

Most days were uneventful. A few were hectic. Holly endured the difficult moments with determination. Proving to Adam, that work at the Art Center was a wise decision, consumed her attention. No matter how hard the challenge, she would show him she could perform adequately.

Her middle name was self-sufficient.

Stan and Rita Miller moved in across the street with four school-aged children. The adults talked briefly, as furniture was unloaded.

When their oldest son Brad suffered a concussion a few weeks later, Rita called Holly. "Brad was teaching a friend to dive after school and caught his foot on the diving board," she said. "Knocked unconscious, he swallowed a quantity of water before being pulled from the pool. Doctors are watching him but additional measures may become necessary."

While Stan and Rita waited at the hospital, their three youngest children needed supervision and meals.

Holly agreed without hesitation.

Brad developed pneumonia and the complications required his parents remain by his side for several days. Charlie was twelve, Rachel was eight, and Rhonda who was almost six, required food, shelter, transportation, comfort, and attention. Their caring neighbor, Holly Clark, helped for eight days, fitting the extra duties into her already crowded schedule.

Lacking much sleep, she trudged on with her responsibilities.

"We can never repay you for your assistance," Stan said handing Adam a basket filled with fruit and chocolate two weeks later. "Thanks so much for your kindness," the note read.

Exhaustion almost paralyzed Holly for a month. Her high standards and work ethic reached their lowest point. Trying to accomplish too much brought her precariously close to serious physical problems of her own.

Four weeks of sick leave resulted in slight improvement.

Holly knew little about realistic planning with her impossibly high expectations. Pretending to have it all together, she grasped at what might give stability and complained to anyone who would listen.

"Adam expects too much from me," she confided to Julie Welch.

"I can't do everything, but I'm unsure what to leave undone—for fear Adam will resent me accepting this job," she told Carissa.

Reflecting about life on the patio sipping fresh lemonade, she observed Lisa watching the sky and stationary in one spot. Approaching the fence, Holly noticed her pink cast.

"What happened?"

"I broke my leg while I was skating—it will take eight weeks to heal," Lisa said. "So we can't visit my grandparents like we planned. They live on a farm and have horses."

"Does that make you sad?" Holly asked.

"Watching birds and listening to them sing helps me forget."

Holly thought back fondly to years in Colorado and remembered things Granny taught her. "Did you know birds use their voices to communicate just like people?" she said. "A baby lets the parents know if it is hungry, frightened, or injured."

"How does the mother know which voice is her baby?" Lisa asked quietly.

"Every bird has a distinct sound. Some birds use a special pattern. Sometimes only the male sings."

"Oh."

Lisa appeared forlorn, dejected about life. Something appeared wrong but she hesitated revealing anything else. Her eyes looked like she had been crying.

To watch this sweet child waiting patiently for her leg to heal, doing nothing for eight weeks, was more than Holly could stand. Without making promises, she determined to get her colored pencils and teach Lisa to draw.

Maybe the peaceful activity together would benefit both of them.

Chapter 7
Wrong Values

HOLLY STOOPED FOR A soggy newspaper before unlocking the front door—kicking off her clogs in the foyer. Adam would be late so sandwiches would suffice tonight. Miffed at herself, she had no intention for conversation with anyone. She sorted through the mail absentmindedly.

Despite her organizational skills, a mess occurred at work. Holly squirmed when her boss approached that morning—with dark eyes squinting. "Scheduling two events on the same day is unacceptable," Theresa Marshall said brusquely. "Dr. Sherman is very busy and is only available for that day. It's imperative he speak as planned."

Because the Art Center anticipated significant contributions that Dr. Sherman might bring, his lecture was vital. Many affluent people in the community already had reservations to hear him talk. In addition, the elaborate buffet before his lecture involved the same area Holly's workshop required. "Paint and formal attire don't mix," Theresa reiterated.

She knew that.

"It's not that I'm incapable," Holly explained, brushing her hair back. "I just got off-tract with these major construction conflicts affecting the whole summer class schedule," She didn't appreciate being reprimanded when the error was clearly not her fault.

The calendar she had been given was inaccurate.

Contacting renowned artist Franklin Valaire to cancel his workshop was also embarrassing. He was cordial in his response to her explanation, but an alternate date couldn't be rescheduled. Holly was disappointed to lose this opportunity and ashamed of her inability to remedy the situation.

Most upsetting, this artist was an expert in the dry-on-wet watercolor technique that fascinated Holly while visiting Adam's friends in Switzerland. Since returning home, she had been unable to master it on her own. Learning this intricate way to paint was of personal importance.

Adding to her frustration, the nasty Artist-in-Residence who was setting up a demonstration took advantage of a disagreement with Holly to berate her abilities as an educator. Not accustomed to being told how to do her job, Holly recoiled and ran to her office. She was humiliated in front of art center patrons by the critical remarks.

Some people are easier to live with than others.

Soothing her anger, she reminded herself artists are well known for being eccentric. A short coffee break became an opportunity for Holly to clean the kitchenette and throw rancid food away. No one would miss the disturbing odors.

Not a thing was left in the refrigerator when she finished.

Attempting to regroup at home, she became annoyed when Jake and Abby started fighting over silly matters during dinner. They bantered on and on about hair styles—and the discussion grew to include sarcasm and insult—with neither interested in making peace. When their mother finally intervened, Jake was shouting and Abby was crying.

"Why does everyone have such huge problems getting along?" she said, sending her children to their rooms before finishing dinner alone.

The silence was especially nice.

Holly relaxed in a soothing coconut bubble bath, before applying refreshing lotion to her arms and legs—pampering her silky skin with additional pleasure—and got in bed with a book. She seldom read for fun anymore but it was the perfect opportunity to forget her cares and escape into her imagination with a new romance novel. The escalating friction between characters proved disturbing, so after enjoying a couple of passionate scenes she set it down.

She missed having Adam's caring attention. His career consumed both time and energy as he gleaned greater wealth.

Creating personal pleasure was her responsibility.

"I have a surprise for you," she announced at breakfast. "My treat—we're going to a cozy retreat up in the mountains for the day. I've reserved a room for tonight. Jake and Abby can stay with Gayle Mint."

"When do we leave?" Adam asked.

"As soon as I clean the kitchen."

Holly pulled out of the driveway an hour later. Music from the sixties' played over the radio and Adam sang along. He thumped his fingers on the door.

"Do you mind?" she asked.

"Sorry," he said. "Does that bother you?" A *what-have-I-gotten-myself-into* look crossed his face.

Holly blew it off and looked ahead intently. Minutes later, she pulled into the Cozy Cove—an out of the way log cabin village. "I thought it would be bigger," she said. They stretched and popped the trunk for their bags. Adam reached for his computer.

"Why did you bring that?" she asked.

"Because I have business to finish," he answered.

"Great! Lot of fun this day will be. What was I thinking?"

"Guess that's the problem. Maybe you don't anymore," Adam said.

Flipping her hair and forging ahead, Holly checked in. Her husband followed. Once in their guestroom she put on her turquoise bikini, grabbed a cover-up, and slammed the door—leaving without saying a word.

Around two o'clock, Adam found her asleep by the pool.

He decided to let her sleep; opting to work out with a curvaceous female dressed in hot pink Lycra that he spotted in the fitness center. He busied himself, proving his prowess with weights when she glanced over. When she needed advice, he was thrilled to help.

Holly poked her head in just as he reached around the voluptuous bombshell to adjust a knob. "Excuse me for disturbing you," his wife said sarcastically. "Do you have any plans for dinner?"

"I just invited him to eat with me," the Marilyn Monroe wannabe said, oblivious to a connection between the other two people.

"Go ahead," Holly said agitated. She left before either could respond.

Adam picked up a sandwich in the café and ate alone by the pool—where assorted females caught his attention. One in particular sat alone in the Jacuzzi peering over from time to time. He decided to join her—hoping his wife would return.

"Hi. Having fun?" he asked.

"Now I am."

A glint of fabric blended with water and he was mesmerized. He hadn't realized her tiny silver bikini strained at the seams before he sat down. Foam floated around them—keeping his curiosity heightened as he tried to see beneath the surface. Her blue eyes revealed interest and her soothing voice exuded warmth. He could barely think.

"Where y'all from?" she asked.

"Local. And you?"

"Savannah." She edged closer, eyes widening, intent on getting to know him better. Her hand touched his arm.

"What brings you to this area?" he asked.

"I'm a travel reporter and check out places to visit." She leaned forward and her plunging neckline revealed more than it should. "What do you do?"

"I'm a banker."

She beamed, rising briefly from the water to scoot closer and rearrange her bikini—high enough to give a better picture of her assets.

"Nice!"

Her leg moved on top of his thigh before he could answer. With the precision of a woman intent on seducing, she continued her advances while he wondered what to say next. What if Holly came in now? He glanced around nervously.

"Uh ... maybe I need to go," Adam finally said.

"We could go up to my room," she suggested.

"I'm married," he confided.

"Well we sure had a nice time together while the party lasted," she said. "I wouldn't mind getting to know you better, if your marriage is truly on the rocks." After drying off, she handed him her business card. "Call me anytime."

He headed toward the exit, glancing back before opening the door. She looked longingly at him. Why were all the wrong females interested in him? Feeling guilty, he returned to his room.

Holly flipped through magazines while her quiet husband watched a tennis match. The frigid air felt like a snowstorm but heat rising from a fireplace made the lodging toasty warm. Wine glasses and a box of Ghirardelli on the counter went ignored.

Fortunately, there were two double beds in the room.

With upcoming Parent-Teacher conferences, Holly scheduled four days off. "I'm going to spend time alone with each child," she told Adam.

Secretly she yearned for time to herself.

"Let's buy basketball shoes and get a pizza," she said to Jake after registering him for a youth-league basketball team. Abby needed new dance clothes and shoes the following day.

"Time off was productive and relaxing," she told coworkers. "I learned new things about my children and gained ideas on how to be a better mother." *With more discipline, perhaps I can put these convictions into practice.*

Despite her struggle to be perfect, Holly saw few evidences of success but persisted in trying to maintain order and please her family. Relegating her personal needs to an imaginary treasure chest in the closet, she dreamed of juggling career and family life.

Rushing to watch Jake's basketball game, she met him in the hall and casually hugged him. A maturing adolescent, he apparently was humiliated in front of friends. "Never do that again," he said back at home. "It was embarrassing."

"I'm sorry," Holly reassured him.

Pondering it later, she regretted having gone.

Jake's awards ceremony followed the final game on Friday. Holly promised to come, knowing she would arrive late. She looked around for Adam. Glancing from door to clock, she fretted the remainder of the game and failed to see Jake make the winning basket. Clapping when he was announced the most valuable player Holly thought, *If only his father cared as much about him as I do.*

Unable to leave an important meeting, Adam realized he would miss the game. With his mind preoccupied, he forgot that the award's ceremony followed. When he arrived home, his entire family fumed.

"Where were you tonight, Dad?" Jake said. "You were the only father missing."

Holly gave him a look of disgust.

"No one seems to care that I work hard to provide for my wife and children," Adam said defending himself.

"But Daddy, he's the most important player," Abby added.

Slamming the bedroom door shut before going to bed, Adam threw his clothes on the floor and his shoes at the bathroom door. "What makes you think you can disrespect me in front of them?"

Holly bristled.

"You have no idea what I spend to make your life good and this is what I get?"

"You couldn't take one hour from your workaholic schedule to make your son feel valuable?" she said loudly. "If I didn't force you, none of us would feel valued."

"People who deserve praise get it," he said with fervor. "I get continuous verbal honors at the bank because of what I accomplish." His pitch escalated as he thought of more to say. "When was the last time you even said thanks? You're an ungrateful, self-indulgent spoiled brat who is only concerned about one person—YOU."

She stood up from the bed shouting in self-defense.

"Nobody cares what you think," he shouted back. "When you learn to consider others' interests, maybe they'll come around."

He grabbed his robe and left the room, spending the night on the sofa.

Pursuing achievement-based actions—with their perfectionist tendencies—Adam and Holly took the results too personal. He blamed her, remaining busier than ever at work, and she resented him.

Hostility increased in their home.

With little support and considerable energy spent working, most days ended with discouragement. Walking by the painting 'Majestic Peaks' by Robert Wood, hanging over the fireplace, Holly longed for solace she could not find.

During a phone call from her mother, Holly realized it had been months since she last saw them. She missed emotional support they provided. Because her self-esteem begged for positive strokes, a weekend visit alone was essential. She made all the necessary arrangements before informing Adam of her intentions.

Holly's father beamed when his daughter walked in.

He adored her as a child; they connected emotionally. "You did things most girls avoided—fishing and trekking in the mountains," he said. "And you were a great asset in my office."

"I miss our lunch dates, Daddy."

Susan Armstrong used her best linens to serve sandwiches and tea so Holly would feel like a princess. Sewing together, while listening to Vollenweider, they seemed caught in a time warp. With no interruptions, they went for walks—to watch birds and sit mesmerized as a squirrel nibbled on a piece of roll. The hours appeared to stand still.

She hadn't been pampered like this for years.

For dinner, they feasted on favorite foods while reminiscing. Climbing into her old bed, she found a piece of candy and note on the pillow. Her mother even tucked her in. *Holly wished she were a child again.*

Reluctantly she returned home.

Greeted with hugs and smiles, Adam pulled her chair out at dinner. Even Jake and Abby acted interested in hearing about their grandparents. Reports about basketball, dancing, and school activities followed.

The serenity was short lived. Red-faced Abby leaped into the car after dance class slamming the door.

"I hate you!"

"I'm sorry I'm late," Holly apologized. "Students' questions caused painting class to go over-time."

Ignoring the reason, Abby expressed her feelings in strong words— and no matter how her mother responded, continued to complain. Confused by her hostility, Holly probed.

"I was scared when you didn't come." Abby finally said.

"I've been late before. You know I'll be there as soon as I can."

"You don't care about me."

"What makes you think that?" Holly asked.

"When I talk, you ignore me."

"I'm listening now."

After an extended pause, Abby decided to share her feelings. "I missed the cue on a dance routine and everyone laughed." She proceeded to give details of the humiliating event.

Thinking they would converse on a deeper level, Holly stopped at a Dairy Queen for hot fudge sundaes. She set aside her plans for the evening to listen. Surprised to have one-on-one time, Abby used it to tell her mother she needed new clothes for a variety of events.

When they arrived home with an armload of purchases, Abby was as happy as a lark—but Jake resented his mother's generosity. "I asked for new basketball shoes and you said we couldn't afford it. Abby gets everything she wants."

He slammed the door to his bedroom.

Holly had no answer.

The sky was overcast and a foul odor permeated the yard as Holly drove in. *I sure hope Adam took the garbage out.*

At least the house would sparkle.

Ranelda had cleaned again today. Her services were excellent the first month—so Holly assumed this petite woman would continue impressing them with her skills. Other customers raved about her work including Theresa Marshall.

Unlocking the door, Holly noticed a gold candleholder missing from the side table. *Hmmm.* The rest of the house appeared normal.

She dropped her jacket on the bed and changed into jeans and a sweater. What a relief she could make dinner and relax in a tidy home. Why hadn't she thought of this sooner? A glimmer of silver under the dresser caught her eye. She bent to pick up a charm and saw a chain behind it. *What in the world?*

Then she discovered her jewelry box was gone.

Panic gripped her as she ran to call Adam. "Call the police," he advised. "I'm on my way home."

A squad car was already there when he pulled in.

"It was our cleaning woman! I knew we couldn't trust her," Holly said to the officer taking notes. She described in detail all of the items Ranelda had stolen. "My diamond bracelet, necklace, and earrings can be replaced—but the multi-stone bracelet and Alexandrite ring were one-of-a-kind."

Adam did his best to calm Holly but she grew more agitated as the loss sunk in.

"They were priceless jewels and memories of each one can never be restored. How could she do it? They meant nothing to her!" Tears erupted and the flow couldn't be shut off.

The officer raised his eyes toward Adam. "We'll investigate and determine whether charges can be filed against this woman."

"I want Ranelda put in prison for the rest of her life!" Holly shouted. "Greed overpowered anything she was capable of doing right. I hope she never sees sunlight again."

"We'll try to get these gems back for you Mrs. Clark," he said before leaving.

Perhaps they never would.

Holly drove to Ranelda's house determined to retrieve the stolen jewelry herself but no one answered the door. A dog barking in the back yard surely protected other unfortunate incidences of theft stashed inside. She talked to neighbors and informed them of major character flaws of this woman—enhancing the story to sound more convincing. The neighborhood needed to know the truth. She made sure her former housekeeper would never be hired again.

"The final report stated nothing conclusive could be proven against this poor immigrant woman—poor my foot!" Holly said to Adam. "Ranelda has gorgeous jewels proudly displayed around her neck. She'll never have to work again."

Eating dinner at a restaurant, the server was slow bringing drinks. Holly glared as she set them down. *Did all foreigners have rotten work ethics?* "I've never heard of iced tea without a slice of lemon," she complained.

Her chicken was cold, cheese stuck to the plate when reheated, and the fries were greasy. She berated the server as they ate. "Did you notice her gold earrings? Wonder how she can afford those."

"We're not coming back," she said to the manager at the door.

Abby's dance recital involved three separate nights at the Civic Center. Ted and Susan Armstrong came to town for the first, which they thoroughly enjoyed before heading back to Colorado. Holly planned to watch the last two shows. She expected Adam would assume primary responsibility for transportation—dropping Abby off and picking her up.

Adam watched baseball on television waiting for his daughter to get ready for the second show. Rushing to arrive on time, they forgot an important prop. He took it in stride; phoning Holly who he assumed could help on her way home from work.

"That isn't what happened," he said when questioned about being irresponsible. All Adam could hear was shouting.

"What options? … No way! Are you crazy? Calm down," he said.

When Holly arrived at the Civic Center, her demeanor wreaked of rage. The tension was intense but talking could only make it worse. She handed Adam a sandwich through the car window; then proceeded to eat silently in the auditorium parking lot alone in her Jeep.

Sitting down in her reserved seat, she later said, "Enroute from work, I picked up dinner from a Deli—with barely enough time to stop home to retrieve the butterfly wings. As I rushed to the recital, a police officer pulled me over for speeding."

"How much is that going to cost?"

"Nothing! I used my charm and only got a warning ticket."

He patted her on the back.

Once the performance started, she settled down and they enjoyed the spectacular backdrops and their daughter's delightful talents. Presenting her with flowers at the end of the program, Adam hugged Abby.

Holly kissed her on the check.

Looking at photos, they laughed at the dancers' facial expressions and sighed at complicated gestures the dancers exhibited in various routines. The colors were brilliant and lighting on the stage was great.

"Not every parent has photos like these," Adam said proudly.

Abby complained about the poses her father captured. "You can hardly see me!" she said about group shots. "Why am I standing like that?" she asked about her skewed posture in another. "The best picture is of Trisha!"—a girl Abby greatly disliked.

Making additional derogatory statements, she sulked to her room.

Passing a family portrait when their children were younger, Holly thought of more peaceful days. Somehow, time spent pondering how to make a good life had been wasted. Choices she made usually backfired, bringing nothing but remorse.

Holly immersed herself in negative self-analyzing as she cleaned the kitchen. A wonderful cook in the past, her family seldom ate tantalizing food anymore. Her home was deteriorating and dirt lurked under the surfaces, she had no time to eliminate. Relating to her children, she bombed more often than she connected. As a wife, she was the most dismal failure. *Abby was learning self-condemnation from the best!*

"What's going on?" Holly asked.

Adam perched on a kitchen stool fuming. "That's what I was about to ask you," he said holding up a bank statement. "How did this happen?"

Color drained from her face.

"Another immature move, I assume."

"If you'd listen, I can explain," she said, trying to think how to best describe the necessary expenditures.

"I have better things to do," he said standing up and storming from the kitchen with his duffle bag. "It's futile trying to get you to change."

He headed to the gym.

Working out improved his hostility—but frustration with Holly remained. He debated the real cause in his mind. *How long had things been going downhill at home? What would it take to remedy the situation?*

He didn't know the answer.

Playing tennis with a friend, Adam asked questions about marriage. Roger had been happily married twenty years. His responses were vague and brief. *Was he simply enduring like Adam?* They stopped for pizza and discussed interesting subjects—like the oil embargo and sending satellites into space ...

Beginning her young adult years with great ambition, Holly's boundless enthusiasm to reach her dreams rivaled sending a rocket into space. What her life had become was nowhere close to the picture she envisioned.

Years before, Holly painted a picture of a little girl smelling a flower in the middle of a field of daisies. The buttercup emitted freshness—while waves of silky grass stirred pleasant memories as they brushed her toes. She loved that picture and the feelings it produced.

Not anticipating her existence could ever be miserable; Holly believed the years would only bring joy and fulfillment.

How had she visualized it so wrong?

Fresh from the shower Holly pulled on a silky white gown, spritzed raspberry body splash on her neck, and rubbed moisturizing lotion on her legs. Her thoughts were a million miles away. She brushed her hair as Adam lay on the bed watching.

Long ago, his bride had been delightful. Once cheerful, caring, and thrilled to be alive, she instilled a passion in him to live life to its fullest. He expected marriage would continue providing pleasure. Her looks were still stunning—but her inner spirit negated the attractive exterior.

He went to the kitchen for a sandwich.

Hoping the problem would disappear he started singing. "When this old world starts getting me down ... and people are just too much, for me to face ... When I come home feeling tired at night ... all my cares just drift out into space ... The stars put on a show for free ... and darling, you can share it all with me ..."

Chapter 8

Resentment

BARKING DOGS PIERCED THE night air as Adam jogged back home. It was crisp outside but not as chilly as the atmosphere inside his house. Two more miles and he could eat dinner. "I wish I'd already eaten so I could go to bed."

Coming home from work late, he shrugged as Holly questioned his apparent selfishness for wanting to run for an hour.

"Jake's school project needs parental assistance," she said.

"What are you inferring? That should be your responsibility," he said. "You spend little time with the kids—why don't *you* want to help your son?" *She has no right to judge my intentions with our children.*

To top it off, Holly knew there was a marathon coming up and he needed to get in shape. He worked long hours at the bank to provide a good life for his family. On rare occasions—and usually at his boss's insistence—Adam participated in physical conditioning. She was the one who stopped at the gym regularly.

Like a tiger at rest, Adam ate lasagna alone.

He had no interest in conversation. Once she started, Holly would continue to badger him until he went to sleep.

When Jake finished the science project with his mother, both laughed. His volcano idea sounded innovative; and the mess actually was acceptable to finicky Holly. *Adam knew it would provide a good bonding experience.*

Abby plopped down by her father in the kitchen. "Dad, where do computer files go when you erase them?" she asked.

"Nowhere; you just cover them up with new files," he answered.

"Oh."

She left to watch a favorite television show. He decided to join her— wanting to appear productive in a relationship with their daughter, if Holly walked in.

"Your hair is getting darker, Abby. You're not a towhead anymore," he said during a commercial.

"Maybe it's just dirty," she said wrinkling her nose.

"You may have brown hair like me when you grow up," he said.

Abby laughed.

"Our eyes are exactly the same baby blue, too." Adam said—noticing the color for the first time in months.

Abby smiled a toothy grin and snuggled closer.

The telephone rang and Holly began talking to her mother. *Good! That will keep her busy for a while.*

When Abby finished watching Kids World and left the room, Adam turned on a season-opener basketball game. Still agitated, he waited for Holly to finish her conversation and find another reason to complain. Adam knew he should step forward but hated confrontation at home. He hoped the dilemma would go away. "One's castle should provide an escape from the world," he believed. Afraid of getting hurt, he protected his emotions by building a wall around them.

He decided to call it a night.

Folding the clean clothes, Holly considered what to say next. Convincing Adam to help with the kids was a chore. She couldn't understand his reluctance to be a physical part of their lives. He worked hard providing money to buy things but had no desire to connect verbally or emotionally.

Disappointments with him were growing in other areas, as well.

When the Grand Cherokee started smoking, Adam promised to have it checked. He didn't. Leaving for work one morning, the Jeep wouldn't start. A simple thing to remedy, that Adam should have taken care of, caused Holly significant frustration. She seethed. Pouncing on him later she said, "I can't understand why you make decisions without analyzing options—or are you simply inept?"

She wasn't afraid to show distain when he failed to measure up.

His silence told the story.

Trying to lighten the atmosphere in their home, playful Jake put Vaseline on his sister's doorknob and waited for a reaction. Carrying a stack of clean clothes, Abby's hand slipped off the knob breaking her fingernail. She yelped in pain and dropped the clothes. Holly rushed to her rescue.

Jake laughed from his room—for a minute.

"It appears you're joining your father in antagonizing others," his mother said sternly.

"I didn't mean any harm, Mom."

"Will you forgive me, Abby?" he quickly asked. "You can play my new computer game if you want." Abby was comforted.

His mother was less forgiving. "You're grounded for a week," she said sternly.

Adam overheard the conversation.

"Holly, you're overreacting—anyway I'm taking Jake to the lake this weekend. That's enough negativity for tonight. Everybody needs to get in bed."

"You're pathetic," she said before falling asleep.

He was already snoring.

"Why would he contradict my decision?" Holly said to Carissa on the phone. "He's making me look foolish to the kids."

"Tell him what you think."

"Conversations with Adam irritate both of us. I don't enjoy talking to him anymore."

"Are you serious? I thought you were in love for the long haul."

"In addition to resenting him, I dislike his parents. Whenever they visit, life is fun and games for everyone except me. His mother had the nerve to say she's intimidated touching anything in my house because it's decorated so beautifully. *What a joke!* I know the truth—she's lazy."

"Sounds like you need a counselor."

"I wish he'd just move out," Holly said.

"Seriously?"

"My own parents are very different. They exude warmth with caring actions and personal questions. Why else would they invite injured strangers to recuperate in their home? Although Adam seems to enjoy their company, he usually spends extra time at the bank when they visit. Probably because he resents my good fortune. Maybe he feels guilty."

"You've got a point. Do you think he will?"

"He's hardly ever here anyway. If Adam had another place to sleep, we would never see him—and that would be fine with me."

"Wow, I didn't know it was that bad," Carissa said.

Adam frequented the airport just outside the city limits when he wasn't at the bank. The hangar became his fortress and he accumulated flying hours. On the ground, he talked to pilots and looked at planes. A peaceful respite from home, it provided a sense of accomplishment separate from his career.

Talking by mobile phone became his preferred way to communicate with Holly. Not seeing her frowns and obstinate glares, he ended conversations when necessary. If she called back, he pretended to be out of range. The men at the airport did the same with their wives. How she observed his aloofness made no difference.

This was the only way he could slow his growing resentment.

Critical and difficult to deal with, her decision-making process seemed wacky, at best. A huge contrast to what she was like in the beginning. Holly was a handful for anyone who dealt with her. *Did she notice the direction and stability he gave—often yanking her back from the edge of a cliff?* How could she miss his parents holding their breath when she walked into the room?

When Holly started working, she vehemently promised the job wouldn't interfere with relationships—him or the kids. She assured Adam she could take care of her responsibilities without jeopardizing anything. Unaware how wrong she'd been, her relationship with him was almost non-existent—and from appearances, she wasn't doing other necessary tasks.

Holly was asleep when Adam arrived home but he shook her shoulder. "Can I talk to you?" he said.

She rubbed her eyes.

"I'm no longer going to feel guilty when you complain," he said.

"I thought you wanted to know what I think," she answered. "Women find it reassuring to know details."

"I'm not interested in that might have been or could be. I deal with facts and think you're impractical and unrealistic," he said vehemently. "My job is to lead this family. I expect big changes in your attitude toward me—and my decisions."

"You're so selfish! You don't care why I need to do certain things. It's been years since I painted, watched stars, or laughed with friends. It's been eons since we even entertained." She reached for a Kleenex.

The last thing Adam remembered was her crying about all she did for him.

Attempting to help, more than most wives, Holly was offended by her husband's coolness. Fed up with overwork and lack of appreciation, she decided to pay him back for his inattention—scheduling a "Girls' Night Out" as she had done years before.

They met at a restaurant each Thursday after work. *Making one dinner a week wouldn't hurt Adam—he could always buy hamburgers.*

Holly lived for Thursdays.

Often meeting new friends while shopping, she invited strangers. "We have the best time getting together. Do you have a favorite restaurant?" she asked. The growing group needed reservations before long.

Adam resented her freedom and resisted the additional obligations with Abby and Jake. His face spoke volumes before she left and when she came home. "I didn't agree to this and don't have time tonight," he said on the phone. "It's a pity you have to miss one dinner."

"I don't recall you asking *my* opinion when you've engaged in stupid athletic pursuits? Or gone to the airport in your free time?" she said. "Why do I need *your* permission to do what I have to do?"

Hanging up possibly gave Adam a smug sense of satisfaction. Holly felt rejected again—his choice to disregard her was a wrong decision.

Calling back, she got his voice mail. "That's fine, Adam. I'll leave a note for the kids that *Dad* will bring dinner home late," she said. "I'm going out. There's nothing you can do about it. Don't wait up!"

Intending to annoy him further, she left a basket of his dirty clothes huddled in the middle of the foyer.

She tripped over the basket, still in the same spot—trying to maneuver through the darkness long after midnight.

And her husband was gone before she awoke. *Thank goodness.* She had an earful to tell him when they talked again.

A pizza box with leftovers remained on the kitchen counter when Holly made breakfast—irritating, but indicative of success. Reassured, she planned her next strategy. When pushed too hard, her stubborn streak turned into a formidable obstacle. Following her inner voice, she became unpredictable.

Holly stayed out later and later …

Bent on achieving greater independence, the free spirit decided to join a bowling league on Tuesday evenings. No longer out to impress, she wore jeans, a favorite t-shirt, and ugly bowling shoes. It didn't matter if she won or lost. This provided a chance to unwind and take a break from productivity. She eagerly anticipated the evenings at Plaza Lanes, refusing to let anything prevent her pleasure—including an uncooperative husband.

"I deserve it!" she told herself. *Adam has his own activities.*

Lindy and Hilda were waiting when she plopped her bowling bag down. "We already ordered a pizza. Get yourself a coke and come join us."

The girls told off-color jokes and laughed about the latest fashions—making fun of a woman or two who came into the bowling center. "I saw that blue sweater at a garage sale last weekend!" Hilda said. "It cost 50 cents and Suzy Q over there must have paid $200 for her shirt with all that bling."

Dark eyes watched from a group of bowlers nearby. His fleeting glances were exhilarating. Occasional comments passed between the competing teams but most of the conversation originated between Holly and the dignified gentleman.

Hank was different from the other men.

He wore a black cowboy hat, respectfully placing it over his heart when he approached with something on his mind. Honesty and integrity were at the core of his soul. A bit of teasing hid beyond his well-thought words. Something inside connected when they first met.

"Howdy, miss. You're a lovely sight tonight."

She beamed.

Confidence spilled over as he threw his bowling ball down the alley with precision. Bam! Right on target. He swaggered off the lane with pride.

He winked when she picked up a spare. "Nice job, young lady," he said with a deep voice.

Holly felt giddy.

The dim lights helped put everything into perspective.

She watched intently as bowlers enjoyed their lives, patted shoulders in support of good frames and great games, and attentively listened as fellow competitors took the limelight. This was the life she had waited for!

She could finally be herself.

It made no difference when she spilled coke on her jeans—reaching for another slice of pizza. *Things just didn't matter much anymore.* She was here to have a good time and that's what she intended to do.

Hank rushed over to help. "Happens to the best of us," he drawled. After wiping up the liquid and checking her clothes for wetness, he bought a round of drinks for the entire group.

To ease her embarrassment, he bragged about his new Ford 150. "You'll be dry in five minutes with a whirl around the block in the box." Lindy and Hilda thought that would be comical and urged her to accept.

"Why not? You only live once."

A ride around the block in the back of Hank's pickup was more hilarious than their heads could handle. When it started raining, they crowded in the front seat—with Holly pressed against Hank.

He rested his hand on her knee.

"We'll see the stars from a remote canyon next week," he whispered after her friends spilled out back at the Bowling Center.

Perplexed by her rebellion and the obvious neglect of their children, Adam confronted Holly. "Surely you have an explanation for your behavior."

"It's impossible, continuing in the same way—when you learn new things," she said. "My daddy used to compliment me for my resourcefulness. You are offended."

"I'm not playing a game of tic-tac-toe. I want simple answers to some important questions." His knuckles cracked as he intertwined his fingers, and then stretched his arms inside out in front of him.

"I despise you!" she said, glaring at him. "You only want what betters your life."

He responded with similar complaints.

"Anything else?" she said taking off her jeans.

"I've tolerated your antagonism for minor grievances but these accusations are becoming unbearable. I give my best to provide—and I'm not valued."

"Neither am I."

A wisp of golden hair fell on his arm as she turned in bed. The silky strands begged to be touched but Adam pretended to sleep.

Abby found an ideal horse camp she desired to attend with best friend Leanne and begged her parents for their approval. When they hesitated, she argued—giving reasons she figured might help. "Jake was picked for the all-star team and I have nothing special to do this summer," she said. "Leanne's parents already agreed she could go."

"You're always too busy to pay attention to me," she continued.

"Or can't afford your desires!" Holly said.

Tired of her persistence, they relented.

Looking forward to this new experience, Abby tried to be more helpful and patiently waited for the day to arrive.

Glimpsing the mares, stallion, and ponies waiting to be ridden excited the novice camper. Their beautiful manes and tails caught her attention as they galloped around the pasture. A field hand showed the expansive stables where each camper would be assigned a specific horse.

"This is so wonderful. I can't wait to begin." Abby said.

"Looks like a lot of fun," her mother agreed.

A drive around the sixty acres to see the dining hall, rec center, swimming pool, hiking areas, and cabins ended abruptly when Holly glanced at her watch. She quickly said goodbye and hurried off, after unloading luggage at the Cabin in the Pines.

Abby chose a top bunk and unpacked, placing her red cowboy boots and new blue sneakers at the foot of her bed. She arranged toiletries in a purple satin zippered bag. Brushing her light blonde hair into a ponytail, she made her way to the barns, waiting for Leanne to arrive.

Realizing her mother left without hugging her, homesickness swept over Abby. She waited all week for a letter—like her new friends received. A short note arrived on the last day of camp.

Sitting on her bunk, she read,

> *Dear Abby,*
>
> *We miss you lots and wish you were here.*
>
> *See you on Saturday.*
>
> *Love ya, Mom*

When her mother returned, Abby insisted they go to the stable to see the horse she rode all week. He was waiting for attention. Abby kissed his nose. "Hey there, buddy! This is my mother."

Pulling a stool closer, she shimmied up on Buckwheat. "I'll show you how he can canter, Mom."

"We don't have time," Holly said. "I need to get back to the Art Center."

Abby patted him goodbye reluctantly, stalling for additional moments together. She cried in the back seat enroute home—dabbing at her eyes and sniffling—as her mother lectured.

"You're very ungrateful after such a lovely time at this expensive horse camp. I can't be responsible for every minute of your life, Abby. You need to appreciate what I do for you—or I'll do less. Next year you can stay home."

A fire alarm pierced the air with a high-pitched wail and Adam leaped from their bed. Holly followed with a sense of apprehension. Smoke poured in from the garage under the door to the kitchen, so

Adam ran out the front door—around to look in the window. *It was too late to get the cars out.* The night was black but the flames were bright yellow and there was no mistaking they needed the fire department's help. He ran back inside to make an emergency call.

"Wake up Jake and Abby!" he shouted at Holly.

Jumping two steps at a time, she complied with his wishes. Groggily they made their way downstairs and into the night as sirens rushed around the corner.

Holly grabbed Butterscotch as she ran.

The feel of soft fur and contented purring caused her jittery stomach to calm a little. Standing on the sidewalk, she watched firefighters attempt to keep their house from burning down. Flashing lights, rushing water, and the smell of charred lumber blurred her senses.

The Stewart family heard the commotion and came outside—inviting the Clarks to their house. Holly's adrenalin was flowing but she encouraged Jake and Abby to get inside out of the cold. "We'll join you after the fire's out," she said.

So Jake and Abby played games with Jason and Lisa Stewart while the fire burned. Mary made popcorn and offered cola, oblivious to the anxieties of her neighbors.

"Lisa's cute," Jake told his sister.

"She keeps smiling at you," Abby whispered back.

Finally able to contain the flames and prevent the rest of the house from burning, the fire fighters put their equipment on the trucks and drove away.

"The garage was severely damaged and the cars are a total loss," Adam said to Pete. "My tools, the bicycles, and our sports equipment melted or are blackened with soot."

"How did it start?" Pete asked.

"Summer heat ignited the dirty rags Holly used to clean her oil paints." Adam told the Stewarts—looking over at his wife in her tie-dyed t-shirt, barely covering her skimpy shorts. He shook his head in amazement. "Sad, isn't it."

"I left them in a container in the garage until I could dispose of them," Holly explained.

It was hard for her to believe something that once brought joy, now brought so much sadness. "Is this a foreboding sign of what's to come?" she wondered.

Damage from the fire had repercussions for the whole family. Jake and Abby were in bad moods for days.

So was their father. The fire destroyed his specially ordered golf clubs—forcing him to cancel an important golf meet. "How could you be so careless?" he asked his wife. Adam continued with comments about Holly's irresponsibility.

"Certain things are better forgotten," she said.

"By whom?"

After waiting for almost a year, Jake had gotten the dirt bike for his birthday—now ruined. His basketball melted so he couldn't shoot baskets. His soccer ball and tennis rackets were also destroyed. With nothing to do, he agreed with his dad about the predicament—and criticized his mother—something Jake had never done.

"When are you going to look at your son and realize he needs positive guidance?" Holly asked.

"You're the one who should look in the mirror," Adam said.

"As long as we're being honest—I'm deeply disappointed in your leadership in this home. You like to point fingers but the buck stops with you," she retorted.

"Your refusal to support me contradicts the vows you made on our wedding night," Adam said, heating the conversation up with his anger. He smacked the kitchen table so hard the dishes rattled. His face reddened.

"Back then, you earned your reputation by doing what was right," she said. "You're never here, Adam. You don't know what's going on with the kids—or me. People act foolish when they don't know the truth."

"Every opinionated comment you express shows your true colors. You want something that doesn't exist. You live in a fantasyland. When you come to your senses, you'll be glad I brought stability to our home."

Holly exploded, saying things she would regret …

Adam's icy blue eyes stared. He pursed his lips and held his tongue—
but Holly could tell his thoughts were not kind.

She squirmed.

It seemed that in being married, one would feel understood as the
years passed; but for Adam and Holly time did not appear kind. Playing
a game of life-sized-chess, they became pawns forcing a checkmate.

Chapter 9

Jealousy

DELICATE SEASHELLS LAY ALONG the winding shore as Holly selected a few unique and colorful ones. Stooping to pick a dainty pink one, the azure water caught her eye. Tide was rising—the ocean was perfect for body surfing. She wasn't a strong swimmer but waves carrying participants to a sandy beach don't require much skill. She and Adam could enjoy this together.

He was already in the water with girls splashing him. Not while she was around. He appeared preoccupied when she called.

"Adam … Adam!"

Surprised, he turned.

"Come in, sweetheart. I've been waiting for you."

Jake and Abby were staying with his parents for a week and Adam found a romantic retreat where they could spend extra time together. From all appearances, this would be a relaxing vacation. With plenty of water, sand, and sun, they were free to frolic as much as they liked. He could unwind from stress at the bank while she relaxed from her hectic lifestyle and excessive obligations.

"I expect your undivided attention for the entire week," Adam said. "For this moment in time, we can have lazy conversations and enjoy impromptu activities. Being spontaneous is something I miss." *Maybe he could rekindle some of the old feelings he once felt for her.*

Svelte as a model from working at the gym, Holly looked better than ever. Adam whistled when the gorgeous honey blonde came into the water toward him. A red bikini matched her nails. With her hair pulled up in a gold scrunchy, it spilled down her face like a Barbie doll.

With a tan, she would look even hotter!

"It's chillier than I expected," she said skipping across the ripples.

He pretended to be a lifeguard, reaching his strong arms out to provide safety. "I'll warm you," he said, grasping her waist to stabilize the situation, before picking Holly up out of the water.

Her giggle started the ball rolling.

She arched her back, sliding down Adam's chest as his slippery skin gave her goose bumps and increased the momentum. "Oooohh," she said, clinging tighter as she slipped lower.

He pulled her down into the water, closer to his body. She clutched his neck wrapping her legs around him like a pretzel, her heart beating wildly. Adam adjusted his feet and regained control. They were in their own world and no one seemed to mind.

On the terrace eating juicy lobster dipped in butter, Adam got her to laugh at his jokes. Holly was still smiling after dinner. They watched a dazzling sunset on the beach with tangerine and orchid fighting for a place of honor among crimson and rose.

It was a good start.

Adam sang love songs under the moonlight. "Only you can make my dreams come true ... For it's true ... you are my destiny..." He couldn't remember all the words but his voice still sounded great. Holly scooted closer.

"That was fantastic, Adam!"

The mocha sand on her feet felt like moon dust. They snuggled, arms entwined, watching the night sky. Foam crashed on the shore as he sang, "For every grain of sand upon the beach—I've got a kiss for you ... and more leftover for each star that twinkles in the blue ..."

Adam reached over to stroke her hair.

Without the usual responsibilities and concerns, she was hopeful. Perhaps they would discover the key to becoming much closer on a permanent basis. Pretending could only last so long.

It was his idea to wake early and watch the sunrise but she agreed. After breakfast, they rented a "bicycle-for-two-on-floats" to pedal around the water. By afternoon, Holly's muscles were aching so she encouraged Adam to para-sail alone.

Asleep on the sand, a shadow covered her body and crushed shells brushed against her leg. Surprised, she looked up.

A friendly lifeguard beamed. "Hi there ... How are you doing today?" She remembered seeing him at the restaurant the night before.

"You have the most beautiful hair I've ever seen," he said.

Holly blushed. *It had been a long time since she'd heard that.*

"What's your name and where are you from?" he said, kneeling down on the sand beside her. She felt like a schoolgirl again. Moist, warm sand pushed up between her toes. She giggled.

Intrigued by his interest, Holly wanted to tell him she longed for adoration from a male. She wanted to hear him say, "You're wonderful!"—and mean it.

Nevertheless, she hesitated.

His eyes penetrated her soul while he listened to the little she could share. She babbled about big waves and dozens of people he probably saved—while they foolishly attempted daring feats to prove his strength and virility. "Your gorgeous muscles and charming smile surely captivate females when you came to their aid," she said.

He looked out toward the water with a boat coming closer to the beach. "It's amazing the silly things people do without thinking," he drawled. "I need to talk to them—but I'll be back."

He winked as he walked away.

"Catch you later," he called a few yards farther down the beach.

"Who was that?" Adam asked, after finishing his swim.

Holly was unresponsive. She didn't want to make him angry and had no idea what to say. Her checks flushed.

"I think I burned today," she finally replied.

After dinner, she took a leisurely cool shower before smoothing aloe Vera lotion over her body. Refreshing her manicure, memories of the afternoon giddiness caused her to smile. "Oops, spilled some raspberry polish on the rug," she said absentmindedly.

Adam watched a hockey game on television.

She went to bed earlier than planned.

"Being in the sun and around water makes me sleepy," Holly said before pretending to fall asleep.

The Amore Resort provided luxurious facilities for honeymooning couples. Lovers wandered arm-in-arm, with stars in their eyes. Females looked ravishing, taking care to impress partners. "Wow!" Adam said turning around to gawk at a cute redhead in a thong bikini.

The males were hunks with nothing better to do than capture their prey's heart. Adam straightened his shoulders and flexed his muscles. "Feel this," he said. Holly reached out impulsively to touch his arm.

She was envious of the past.

Adam was once romantic and attentive. Now, he appeared to be making gestures out of duty—or maybe a challenge long overdue.

With their minds a world apart but bodies in close proximity, Adam and Holly connected superficially. He enjoyed the water—while she relished being around it. Occasionally they swam together or sat in a Jacuzzi to soothe their aging bodies. Sometimes they rubbed suntan lotion on each other.

When Adam involved himself in other activities, Holly looked for her lifeguard friend. If she found him, they had brief conversations. He called her Goldilocks and winked before parting.

Building a castle in the sand one afternoon, Adam begged Holly to help. "You're the artist who likes to create. We could make an impressive work of art. Where's your sense of adventure?"

"I'm almost done with this book and really want to finish it. Sorry!"

He captured Holly's attention by throwing sand on her legs.

"Hey, that's a remarkable structure—exquisite in its detail and handiwork," she said after catching a brief glimpse. It reminded her of the enchanting castles of Europe. That seemed like centuries ago! She joined Adam immediately.

Working together, they made it elaborate and stately. Adding windows and doors, towers and balconies, they carefully finished the project. Holly gathered seashells and placed them inside the fortress as furniture. Laughing, they agreed this was the finest architecture ever designed. "The only problem—we made it entirely from sand," he said.

Leaving their creation, they went to eat dinner.

Waves demolished part of the castle during the night so Adam knocked the remainder over the next morning. It had been a stronghold during its fleeting hours standing. Lovely in the sunlight where everyone could observe its beauty, the stronghold disintegrated when darkness and tide came in. A crab burrowed its way into the castle's dungeon.

"My life is like that castle," Holly said.

"Life isn't about getting what you want."

"A dreamer—when somebody believes in her—can do great things; kind of like the prolific growth in a forest after a wildfire."

"You're unrealistic," he said, ending the conversation. "Let's go eat breakfast."

At the café, Adam flirted with a server. She wasn't exceptionally friendly to other customers but he engaged her in conversation and discovered multiple areas of mutual interest. Bubbly and full of enthusiasm, Stacy explained her father owned a boat and she loved water-skiing.

She came back often to refill water glasses.

Impulsively, Stacy invited him to join her for a spin around the lagoon in the afternoon. Holly protested quietly—trying not to look fussy or negative next to Miss Cheerleader—with absolutely no desire to participate while confined in a perfect stranger's boat.

However, Adam loved water skiing and it was obvious he longed for a chance to show off.

The afternoon turned out fine, with a sunny sky before cumulous clouds started to build. Adam showed his athletic abilities and challenged other guests on the boat to a skiing contest using only one ski. Stacy was cordial, providing cold drinks and plenty of snacks. Her girlfriend Beth was more of a flirt.

When it started to rain, the party ended abruptly much to Holly's relief.

A fireplace was crackling and the mood mellow back in the lodge—with bored vacationers unable to participate in outdoor activities due to the storm. Deep in thought, Holly pondered her marriage. Lighthearted fun with Adam was a refreshing change but questions about their rocky relationship remained unanswered.

She had no idea what the future might hold but one thing was certain, she would never give up her dreams.

Evaluating the week back home, Holly polished her souvenirs. The scallop was fan shaped with a delicate, fluted pattern around the edge. The starfish was more solid. The color inside a conch shell was brighter than the outside. Her favorite was the triton—a turreted shell with colorful, twisted spire. She put the beautiful seashells away in a box and pushed it under her bed.

Adam put his sandals in the closet—grateful for a relaxing break—eager to get back to work. Being in the water and sun reminded him of his youth, invigorating to his soul. He wanted to continue connecting with Holly but was disturbed to discover her interest in other men. He determined to find her intentions.

"What was going on between you and the lifeguard?" he asked.

"We see the world from a certain point of view," Holly said. "Sometimes the window is clean; other times it gets dirty."

"You don't remember what happened?" he asked again.

"Of course, I remember. I write everything in my journal. The pages are overflowing with interesting details you probably know nothing about."

"Your secrecy tells me a lot, Holly. Next time you fall off a cliff, you'll wish I was nearby" he said.

Adam secured a prestigious trip to New York City as top financier for the region. Hesitant to stay home while he mingled with executives, Holly convinced a co-worker to handle her extra duties at the art center.

Arriving at the Conference Center, she became uneasy when the younger wife of a balding man approached Adam with questions about optional activities. Naïve to her advances, he answered while the striking southern belle leaned on his arm.

"Thanks, sugar. I hope to see more of you," she said, obviously unaware Adam had a wife by his side.

"Who is she?" Holly asked when she left.

"The wife of the most influential investor in this country—Nathan Edwards."

"Why would she think you knew the answers?"

"My assistant was involved in planning the excursions for our free-time. She needed Kate's approval before finalizing everything."

"I don't understand how you're involved."

"Neither do I ... but what Kate wants, she gets. Nobody messes with her!"

Determined to stay close to her husband the entire weekend, Holly chatted non-stop. "I love being in New York with you," she said as they watched the city from a balcony outside their suite.

"You're not saying much," she said.

"I have a presentation in the morning. Guess I'm thinking of that."

Holly soaked in their private Jacuzzi, bathed in candlelight, while he went over paperwork. She determined not to let it bother her.

Meeting outside the conference room for lunch, Holly looked striking in a shimmering green top ... with emerald heels strapped high on her ankles.

"Wow!" he said.

Pressing against her husband in the elevator, his hand brushed her silk blouse. Anjali perfume penetrated his nostrils. "I like being with you," she whispered.

"I'm glad you're here," Adam said—checking his schedule. He hoped her good nature would continue.

A ferry from Manhattan to Liberty Island was the afternoon excursion. "I'm a little chilly," she said to Adam, who moved closer and put his arm around her, unaware of her intentions.

Behind them sat Kate Edwards.

Holly was elated with the breathtaking view from the Statue of Liberty. "Have you ever seen such beauty?" she gushed. "Look Adam, the base is a star. Imagine standing on a massive pedestal—holding the torch of liberty—promising freedom to millions of immigrants. I wonder what our lives offer in comparison?"

They moved to a different vantage point.

Trying to separate from Kate, Holly pulled Adam aside to show him a small boat. The affectionate couple inside seemed oblivious to onlookers. "Can we do that after we finish here?" she asked.

"Not enough time."

She massaged his neck and shoulders. Impulsively she planted a kiss on her husband's lips.

Back in their hotel room, Holly changed into a seductive gold gown with plunging neckline—perfect for her plans—intending to guarantee her husband stay attentive all evening and pleased she accompanied him to New York. Her glamorous honey blonde tresses spilled down from a glittery barrette, with wisps of tendrils highlighting her sparkling brown eyes.

She used her female charms like never before. Touching his hand when he talked, she exuded a sense of warmth he forgot existed. She giggled at his comments, fingered his buttons, and looked in his eyes.

"I have a good job and a beautiful wife. What more could I want?" he said.

When Kate arrived for the evening reception, in a stunning black mini-dress with dark hair tumbling in curls, Adam excused himself and greeted her warmly. Finding a place to sit, they spent several minutes in a deep discussion. He patted Kate on the thigh and started laughing. After refilling their drinks, he touched her shoulder affectionately and bent close to her face—surely not to ...

Holly interrupted the conversation.

"Hello again, Mrs. Edwards," she said cheerfully. "You surely have other friends waiting so I'll take this incredible husband of mine back to greet more people at this reception." She kissed Adam on the cheek and reached for his hand. "We really should circulate, sweetheart, so we get a chance to include everyone. This is the business part of your life; the intimate part happens when we're finished here."

Kate was speechless.

Adam enjoyed the act more than he let on. He played coy. His animal instincts were aroused ...

In their suite, he allowed the drama to continue.

Holly stroked his chest as they lay on the bed. "If you succumbed to my desires, you would probably worry about having a heart attack."

Adam couldn't remember the last time she talked of such things. Enticed to hear more, he mentioned her rival again—knowing flames of jealousy would pump her higher. Holly would stop at nothing to succeed. Neither would he.

"I met Kate during that convention in Phoenix. Her husband was preoccupied with some business ventures and asked if I could entertain his wife. So I did. At first, it was just breakfast and lunch—keeping her from being lonely. It expanded to spending time together in the afternoon. Nothing significant. Just business. You know what I mean."

"You've been unfaithful to me?" Holly said, jumping up with rage.

"That didn't happen … You're not listening."

He reached for Holly's waist and pulled her closer. "She's not important to me. You're my wife." His lips were moist, kissing her as if he meant it. He nibbled her neck, pausing as he continued slowly down past her shoulder. His fingers gently stroked her skin—dancing here and there in a game of cat and mouse. She arched her back and quivered from his touch. A smile crept over his face. She may continue pouting or fighting with words, but she would always tremble at his touch.

Adam anticipated Holly would pay attention to his needs when they returned home. Regardless of her intent, she understood there was competition. That lit a fuse! In addition, her heart longed for an intimate connection only he could provide.

Accidentally finding her journal under the bed, he looked inside. Horrified, he read more.

> May 14 *Hostility has created a wall so high, I've chosen to move on and find someone who can satisfy my needs. My heart longs for more than what Adam can give me.*

> November 8 *I was giddy with desire tonight when Max touched me. My longings crescendo when we spend time together.*

April 29 *Scintillating touch means so much when it comes from a paramour you didn't expect—and in a pickup truck? His drawl and earthy demeanor keeps me begging for more.*

Adam seethed with animosity.

She had changed like a chameleon since pledging vows to him—with no apparent need to enjoy his affection any longer. It was her responsibility to provide a loving environment where he could be himself. This was like a slap in his face, especially after allowing her to find personal fulfillment in a career. Her needs were being met—his were not.

Was he simply a male to be toyed with?

"Can this marriage get any worse?" he shouted. "It's inevitable!" His intention was to confront her the minute she walked in the door.

A call from his boss changed everything.

"Can you fly down to Miami tomorrow to meet with investors? We've been working on a project that needs hands on involvement; and I'm scheduled to present awards at a conference in California?"

Adam had no recourse. His career demanded the best he had to offer.

It would have to wait. He needed Holly to take care of things back at home … temporarily.

Chapter 10
Disillusionment

SWATTING AT MOSQUITOES, HOLLY loathed being outside at the hot, sticky ballpark. She regretted having agreed to come—impatient for Adam to finish his game. He asked her to watch one of his baseball games for weeks saying, "You're absorbed in your own affairs and no longer interested in me."

That was simply not true.

Holly painstakingly scheduled her days to take care of Adam, the children, and their home. Often that involved going out of her way so he could have freedom with his career. "I systematically take care of his needs *before* paying attention to my own," she said.

Yesterday, for example, Adam misplaced a folder he needed. He left relieved after Holly found it—but caused her to rush to work late without even a thank you.

And this morning, he forgot the dirty baseball uniform in the back of his car. "I need it for the game," he said. Aware her husband was in a jam; she offered to launder it—and in addition cleaned mud off his shoes. Going the second mile indicated true loyalty in her book.

There was much to do at home so she left the game early ... guilt free.

"You have every right to tell him the truth," Carissa said while they chatted on the phone. "Confronting him is the only way to stop rude behavior."

Holly mulled her options.

When Adam returned home after the game, she let him have it. "What are we going to do about your irresponsibility and passing the blame on to me?" Holly enquired with eyes blazing as he walked in the bedroom. She expanded on the subject of respect.

"This is not a good time, Holly."

"Not good? ... Why? ... What do you mean?" she didn't pause for answers. "You're an inconsiderate fool!" she said slamming the door.

Storming into the kitchen, she was shocked to see Jim sitting on a chair.

He raised his eyebrows as she passed. Holly had no idea he was there! It wasn't her fault Adam brought a friend home—to overhear this tirade. *Maybe Jim needed to learn the same lesson.*

Repeating how offended she was to Julie on the phone, Adam looked over with a disapproving stare. *At least I'm honest*, Holly thought.

"You don't get it," she said to Adam after hanging up.

"What is it now?" he asked. "Is there anything I do right?"

"I expect certain actions from you as my husband," Holly said.

"Like what?"

"You don't appreciate my efforts—I work long into the night, if necessary. Nobody helps me when it's obvious there are tasks to finish. It's like a contest the ancient Greeks might have enjoyed—you appear to scrutinize how much I can accomplish and bet on how worn out I'll get before falling down exhausted," she said.

"You're wrong ... and there are things I expect that you blissfully ignore!"

"With all my heart, I try to make your life the best I can. I devote hours, days, and years—literally preoccupied with your needs."

Maybe wanting to help Adam, she had hindered him instead.

"Do you think we'll ever bond emotionally?" she asked changing the tone of the conversation. "Maybe we need counseling."

"What good would that do?"

"It's hard connecting with you," she said.

"Okay. Don't. I'm leaving and won't return until you're asleep. Save your words for someone who can feel sympathy for you." He sauntered out of the room with a gusto that blew her back in the chair.

Fear had never paralyzed before; but at that moment, none of her dreams would ever become reality. Was it time for Adam to look for another place to live?

Holly admired a large church down the street from the Art Center with exquisite stained glass windows. Colorful scenes filled the lobby at the entrance; a second group of vibrant designs was higher on the right side of the building. The works of art were breathtaking, gleaming in the sunshine—perhaps how paradise might look to dreamers who make up theories of an afterlife.

Passing by on difficult days, she often thought about stopping.

Congregation members raved about the new minister, Reverend Jeffrey David, but Holly rejected meeting him in person for fear he may try forcing meaningless opinions on her. Avoiding his lectures was imperative; but seeing the beautiful windows from inside the structure piqued her interest. Something within her spirit urged her slow down.

Would the door be open?

Not accustomed to churches—except for weddings and funerals— she was uncomfortable actually going in—but she longed for the serenity she might find inside. Would she be welcome, or considered an intruder? Explaining how she felt, arguing her point of view, and answering lengthy questions seemed overwhelming.

Her discomfort increased and she got back in the car. Feeling awkward and out of place, she drove away.

Adam went to the airport early on Saturday after an extra-hectic week. It was a beautiful day with scattered clouds but no hint of any past or looming storm. Isolated from his wife's hostility, he would again be the master of his life.

He strolled down the taxiway to the hangar greeting friends already engaged in aviation related activities. Rolling the Cessna 182 out of the hangar door, he performed a pre-fight and then climbed in. Taxiing the plane to the end of the runway, his energy soared. Seeing the beauty of the earth—with snow-capped mountains, lakes, farmland, and a new perspective on cities—thrilled him each time he took off.

Climbing through a hole in the clouds, Adam breathed deeply. The transition from earth to sky was unmatched by anything he knew.

"I'm not alone up here ..."

On top of white wisps of cotton at 6,000 feet, a rainbow appeared—not just any rainbow. The horizontal colors, less than 200 feet below the Cessna 182, completely encircled the plane. Wherever Adam moved, the multihued phenomenon followed. The airplane was its focus. He looked around in awe. "This is *not* a common occurrence—it's definitely not the norm." It was a humbling experience for a moment.

"There's no reason for this!" he said out loud.

As he continued to climb, the stunning colors slowly dissipated.

"I've never heard of anybody seeing a 360° rainbow!"

Seeing the small towns with little cars and roads connecting below, Adam smiled. There are many people on this earth but the cities aren't as enormous as one believes down on a crowded street corner. *All of these individuals must have a purpose for something.*

Bringing the bird back to home base, Adam controlled his descent by monitoring altimeter and vertical speed—working in concert together. He arrived at just the right altitude.

Every pilot wants his landing to be textbook perfect.

"One way to tell—is how the tires touch the runway. It's not just a skireech-skireech, but you hear a long screeeeech—with no thud when meeting the pavement. If you do it right, you can't tell the difference between actually flying and being firmly on the ground," Adam's flight instructor said. "You just know it's good!"

Adam greased this one and waved to Roger as he sailed down the runway. The tension freeing exercise proved successful. "You've achieved every man's dream—flying!" his airport buddy said. "Are you coming to the flight breakfast tomorrow?"

"Wouldn't miss it!"

Unless his wife had other plans ...

The way Adam spent free time at the airport was a gratuity Holly believed she provided. *Though she didn't relish Adam enjoying himself away from her, she allowed it.* It was her duty as a good wife to give him that freedom—but what she wanted in return was a husband who cherished her and let her know how important she was.

"I'm in a quandary and don't know what to do," she said to Carissa. "Everything was perfect in the beginning! Adam made me feel special early in our relationship. He couldn't do enough for me; but his heart has turned to stone and his lips are sealed. You won't catch him complimenting me even on my birthday."

"For a while I thought you were the marital exception," Carissa said. "You used to be so radiantly in love; it made me envious."

"Adam has a problem sharing deep thoughts. I hoped we would become closer—but after that week at the Amore Resort, things got worse," she confided. "Ever since we returned from New York, he's been antagonistic. I'm not sure if I care anything about him anymore. Guess it would be more honest to say I abhor having him in my life. There's nothing left in our relationship."

"You're moving out?" Carissa asked.

"No, I'm hoping he will. I could never leave this house."

"Are you considering marriage counseling?"

"Adam refuses! I thought it might help … but I really need to move on with someone who can provide a stronger relationship and the deep meaning my heart begs to enjoy. I already know a couple of delightful men whose chemistry sends me soaring but you never know how long that will last," Holly said.

"Just be careful. You can't trust anyone but yourself," Carissa encouraged her best friend.

Holly watched in amazement as her tapestry, woven in multiple colors with intricate detail, started to tatter. In a daze, she polished silver and washed windows. Her oak floors gleamed.

Her accent table and storage bench in the foyer with carved pineapple designs symbolized hospitality and a warm welcome—but instead of the refreshment, they should offer; they exuded a sense of sadness. The wall hanging above with a picture of a Spanish-style residence and vineyard situated on a lake, bordered by majestic mountains, once offered hope she intended in her own house. Similar to her home, this structure in the middle of creation silently failed to inspire anymore.

He had turned her dreams to ashes. The tropical flair offered no escape from despair.

Once Adam left, she would redecorate in navy etched with ivory scrollwork and porcelain. Purity and peace would reign.

Wedding pictures, photos of the couple on vacations, and mementos she no longer cherished were relegated to boxes in the garage. She couldn't throw them away but didn't want them in the house.

Wanting to feel life made sense, she called her mother.

"Yes, I'm coming for your fortieth Anniversary celebration," she promised. "I miss you and can't wait to see Granny." Adam had other plans so couldn't attend.

Luckily!

Visiting her parents, Holly observed their responses with more interest than usual. Married for forty years, they exhibited deep respect for each other—having developed an uncanny ability to understand and be supportive.

Following their intuition appeared to please each of the soul mates.

Curiosity got the best of her. "What are the components of a good marriage?" she asked her mother.

"Why do you still love Mom?" she asked her father.

Their answers were things she had never considered before.

Lying in bed, Holly contemplated the circumstances that ruled in her own home. *What happened to Adam's concern and his desire to spend time with her?* Driven to succeed in his career, why was her husband content to let his marriage become estranged?

"Come outside, quick!" her mother said knocking on the bedroom door. She pulled on her robe and shoes.

"Isn't the sky awesome with the aurora borealis producing a spectacular show—just for you?" Dr. Armstrong said seated on the porch. "Sit here, Cupcake."

"Why are you still awake? It's after midnight," Holly asked.

"I got a drink of water and saw the colors shifting through the sky," he said.

"We know how you love seeing the northern lights," Susan Armstrong added.

Holly watched the dazzling display in the night sky. Constantly moving waves of red, green, blue, and purple—mixing randomly and sometimes glowing—looked like draperies on a stage. They fanned outward with brilliance, rescinding under a compulsion to regroup before pulsating upward with passion that knew no limits.

"I've given lots of injections in my life," Dr. Armstrong said. "But there's nothing like nature injecting these charged particles into earth's magnetic field. What power! Isn't this worth waking up to see?"

Holly reflected on the awesome natural spectacle that couldn't be duplicated. She considered how life could be an object of beauty for those looking on. Once, her future glowed like an ocean filled with gold. For all her brilliant strategy and tactics—so far she wasn't accomplishing what she intended.

She contemplated creation.

After storms, the rainbow with its brilliant color inspired her. Awesome star constellations lit up the dark sky with billions of sparkling lights, providing a sense of deep satisfaction.

Maybe she should continue pursuing her fragile dreams.

Back at home, when she got in bed with her husband, Holly longed to lean against Adam's body and feel warmth. On rare occasions when he slept, she touched his back or shoulder until he moved. She just needed a male to care about her.

The coolness of his attitude remained unchanged.

Adam furrowed his brow. Holly resisted his topics of conversation yet whined when he wouldn't discuss subjective issues. Laughing, he told jokes and tried to have fun but she ragged about his needing to discuss problems. He tried to be the host she demanded at social events and provide the solitude she enjoyed in childhood—yet she complained, criticized, and demanded more.

He couldn't offer the direction she required.

One day while home with the kids, Adam washed towels. He failed to notice her red blouse fall into the machine. Throwing in soap and turning it on, he watched a tennis match while waiting. Returning to put towels in the dryer, he discovered the once ivory towels were pink.

"You have no sense of humor," he said when she blew up.

She continued ranting.

"This is going to stop right now," he yelled, grabbing her shoulders. "I'm beginning to despise you. I don't know how much longer I can tolerate your hostility." He rushed from the laundry room, picked up his keys, and turned toward the door—noticing Abby and Jake watching silently.

"I'll be back in a little while. Don't worry. Everything will work out," he said.

Holly came into the room with her fake little voice and pretended to be a caring person.

The door clicked.

Adam started singing as he drove away.

"Yes, I'm the great pretender … pretending that I'm doing well … I play the game but to my real shame …"

"This is what life's like with her," he confided to Roger. "What a relief to be out of there. I can hardly stand her today."

"Could you have done anything different?" Roger asked. "Maybe you should cut her some slack."

"Never! She's a free spirit who needs to be reined in. Instead of accepting my decisions—Holly chooses her own selfish endeavors," Adam said.

"Maybe you should talk to her," Roger said. "You're the man of the house. Stand up for your convictions. Don't let her destroy you."

"Yeah, sure. You don't know my wife."

Flying brought him little relief from the hostile confrontation. He replayed the conversation and debated her negativity. He had several options but a divorce might escalate his problems. If he were smart, he should start the process of finding a place for her to live—away from him, if necessary.

Dinner was polite but quiet. The tender roast beef slid down with luscious whipped potatoes—Adam's favorite—followed by a decadent chocolate cake. Jake and Abby chatted about friends and left to finish homework.

Holly stood to clear the dishes.

"I've been thinking," he began. "People pretend life is great but lose sight of the goal."

"Are you apologizing?" she asked.

"I'm just trying to figure a solution."

"What are you doing to make our relationship successful?" she countered.

Adam considered the obvious. There was no sense talking. Self-centered Holly was determined to pursue her own goals. Respectful in public, she looked for ways to usurp his power in the privacy of their home. If she were a lion, her tail would be twitching ...

When Adam turned out the light, Holly scooted closer. He re-adjusted his position as far away as he could get. His rejection made her feel lonelier.

He never touched her anymore, not even her hair. She once teased, "When my hair turns gray, you'll have no interest in touching it." He assured her otherwise. Not yet gray—he hadn't found it appealing for a long time.

She couldn't remember his last tender gesture.

The vacation at the Amore Resort gave her a sense of hope, for a while—but that was short lived. "Did the love songs mean anything to him?" And the trip to New York? Even though Holly was deeply concerned about that other woman, the intimate sparks and romantic moments were real.

But back at home, a different story unfolded.

The things they once loved about each other—they now hated. Instead of building each other up—they looked at imperfections and tore each other down. As if in a fish bowl and open to criticism, the colors, stripes, and patterns of each fish blurred.

Holly dabbed at her eyes with a corner of the sheet.

She used to sit under an apple tree with sunlight glimmering on its fragrant blossoms and dream. Now she felt like a dismal failure as a wife. *The bareness of their souls indicated something was missing.* Would eternity be any better?

Pondering her fate, Holly began to weep.

Chapter 11
Desperation

BUTTERSCOTCH LEAPED FROM HOLLY'S lap with a screeching meow and flew across the room to the safety of her bed. Rain poured down and the deluge from this cumulonimbus cloud was enough to fill a lake. Thunder rattled windows and doors shook as excessive wind howled through the house. *The storm had been brewing for quite a while.*

Abby listened to music upstairs; Jake was spending the night with Joey.

Adam read the newspaper agitated. Because of the storm, his golf meet was suspended and he waited to get back—in second place, one shot from tying the leader! His drives were right on target. It seemed he could do nothing wrong.

Until he got home.

Holly was in an argumentative mood and disapproved of the way he parked his car in the garage. *Why did she even go out there?*

Apparently, she tried going to the store earlier but came back drenched. Her hair was wet and shoes lay in a pool of water. "Abby's bicycle was in the driveway and I needed to move it before I could back out," she said. "Just as I reached her handlebars, the downpour began."

"That must have been when we ran for cover," Adam said. "You're not the only one who got wet."

When he asked about dinner, she snapped again. "We already ate, Adam. Wasn't there supposed to be some kind of shindig for golf pros at the country club?" She crossed her arms and glared.

He didn't like the tone of her voice.

"These men aren't professionals who golf, but amateurs like me who take the game seriously." He tried to participate in meets as often as possible for the challenge. Playing an 18-hole game usually provided little competition.

She would never understand.

Adam went to the kitchen and found a frozen pizza he could bake. Placing it on a baking pan, he turned the oven on and set a timer. "What a tough job," he said to himself mockingly. Holly sure had it easy all these years.

He enjoyed the silence as he ate.

Complaining about simple tasks, she made her chores more difficult by unrealistic pursuits. Her exhaustion was a self-secured trophy—so he might feel sorry and perhaps give her a reward. Thinking about how he gave in—just to please her—made him angry. Her thank you was to attempt goals that are even more selfish.

He put his plate in the sink and looked out the window.

She added unnecessary burdens to both of their lives with her endless pessimism. *Holly once was optimistic and cheerful, full of positive energy. He loved being near her because she invigorated his spirit.* A bolt of lightning hit the ground with a flash.

Adam lurched back and moved into the hall.

Clever and ambitious, she figured out how to control her husband. Harsh remarks replaced the soft caring responses he originally heard. Hardly a day passed anymore without Holly expressing a stinging complaint or negative opinion. *With a little self-discipline—she should be able to control her tongue.*

Finding a good football game to watch, he hunkered down in front of the TV. Enough of her—life moves on. One of his favorite teams was losing but only by a field goal.

With three minutes left, Holly interrupted … "Adam!" He leaned forward to hear the TV better. "The ceiling in the bathroom has a leak," she shouted louder.

Adam went to see.

The growing puddle on the floor found a path of its own, escaping down a laundry chute. Dirty clothes were getting wet but nothing electrical was involved. He couldn't be sure. The only thing to do was wait for the rain to stop. He leaned back in his recliner engrossed in the game again.

Annoyed that her prized bathroom might be ruined—maybe displeased at his lack of concern—she started to grumble. Adam threw his hands in the air. "What would you like me to do?"

She didn't answer. That annoyed him even more. He had no idea what her problem was. The minutes were running down and the Cowboys had the ball. With his eyes glued on the next play …

The electricity in the whole house went out with a bang.

Abby screamed upstairs as Holly groped to find candles in the kitchen.

Adam thought about where he last saw a flashlight. The batteries probably didn't work, even if he found one. Back when he cared more—he knew where stuff was stored. Before the fire, everything in the garage had been carefully arranged with tools and sporting goods neatly displayed.

Adam even stocked a closet in the kitchen with items for an emergency. The first aid kit was in there, along with a pair of crutches. There was a personal care kit with nail clippers, tweezers, files, and a magnifying glass. Next to the sewing kit, was a shoe polish kit. Computer cleaning supplies, photo equipment, a star gazing kit with binoculars, and other less used objects filled upper shelves. Waterproof matches and lanterns were on the top shelf with bottled water, cans of food, and a blanket. Holly laughed at him when the kids were small, wondering how that one blanket would keep their family warm. *He joked about them being warm—all huddled together under it—telling stories by flashlight.*

Abby sobbed so Adam gingerly crept up the stairs. It didn't matter if he could see. His daughter needed him. He calmly called out her name, soothing her with the sound of his voice as he approached. They hadn't experienced much bonding recently.

Both felt great relief when they hugged.

"It's okay, Cream Puff. You'll be fine now." She clung to her dad as he maneuvered along the hallway wall. Helping her downstairs, they met Holly at the bottom—with a candle.

"Thank you for rescuing Abby," she said.

"And thank you, too," Adam said back. It was remarkable what one little flicker could light up. He was astounded!

The entire room was visible—even to the top of the stairs. Expecting the beam to stop a few feet away, it went around the corner and spread light into the adjoining rooms. "Amazing isn't it," he said.

With the candle on a table, they stretched their comfort zones and started thinking creatively. Holly got nachos chips and Abby found playing cards. The candlelight was bright enough to play a game—barely. Few words were exchanged besides the necessities as they played.

No longer afraid, Butterscotch sauntered in. She purred on Holly's lap watching tantalizing patterns on the wall. As wild as a tiger a few hours ago, she was now an adorable, friendly pet that soothed. "How ironic—just like Holly," Adam thought.

The rain stopped and all three started telling jokes. It had been a long time since Holly laughed at one of Adam's jokes. Abby was even funnier. Once they adjusted to living without electricity, they started to enjoy it.

What a difference an hour and one candle made!

The storm stopped inside their house, too. Though they weren't acting like courting lovers, Adam and Holly had a brief respite from their normal animosity. The night was turning out better than it started.

Adam found sleeping bags he used years before and spread them on the living room floor. "We can sleep here if the lights don't come back on," he said.

"That's a great idea, Dad." Abby said, with minimal exposure to such an activity. "I read a book about a family camping in Wyoming on a vacation—where the dad chopped wood to make fires and taught his children how to make birdcalls. The mother cooked food over the flames and they took baths in the river. At night, they listened to crickets and owls while talking in their tent."

"We won't go that far," Holly said clearing her throat.

"Leanne went on a Girl Scout campout once but didn't have a good experience with the bugs and all," Abby informed her parents. "She showed me pictures and it looked kind of scary."

"That's too bad," Adam said.

With a flash of lights, the electricity came on just before bedtime—so they ended up sleeping in bedrooms. "Sweet dreams, Abby," Adam called. "Pretend you're in a tent."

As Abby lay on her bed thinking about the fun evening, she missed her brother. Jake would have enjoyed being here; and probably added some amusement of his own. She couldn't wait to tell him about it.

"Tonight was a memorable experience," Adam said pulling the covers up in bed. He appeared calmer and his gentle touch indicated he still had feelings. *She could almost imagine riding in the horse drawn carriage around Salzburg.* His snores soon replaced the peaceful moments—but that was okay.

Holly savored it in her mind before she fell asleep.

She contemplated what happened while rushing around the Art Center. The hectic pace at work was in sharp contrast to the tranquility they experienced after the storm. The illusive joy was short-lived, however, and Adam returned to his own concerns with no interest in hers.

Most days Holly wished she had never married. She felt a stinging void. Daydreaming about romance, she couldn't endure eating lunch in the park where couples shared intimately.

Adam meant nothing to her but was rather a burden to bear. If he would only find someone else and move out like thousands of unfaithful spouses. He seemed determined to stick it out just to watch her drown in misery.

Max—the guy who persuaded her they were two peas in a pod with a bright future—chose a younger client to pursue, doing everything in his power to make Holly so uncomfortable that she stopped working out at the Fitness Center.

Rich cowboy Hank hooked up with Hilda and ran off to live on an island he owned. He was deceptively searching for fleeting good times with as many suckers as he could ensnare. Luckily for Holly, she came to her senses early enough to prevent a huge fiasco with the eccentric millionaire.

There were other fish in the sea.

With certain standards in place for success, weeding out the self-centered and mediocre suitors would take time. She would eventually find another hunk that could make her happy permanently. This time would be different.

In the meantime, whenever attractive men approached, Holly fumbled for words, her face flushed, and she forgot what she was doing. What was the key to a successful courtship? Could she be duped again? Once capable of interesting conversations, expressing simple greetings became awkward.

"I'm usually alone anyway—accomplishing routine tasks," she told Carissa. "Living as a single person would allow more freedom. No matter how hard I try with Adam, I never do it good enough. With one less person to take care of, my workload will decrease significantly."

"So who is moving out of the house?" Carissa asked.

"That's the only detail still to be resolved. For the time being we're co-existing."

🍎

Holly received a phone call in the middle of the night informing her Granny died. Her heart grieved as she listened to her father share details.

"It was a heart attack," Ted Armstrong said. "When I talked to my mother earlier in the evening, nothing appeared wrong. She called back at midnight with intense pain in her arm, and then became unresponsive before I could ask any questions. I drove over immediately but it was too late. Her body has been transferred to the morgue."

"A frantic call at midnight changed everything for that lively woman," Holly told Adam. "At least Granny wasn't in pain for long."

Knowing her loving grandmother, who was so full of life, had taken one last breath and would decay into the ground like a weed—caused Holly to sob.

She arranged time off from the Art Center to attend the funeral. Gathering schoolwork, Holly signed her children out of school. Details were a blur as they packed and left. Adam had important business out of town so was unable to accompany them. *What emotional support he might have been was unknown.*

The air was crisp—with autumn turning into winter—as the Jeep pulled into the funeral home parking lot. "I forgot snow was possible this early in the year up in the mountains," she said to her father. "I neglected packing heavier clothes for the kids—but they'll be spending most of the time inside, fortunately."

This day was colder than usual.

Hugging others brought a sense of warmth. She mingled with a crowd of friends offering their condolences. Comforting words were shared but her spirit felt deep sorrow.

"No one knows what to say at a funeral," Carissa said.

Holly longed for the things that used to be a source of strength in her life—like Granny's smile and wise words—but she was gone forever. Family members reassured each other she "left a rich legacy" to ease their pain.

Noticing Abby, in the corner with downcast eyes, Holly sat beside her daughter. They talked about life's hardships especially death and how humans struggle overcoming obstacles. It was a deeper conversation than they had shared before.

Guilt began to overwhelm Holly and she burst into tears. Putting her arms around Abby, she sobbed even harder—mostly for her failure as a mother. All she could do was weep on her daughter's hair.

"I wish Adam was here," she finally whispered.

The minister began the funeral by reading John 14:1 from the Bible. "Do not let your hearts be troubled. Trust in God; trust also in me." It sounded comforting but Holly was confused. She couldn't hear the rest of what he said—trying to figure out what he meant. Her eyes rested on the coffin.

Jake and Abby fidgeted by her side.

The soloist's voice sounded like an angel. "I sing because I'm happy ... for his eye is on the sparrow ... and I know he's watching me." Thinking about bird watching with Granny made Holly happy for few minutes.

After the service, the extended family gathered at Granny's house to dispose of her belongings.

"Granny wanted relatives to have a special reminder of her life so she carefully made lists," her oldest son Ted said when everyone arrived. "We're going to work together. Females collect items in the kitchen, bedrooms, and living areas. Men go through the basement, yard, and garage. Holly will check each of those articles off on her list—to confirm who the specific item goes to—before we set it aside."

"Let's use our cars to store personal heirlooms," a nephew said.

"Put unmarked *useful* objects in these boxes. Junk to be discarded can be relegated to the back porch," Phil Armstrong said.

Holly looked at the garden with sadness.

Even the forlorn birds had stopped singing. What would they do at Christmas? She wiped her tears, blew her nose, and began to study the items listed in Granny's notebook.

Tired from the extra activities and drained of emotion—family members used the last of their energy to accomplish this final task. When everyone finished, Holly's father brought in dinner from a deli. Sad faces mourned around the living room as they ate. The delicious flavors of the food went unnoticed.

Most relatives were unusually quiet.

"Granny's gone and won't celebrate here ever again," Holly said suddenly. "She would want us to be happy. Who has a story to share?"

Jake began to tell what he enjoyed about his great grandmother. "Gigi jumped rope until she sat down puffing … and she smiled no matter what I did." He retold some of her exciting tales. Holly's eyes glistened as he talked. Abby joined her brother in retelling the story of the cookies.

Others followed with their own stories. Soon everybody laughed with delight at the joy Granny brought.

"Taking nature walks with her was always enjoyable for me," Holly shared.

"This incredible woman cared more about others than herself," Susan said about her mother-in-law. "I knew how much she loved me."

"She called on the phone to keep up with my current travels," Shari said. "Her notes in the mail cheered me up."

"Granny never forgot anyone's birthday," Lori added.

"Working out in her garden was a good example for us," Ted's brother Phil said. "Still living alone at 84, she cleaned her house like a young maid and picked her own green beans."

"Never ill or needing medical intervention, I've been amazed at my mother's health," Ted said. "Her positive outlook and cheerful countenance benefited Granny, as well as others."

Holly decided to become more like her grandmother.

When I reach the end of my life, it needs to count for something other than myself, she thought driving home. She smiled at her children. With or without Adam, she would provide all the joy a mother could offer. She couldn't wait to get started.

Waking early, she retrieved oil paints stashed in a corner of her closet and set up an easel in the kitchen. Humming, she mixed colors and created Granny's garden. From the bay window, she looked outside at her own.

Birds frolicked as she painted.

Determined to spend less time cleaning, she designed an innovative schedule. The detailed lists were color coded and beautifully adorned. Her new strategy allowed for gardening and working outside on Saturdays. Sundays were art days.

Colorful paper plates were perfect for meals. *She had little appetite for food but craved something that would satisfy a deeper hunger.*

"Adam's away on business trips and hardly eats at home, even when he's around. Jake and Abby are preoccupied adolescents who usually just snack," she said to Carissa. "Everything's going to turn around now that I'm figuring my life out. Next item on my agenda, find someone who I can bond with for life."

Wondering about the scripture from Granny's funeral, she searched for the red Bible that Gramp and Granny Armstrong gave her as a child. It had been years since she looked at it. Opening it, she hesitated—but spotted a table of contents.

Finding the reference was easier than she thought.

John 14:1 said, "Let not your heart be troubled; you believe in God, believe also in me."

"What does it mean?" Each word seared into her mind like a tattoo.

Holly loved the first part, *"Let not your heart be troubled ..."* That had been comforting at Granny's funeral and was soothing right now—with her messed up life; but she had no idea how one goes about doing that. You can't magically forget your problems. It was baffling.

And to *"Believe in God?"* She opened her dictionary. The word *believe* means: to accept as true or real, to trust. She believed there must be a god out there somewhere. The world was amazing—and the order of the universe too detailed and technically spectacular—to have just happened with a bang as they explained in school. *It couldn't have been an accident.* Someone must have planned the solar system.

How can you *rely* on someone you can't see? Is that like expecting Santa Claus to come with presents every Christmas?

Two gods? That was hard to accept. If there were two different gods—which was superior and what did the second one do?

Holly had no answers.

Tucked away in her old Bible she found a fancy piece of paper, 6 *Rules Children Live By.* It was unfortunate she misplaced it until now—it could have been useful years ago. She read it again.

Rules Children Live By ~ Children Learn by Your Example

1. Children who live with criticism learn to condemn ...

The words went on but Holly's tears kept her from reading them. She set the Bible aside and went to get a cup of tea.

Her life was painful enough.

Summoned into the Administrator's office, Holly shut the door and sat down. Judging by Theresa Marshall's serious facial expression, something was dreadfully wrong. They had laughed together just minutes earlier in the break room.

Theresa Marshall started speaking and broke down in tears. Holly could hardly understand what she was saying. Filled with compassion, she leaned closer—desperately trying to understand.

Something terrible has happened to Theresa.

With a contorted face, her boss mumbled some words. "On his way … he might not make it … Adam … someone was waiting …" Her red and puffy eyes filled with tears.

"Did you say … Adam?" Holly asked, her eyes narrowing.

Theresa nodded. Regaining her composure, she repeated the information.

"On his way to the airport for a business flight, Adam was involved in a terrible accident. He was rushed to the hospital—they don't know if he'll make it. He may already be gone. I'm so sorry."

Holly was numb with shock. Part of her wanted to rush to Adam with open arms and cling to him. Part of her had no desire to see him again and wanted to be alone for a few minutes.

"Do you want to drive to the hospital yourself, or would you like a ride?" Theresa asked.

Holly slowly stood and then sat back down, slumping in her chair. "I need someone to take care of Jake and Abby," she said with a lump in her throat.

"Beth agreed to watch them until you can make other arrangements. You can take as much time off as you need," Theresa said, coming around to the other side of her desk. "Stella can drive you over there."

Arriving at the hospital, Holly filled out paperwork before going to the ICU waiting room. She had eaten nothing since breakfast and had no appetite now—but a nurse brought a sandwich and coke. Her thoughts were jumbled. She forgot to call home to see if things were okay there.

"Mrs. Clark … Come this way," a nurse announced.

She stood and followed as if in a trance.

Holly stared at the gauze-covered figure, unable to recognize one familiar feature. Ugly tubes protruded from the nose, mouth, arm, and groin. Contraptions pulled his extremities into contorted positions. The body lay motionless except for an occasional rising of the chest.

Was there some mistake? Could this possibly be Adam?

Her lips were parched, her throat ached, and sweaty hands trembled. Fluid oozing from his head caught her eye. Aaugh! An offensive smell gripped her nostrils as waves of nausea overcame her senses. IV's, blood, anesthesia—it didn't matter. Holly clasped her hand firmly over her mouth, pivoted, and rushed from the room.

Just in time.

Her knees buckled when she reached a chair in the waiting room. Was this the end of a miserable relationship? Was her marriage ending abruptly without a divorce? Having her independence somehow seemed catastrophic instead of offering the exciting future that looked so promising yesterday.

She struggled to maintain control but memories of the past flooded her mind.

Adam had been a tower of strength—so energetic no one could beat him physically. After the ski accident in college, he hiked with his leg in a cast before the week ended.

Oh, for one more laugh together.

Her loneliness escalated as the clock ticked. Suddenly the starkness of the situation gripped her. She was the one without life! Nothing she attempted had meaning—it was all in vain.

"Oh God … I need somebody to help me!" she cried.

A nurse appeared and informed her Adam had suffered multiple internal injuries, broken bones, and facial lacerations. Once stabilized, his face was sutured and bandaged. Emergency surgery stopped internal bleeding. With that corrected, they could set his bones.

His fragile condition was prolonging efforts to help him, however.

Once every hour, for five minutes, Holly could go in and stand by Adam. The first time she just cried. Then she had to wait for another opportunity. There was uncertainty whether he would make it, but he was still alive an hour later.

Holly sat patiently in the waiting room day and night—only leaving her chair to use the bathroom, get coffee, or call Jake and Abby. Her mother flew in to care for them.

At night, Holly slept with her head propped against the wall.

She tried to appear strong each visit to his room. Reaching down to touch his hand, she prayed Adam would live. Once she whispered, "I'm glad you're alive." She tried to be creative. Smiling, she told him that his children loved him.

The stranger peeked at Holly thru bandages—looking nothing like the Adam she knew. He couldn't talk. "Was it even the right man?" Holly didn't know but she continued to go in and stand by his side.

Occasionally, she said other things to him.

"How are you doing, today? Jake and Abby are planning a trip to Disneyland when you get home. They are busy playing tennis these days." He didn't respond; but surely wanted to hear about his children.

Waiting for the hours to pass, Holly attempted reading magazines— usually in vain. Most daylight hours included fidgeting with her purse and pacing the hall. Preoccupied by his condition, her mind jockeyed with assorted scenarios.

Various people entered and exited the waiting room giving ample occasions to observe character. Holly withdrew emotionally but watched with curiosity. Their interactions fascinated her and reading people became a new pastime—looking for patterns in body language, speech, and appearance.

One frantic female cringed in the corner. Another aggressively interrupted family conversations. Common sense, foolish judgments, and guilt about the past spilled out unknowingly to innocent bystanders. Many conversations were hushed or muffled by tears.

"I just don't understand why this is happening ..."

"Would you shut up," a mother said to her child.

"What if she doesn't make it?" one man asked his wife.

Holly noticed a dignified older woman who exuded a sense of peace—strange for such a setting. Nothing seemed to change her serenity. Family members interacted with her and she offered solace the others craved.

Reflecting on personal strategies and her own responses to problems, Holly was intrigued. "Do you have a family member in ICU?" she asked.

"My son ... who isn't expected to live," the woman said bravely.

"How can you remain so calm? Were you emotionally close?"

"Absolutely! He has been a delight for 40 years."

A nurse interrupted the conversation. It was time to see Adam. "Good news," she said as Holly approached the door. "After 6 days the endotracheal tube has been removed."

Holly looked around the corner with curiosity.

It was still the same immobile patient but now he had lips. For some reason it appeared funnier. With one leg in a cast pulled up in the air, Adam looked like he was trying to fly. Both arms were broken so his extremities protruded. Holly giggled at the profile. *Here was a gifted athlete—capable of doing almost any physical feat—looking like a mummy.* Grinning, she squeezed the big toe on his right leg … his toe twitched.

"Ouch!" he said.

Holly jumped backward and ran to the door.

A nurse, walking through the doorway heard Adam say, "Please stay?" Astonished, she called the doctor who came right in to check his patient.

"Adam's going to make it," Holly told her mother on the phone.

"When can we see Dad?" Jake asked.

"I don't know—but I'll tell him you want to come."

"Can I bring some cookies?" Abby asked. "I made some with Grandma."

"We'll see," Holly said.

Back in the waiting room, the older woman noticed her smile. "Looks like good things are happening … I'm Libby Thomas, by the way."

"Life is a lot more difficult than it looks. I'm not sure if that's good or bad," Holly answered.

Over the next week, Holly continued to seek answers to her questions. "Where do you turn in times of difficulty—when you're overwhelmed and feel helpless—hopeless?" she asked Mrs. Thomas.

"I may feel lonely but I'm never alone—I can't be even if I want to," Libby said.

"How nice," Holly answered, believing the Thomas family surrounded their matriarch all the time.

"Lift your eyes and look to the heavens," Libby said pointing.

"I love creation!" Holly exclaimed. "I've never known for sure—but there must be a god who made it all."

"Since the creation of the world, God's invisible qualities have been clearly seen," Libby said. "There's a verse that says men are without excuse … Although they claimed to be wise, they became fools, and denied that God exists. Look it up in the Bible. It's true."

She scribbled verses on a piece of paper and handed it to Holly.

When Mrs. Thomas went in to see her son, Holly picked up a Bible on the corner table and opened it to Romans 1:20-22. Bewildered, she read the words again. Then she found Isaiah 40:21-26.

"How do you know the Bible is true?" she asked, when Mrs. Thomas returned. "Do you really believe god calls each star by name?"

"Yes—and He feeds the birds," Libby said. "He also cares about your needs and what's going on in your life. We were made to connect with our Creator."

She reached for a cup of tea.

"When I star-gaze or listen to birds sing, I feel a special warmth—but I'm confused by what my emotions tell me in other areas. I've gotten into huge problems paying attention to how I feel."

"I don't let feelings guide me," Libby explained. "Our emotions are like the gorgeous creation around us—God provides them to make our lives richer but they shouldn't become a god, or control our responses."

"How do you know this?"

"I don't have all the answers but I know who does. You can find lots of important clues about living in the Bible."

"People say we're supposed to let our conscience be our guide. Doesn't that mean listening to your feelings?" Holly asked.

Libby readjusted herself in the chair and leaned forward with a smile.

"Every baby is born with the ability to discern right and wrong. Watch their eyes when they start moving around. Alarms go off if they head in the wrong direction. We're all tempted to misbehave—telling lies, serving our own interests, allowing longings to become more important than character—no one is immune. When you disregard warning bells meant to protect and accept distorted reasoning instead, your seared conscience will be muffled, stifled, silenced over time. When your alarm system becomes damaged and can no longer grasp wise insight, you're in big trouble."

"Is that why the Ten Commandments are important?" Holly asked. "I don't really believe in them … but the principles seem beneficial. Didn't people in Mesopotamia have trouble obeying them? No doubt, they couldn't figure it out with the societal unrest and constantly changing political scene. Their altered thinking wasn't a personal choice so I don't hold them accountable. If there was a supreme being guiding them, surely they would have made different choices."

"There's a difference between my conscience dancing around truth and His sweet Spirit guiding me that will never compromise. It all goes back to what you believe about a carpenter who went to the cross."

Holly was disappointed when Mrs. Thomas announced her son was being transferred to another wing. "There are more things I wanted to ask you," she said.

"Don't be afraid to talk to the Almighty Creator. He is waiting for a personal relationship with you. Scripture will also open your eyes to many things. It's a guide book for living—just like a map when you head out on vacation."

"Thank you, Mrs. Thomas. You've given me hope," Holly said, hugging her new friend.

"I believe in miracles," Libby said before she left.

The next morning, Adam was transferred to a private room where Holly could stay all day. At night, she went home to sleep in her bed. Grandma Susan continued to take care of the children and manage household chores.

"When can we go to the hospital?" Jake asked.

"We'll see," Holly said.

Since both of Adam's arms were in casts, his wife held the glass of water so he could drink with a straw. It seemed to soothe his throat because he smiled at her. The only thing she could think to do was smile back. "You're making great progress," she said hesitantly. He looked frail with his body ravaged by injury. She wondered what the future would hold.

Most days were pretty quiet.

Haltingly, Adam began speaking. He only answered her questions at first, with brief answers. Holly usually lost track of what the conversations were about. It was like talking to a newborn. He remembered nothing about the accident but seemed aware of his injuries. Slowly, he started asking his own questions.

When Holly left, he would cry.

She could do little for him—but pictures of Jake and Abby around the hospital room brightened his spirits.

Arranging for a brief visit, Holly finally brought her children to the hospital to see their father in person. Stunned to see his helplessness, they stayed by the door for several minutes. Abby started sobbing, hiding her face in her hands. Holly coaxed them in with a conversation about Disneyland. Jake remained stoic, preoccupied with becoming a teenager soon. After enduring the awkward situation for an hour, they said goodbye.

"See you again soon, Dad," Abby said before leaving.

His eyes looked fearful and began to moisten …

Adam wanted to be significant to Holly. There was no way to convey his wishes though. Speech was difficult—and sharing his emotions had been almost impossible before the accident. He couldn't reach for her hand either; but whenever she touched him, he said, "Thank you."

He wished just once he could touch her lovely hair again.

Or her body.

She looked more beautiful than ever with her sparkling charm dressed in cute sundresses, striking capris and knit tops. The way her shirt clung to her chest was more thrilling than any movie he could remember. He watched a lot of them when she chose to ignore spending time together—in the interest of helping him out.

"Haahhhh!" he said.

"Are you uncomfortable?" she asked.

He looked deep into her eyes and wondered why she rejected his love in the first place. How could she turn to other men to fulfill what he longed to give? What did she see in them that was more desirable? Hadn't he proven his love; shown how much he cherished her? Why was it never enough?

She gave him another sip of water. *Maybe this was her way of saying that she still really cared.*

When she left, his tears started again. It was lonely without her.

Finally, the day came for Adam's release.

"Take it easy," his doctor said. "Skiing and marathons are out! You need extra healing before you can even do much physical therapy."

Holly understood there would be months of recuperation but he could mend in his own house—and cheaper. Regardless of the challenge, it would be a wonderful change in environment.

She was relieved to get back at the Art Center. The months had taken a toll on her emotions. "I'm only working part-time—to be available for you," Holly said to her husband. "And some of it can be done at home."

Jake and Abby sat by their father in the evening, chatting instead of going to their rooms or spending time with friends.

They enjoyed him more than they expressed.

Costly medical expenses had strained the Clarks' finances to the limit—even with insurance paying most of the bills. With Adam unable to return to work for an indefinite period, they lived frugally as possible. Maybe they could sustain themselves until these desperate circumstances changed for the better.

If not, they would have decisions to make.

Chapter 12

Redemption

ADAM HOBBLED TO THE front door—perplexed by insistent knocking. A mail carrier handed him a form to sign and registered envelope.

"Thank you, sir."

"Hmmm ..." he said shutting the door. Adam opened it gingerly— apprehensive of what could be inside. He pulled out a letter.

> *To whom it may concern:*
>
> *The Desert State Bank is currently under scrutiny by the New Mexico Department of Banking Authority regarding questionable lending practices. You will be notified of probable closure pending outcome of our final review.*

The news was shocking. He was aware of nothing during the past twenty years that would have contributed to this outcome. His last conversation with Tom Mitchell had been upbeat. "The bank's doing fine and we're eager to have you return," Tom said cheerfully.

With his hand shaking, Adam dialed the bank.

"Mary, can I please speak to Tom?" There was a brief pause before his boss answered.

"Tom Mitchell ..."

"Tom ... Adam Clark ... I just received a letter from the State Banking Authority. What's going on over there at the bank?"

"Oh, hello Adam … Sorry I didn't share more with you earlier. I was hoping to keep your spirits high so your recovery would be quicker." Tom said. "Unfortunately, without your expertise to keep things on target, our bank has taken a nosedive."

"A nosedive?" Adam said, waiting to hear more.

"Your temporary replacement was actually inexperienced in speculative loan skills. I assumed it would blow over," Tom explained. "Norman lacked your capabilities as CFO. I can't go into more detail." Adam's intuition indicated he withheld pertinent information because of the nature of the situation. "We'll let you know more, as soon as this can be resolved. Don't worry about us. Just get healthy."

Not prone to analyzing theories, Adam had nothing better to do than his physical therapy. What would he say to Holly?

The hours crawled by slower than ever.

Returning from the Art Center, she encountered car problems. The Acura stalled in the middle of an intersection. Holly had the car towed to a repair shop; calling Adam to give an estimate for replacing the computer module—and to say she would be late.

"If it's got to be done, then do it," he said.

He decided to withhold his news until later.

Shocked by the final charges, Holly arrived home discouraged—suspecting they would have trouble fitting this bill into their already tight budget. Getting a drink of water, she sat down by Adam who looked ashen. Holly suddenly remembered he had been home alone the entire day.

"Oh, I forgot you might need help. How are you doing?" she asked.

"I managed to eat some lunch and complete my physical therapy."

"That's good. I'm sorry I wasn't here," she apologized. "I intended to get back hours ago—the car took longer than I expected."

"Where are Jake and Abby?" she asked, noticing it was quiet upstairs.

"Didn't I tell you? They're spending the night at Julie Welch's house. By the way, I got this letter in the mail."

He handed her the envelope.

"What is this about?" she asked. He tapped the table while she read. "How can this be?" she said, looking up completely confused.

He shared what Tom Mitchell said. "Now it's a waiting game."

After Adam went to bed, Holly went to the kitchen to try to calm her stomach gnawing on itself. Distraught by months of emotional upheaval following Adam's accident and the agonizing recovery process—followed by reduced income and financial problems—this was the final blow. Adam would be unemployed permanently. They would lose their house. Financial devastation was knocking on their door.

She could no longer take care of anyone, including herself.

Holly paced back and forth deciding what to eat for dinner, wondering if there was another option for solving the ongoing financial mess. Fighting about money had consumed so many years they should have enjoyed. If God cares about feeding the birds, why didn't he care about what she had to eat? She made a sandwich with turkey and cheese—dropping it on the floor before she could eat a bite.

"All of your useless strivings have been in vain."

She already knew that. It was obvious to everybody how miserably she failed at everything she attempted.

She poured a glass of water and gulped it down.

"You try to quench your thirst, but nothing ever will ... It's not water you crave," a still small voice said.

Putting her elbows on the table, hands covering her face, she sobbed.

"I don't know how to express my thoughts anymore but I'm speaking from my heart. Can anybody hear me? Please ... someone listen," she began. "I've made a huge mess of my life! Everything good, perfect, and noble I have tried has turned into ashes. My attempts to do right are like those filthy rags that caught fire in the garage and burned it down—I thought they would bring joy but they brought great sorrow instead."

"I'm desperate for answers I can't find—although I know a million interesting facts that are useless right now," she pleaded.

"Hmmm," she said standing. A longing to read scripture—and understand what it meant—was growing in her brain. She ran to find her Bible. Opening the pages at random, she read Proverbs 14:1, "A wise woman builds her house, but with her own hands the foolish one tears hers down."

It couldn't have been said more clearly. Tears filled her eyes.

"Please forgive me, God—I tried to usurp Adam's power in a selfish struggle for control. I'm also sorry for being a terrible mother, failing to be a good example for Jake and Abby. I was obsessed with my capabilities—egotistical—and drove others away."

"I'm a failure and don't deserve a second chance ... but I need one."

As Holly drew near to God, He comforted and wrapped his arms around her—just as she had held Jake and Abby years ago. Breaking into a smile, she thought about people placing a baby in nativity scenes at Christmas. Holly always assumed that represented a symbolic family unit—important for bonding over the holidays. Christmas seemed more cheerful with a newborn.

Old Christmas cards Granny sent were still in the closet. Holly retrieved the basket and sorted through a few. They always mentioned Jesus ... she seemed to remember.

"Humble shepherds worshiped Him in the fields when they saw the star," one card said.

"Angels sang, *Glory to God in the Highest!*" another declared.

"Wise Men traveled from afar to present Him the best they could offer," a third announced.

The baby Jesus suddenly acquired new significance. It all made sense after years of wondering. Her brilliant mind missed an important event in history. *What else did she skip over unknowingly?*

Reading John 14, the verses shouted answers Holly searched for her whole life. She touched the words as she read, "I am the way, the truth, and the life. No one comes to the Father except through me ... Because I live, you will live also... But the Helper, the Holy Spirit will teach you all things ... My peace I give to you ... Let not your heart be troubled, neither let it be afraid."

Falling on her knees, she acknowledged that only Jesus could give what she desperately needed. In the middle of her kitchen, Holly accepted the gift He waited to give.

She begged God to teach her the proper way to live—how to please Him instead of herself. Filled with joy, Holly turned the light off and went upstairs.

Tiptoeing into the bedroom while trying not to disturb Adam, she bumped the bed. Restless, he woke and rubbed his eyes. "I wondered when you were coming to bed," he said. "It's after midnight."

"I didn't realize it was so late."

Adam did a double take. Was he was seeing things? *She changed dramatically since he went to sleep.* Puzzled he sat up and turned on the lamp. Holly seemed to sparkle! Adam couldn't take his eyes off her. "Look in the mirror!" he said.

"Why?"

She glanced in the mirror but didn't understand what he was saying. "Perhaps you had a bad dream," she said.

"No, something is different—even your voice has changed."

Adam started weeping so Holly cradled his head in her chest. Maybe the shock of losing his job was making him crazy. Possibly the accident had done more damage than the doctors estimated. She was unsure how to respond but a transformation within her was beginning to build—like steam, when a teakettle is about to start whistling.

Words began to slip out of her mouth.

"Oh Adam, I've had such guilt and desperation. When I was up in Colorado for the funeral, I tried to find solace but there was none. I remember touching Granny's hand after she died. The warmth was gone—it felt like stone. Then I realized she was never coming back."

Adam listened in silence, wiping his eyes.

Holly continued. "You know how I love being in the mountains? This time, the lavender mist at nightfall frightened me. I watched pieces of cliff separate and plunge thousands of feet below, shattering on the bottom. One thought gripped me—what will happen to me in the end? That's it … I'll lie in the dirt with maggots eating me?"

Adam couldn't formulate words fast enough.

"At the hospital after your accident, I didn't recognize you. It reminded me of a terrible nightmare that paralyzes—but you wake up and find it's not real—only this was! The awful smell reminded me of death and I realized our marriage *hadn't* turned out as expected … and it would be better if you didn't survive."

Adam sat wide-eyed. "Have you hated me all this time?"

"I recognized the problem was me—I was the one without life. The world couldn't provide what I craved. I rushed to grab my desires prematurely and they all turned to dust. It's like planting seeds in a garden. You need to let them take root and grow the way God intends."

She took a deep breath.

"Don't stop! Tell me more."

"I don't know if it means anything to you but I prayed you would someday see the truth about my new decisions and give me a second chance. Will you ever trust me again?" Holly asked.

Choked up, Adam reached for her hand. "I'm not saying things were perfect—but our relationship is worth rescuing," he said. "I remember when you used to respect me. I'd give anything to have your love again."

"I promise—with God's help—to be there for you," Holly said. "We need to pick ourselves up and move on. Ultimately it's an act of commitment."

They snuggled together for the first time in many years, at peace with each other and hopeful about the future.

A glorious sunrise surprised Holly as she tiptoed into the kitchen eager for a cup of coffee. Most shocking was the variety of swirling colors, with ochre, tangerine, and peach shooting rays into the darkness of heaven. Seeing the brilliance, she let out an audible gasp. Surely, God meant it as a fresh reminder that not everything was, as it seemed.

Wind woke her earlier—still blowing tree branches after an eventful evening of storms. She fully expected to find rain and a cloudy sky when she peeked outside. Patio furniture lay askew and a container of flowers had tipped.

A dazzling ball of gold made its way to the horizon—popping its head to say, "Good morning."

"You're sure cheery!" Adam said when he shuffled into the kitchen.

"The day is beginning great! I'm anxious to see what it holds."

Holly made cheese blintzes and ate breakfast with her husband, smiling for a change. Lighthearted, she tried to figure out why she felt such peace. Adam's letter on the counter made no difference. "Something changed in me," she said. "My brain feels like I'm at rest—no longer searching for meaning to life."

"What a relief!"

Adam smiled, finishing his enjoyable breakfast.

He thought about the night before … and the letter. It was all a mystery. His wife mentioned a brain change; maybe his brain still needed healing to understand what was happening—but he liked where things were headed; or maybe not. What would happen if he couldn't return to the bank?

Talking to his parents on the phone, he made some decisions. He gave Holly a summary.

"My parents invited Jake and Abby to visit California for the summer. I promised they could. Do you have a problem with them leaving next week, after school ends for the year?" he asked.

"How long are we talking?"

"A couple months …"

"That's a good idea, Adam. It will give us time to regroup here."

So Jake and Abby excitedly packed—eager to see grandparents, uncles, and cousins for two wonderful months.

Ready to surf in the Pacific Ocean, they climbed out of their grandpa's car. "I can't believe we're on our own," Jake said with a grin.

Life by the ocean—away from hostile and overprotective parents—presented more opportunities for fun than recent years offered. He grabbed his surfboard from the back of Grandpa Clark's Prius and raced across the parking lot in his bare feet. Abby followed behind, struggling to keep up.

"I'll be back at seven," his grandfather called from the car window, almost out of hearing. Jake turned to wave.

"Thanks for bringing us, Gramp."

"Come on, slowpoke. Race you to the shore," he said taking off.

Abby leaned on a post—briefly adjusting her flip-flops—before trying to catch him. She grasped the surfboard tighter and ran a few steps, dropping her bag of belongings on the sand. By the time she got to the shore, he was headed toward her on a huge wave.

"Yay!!!" he yelled.

She pulled her camera out in time to catch him going headfirst into the surf. "Dad's going to love this," she said.

By the time he regrouped, Abby was attempting to get the hang of staying upright herself. She struggled to stay on her board.

"My feet keep slipping when the wave begins," she complained. "First I go forward on my knees; or I lose my balance and fall off the side." She landed on her fanny with a thud and decided to give up for the day.

Before long, her brother was sailing down the surf having the time of his life.

"It's going to take time," he said, sitting beside her for a break. Jake watched the other suntanned kahunas for ideas. "That guy in the gray shorts is pretty good," he said with envy.

Abby had already wasted too much time, and was getting sunburned, so needed an exciting alternative. Watching people come and go from the corner store with their purchases was more enticing. Fortunately, she brought some money.

"Wanna watch this stuff while I go in the little shop?" she asked.

He nodded.

"Bring me a sandwich when you come back."

Over an hour passed before she returned with a new bathing suit—a floral bikini—that caught her eye. She also bought a chick lit story about three girls marooned in Hawaii during a storm. "Where's the sandwich?" he asked.

"Oops."

"I'll get one myself," he said jumping up. Want anything to eat?"

"No thanks. I ate a Snickers while I shopped."

Jake returned within minutes—with a burger, two wine coolers, and a big smile. "The guy looked at me and said to enjoy. He thinks you're cute."

She blushed. "What will Mom and Dad say?"

"How will they know? We're growing up, Abby. They aren't going to know everything." He unscrewed the top and handed her one. "Strawberry Fields ... I figured you would like this one since you like strawberries."

She felt guilty taking a sip but the sweet flavor slid down her throat with ease. Before long, the bottle was empty. The smoothness was amazing. She tingled with a feeling she'd never experienced.

"Want another?" Jake asked, already finished and counting his change. "Life's too short to miss opportunities when they jump in your lap." He stood up and headed back, eager for a greater thrill. Abby could hardly wait.

She watched the surfers, so confident and in control of their lives, and determined to become an expert herself.

Jake returned empty handed.

"The younger guy was gone and this man told me I needed to be older to buy those drinks," he said. "Sorry to disappoint you Abby. We can get more coolers another day. The best part of this vacation is that we won't hear people screaming at each other; and telling us what to do."

"Yeah, it's going to be fun," she said. It didn't really matter what happened this summer. They were growing up and needed to learn to be independent. And they wouldn't get in trouble!

Gramp Clark drank cocktails every night around the pool—even offering Jake a taste of his highball. "Now that you're a teenager, everything's going to change," he said. "We'll teach you a few things about the good life and get you ready for manhood. By the time you get back to school, other boys will look up to you."

Maybe boys would think more highly of her, also. She could wear her colorful new bathing suit to test the waters. Since her body was maturing, she was beginning to stand out from other girls.

When Jake returned to the water, she went to the restroom.

Her bikini was adorable with tiny bows at the sides of the panties—and another where the top scrunched together at the cleavage—with piping around the edges. It plunged a little lower than her mother would appreciate but that didn't matter this summer.

Sure enough, it worked like a charm!

While Jake perfected his surfing talents, curious teenage boys crowded around Abby as she sat on her beach towel. "Hello there," a muscular blonde with attitude said, sitting down on the sand. His friends chatted about surfing while Zeke got to know her better. A boy with glasses moved in when Zeke left. He was more interested in looking at her bikini than finding out about where she came from.

Rusty—a fifteen year old with red hair—was the most fun. He teased Abby and tried to tickle her. They wrestled on her towel until it was full of sand. She never had a boyfriend before and imagined what it would be like. When he invited her to take a walk on a trail, she jumped at the chance.

"Come this way; there's a better view of the ocean," Rusty said. Abby followed close behind. They hiked up a hill and the path narrowed. Rounding a group of trees, he pulled her up beside him. "I think you're beautiful," he said. She smiled.

"Are we almost there?" she asked.

"You've never seen anything like this before. You'll be glad you came." They went around some bushes and he stopped suddenly, wrapping his arms completely around her body. "Ready for the best part?" he said.

"Am I ready to see the great view?" she asked, a bit confused. "Yeah ... I'm ready."

Rusty pressed his lips against hers, holding her in a warm bear hug. It felt sweet. His mouth opened and he gently sucked her lip. She giggled. He paused for a second before kissing her again even harder than before. He pressed his tongue onto her teeth, trying to make an opening. His hand slid under her bathing suit. Abby tried to turn but he pulled her down on the ground and began groping her body.

"I don't want to do this," she cried out.

"You know what you want me to do," he insisted, continuing to touch her torso—moving his right hand down to her thigh and fondling sensitive areas.

"Please Rusty, I just want to be your friend," Abby said, with fear growing in her throat.

"That's a lie," he said, pressing his lips against hers so hard she couldn't talk. He continued to touch her while bearing down on her lips with such passion she could hardly breathe.

He readjusted himself over her body and she began to cry.

"Why would you throw yourself at me, driving me crazy with desire for you … if you had no intention producing rewards?" he said, pulling back. "You little tramp!" He slapped her in the face and stood up.

Adjusting his clothes, he walked away.

Abby lay on the ground in disbelief. How did he get such a wrong idea of what she wanted? What was it that caused him to treat her this way? Maybe she was an awful person. She would never tell a soul about this situation—including Jake. The secret would stay right here under these bushes.

She stood and adjusted her bikini, trying to brush off dirt and leaves. Retrieving a flip-flop, she noticed a dark smudge across the leather. Her mother would be so upset; these were expensive. Why had she insisted on spending birthday money on something so stupid? Oh well. Right now, there were more pressing matters.

What if Jake noticed she was gone? Where could she say she had gone?

Frantic to find her way back to the beach, Abby rushed down a path. A rustle in the weeds startled her and she jumped. "Oh god … not again!" she said. A squirrel darted up a tree. Tears resumed and she brushed them away, hoping her nightmare would end.

She looked around cautiously, glanced back, and hurried on. Stepping over a Pepsi can in the clearing; she remembered the trail and picked up her pace. Compulsive thoughts of how to explain her actions superseded any pain she felt.

When she reached the bottom, preoccupation with finding a restroom overcame her senses and she bolted in.

No one was around.

She sat in silence, her heart beating faster than ever. She leaned forward with her head in her hands. Why did she come to California with dreams for a wonderful summer? Why did she buy the stupid bathing suit?

Remembering her brother, she washed her hands and splashed warm water on her face. Her lip was bruised. She touched her lips—reminded of the sordid kiss she enjoyed in the beginning. A scratch on her arm and red mark on her thigh couldn't be disguised. Too bad, she didn't bring a cover-up. If only she could make it back to her towel without being noticed.

"Where have you been? I've been looking all over for you," Jake asked as she hurried across the sand.

"Uh ... Oh, I decided to take a hike, and got lost," she said, brushing dirt from her forearm. "I fell down on the trail." She bit her lip, struggling with emotion.

"You look terrible, Abby. Are you okay?" Her tear-stained eyes brought feelings of compassion and he reached over to comfort her with a hug. She broke into tears as he stroked her back.

"Shhhhh ... It will get better," he said.

Jake held his sister in his arms until her sobbing ceased. "It's time for Gramp to pick us up. We need to get our things and head over to the parking lot."

"Don't say anything about this. Promise me? I don't want them to worry about us out here. I want them to trust me," she said.

"I do, too."

Abby sat by the pool alone after dinner deep in thought. Sunburned, she felt like she was on fire. Her body was beginning to ache but her soul was distressed. Hearing her parents argue, shouting hostile things at each other—hateful and full of revenge—was a lot to take in, but this was worse. Dreaming about having a loving husband someday once gave hope to the dreary reality of marriage.

Maybe it would never be a good thing!

Trusting another guy with her heart someday? No way! She would never give another person the chance to take advantage of her.

Watching a half moon, so detailed on the curved left—with a blurry right side melting into the sky—caught her attention. She could almost see the craters. It stood at attention like a photo as filmy clouds passed below.

It moved slowly; the only way you could tell was where it hung in the sky an hour later.

Why was there so much evil in such a beautiful world?

Her parents probably loved her but she felt like a wretched failure. Maybe she was the reason they were unhappy. Nothing made sense!

Would tomorrow be any better? Jake was excited about being a teenager but the thought scared her to death.

No matter how hard she wished, no place on earth would welcome a tramp. Everyone said, "Go for your dreams, Abby!" but right now, she had none.

Chapter 13
Joy

HOLLY SEARCHED SCRIPTURE BEFORE the sun woke up, sipping hazelnut coffee and feeling giddy. Her favorite verse was Psalm 16:11, "You will make known to me the path of life ... in your presence is fullness of joy." Spending time in His presence was the best thing she could imagine. With good time management, she also could enjoy her husband—who was becoming a better friend.

Adam remained quiet most days. He seemed preoccupied.

The daily struggle to complete physical therapy—regaining only minimal use of his limbs—required more motivation than he could muster, with dimmed hopes of reclaiming his former athletic prowess. He did little else with his time.

"I found the most amazing thing," Holly said when she returned from the Art Center. "Can I take a minute to show you?"

"Sure."

She opened her Bible to Genesis 3:16. *"To the woman he said, your desire will be for your husband ..."*

"The minister read that when he married us," Adam said.

"Yes, I know. I believed a wife was supposed to enjoy her husband—but didn't after a few years. Now I realize it means that wives would try to usurp their husband's power for selfish purposes. Who does that remind you of?"

"Surely not *my* charming wife?"

Holly continued reading. "And he said to the man, you listened to your wife and ate fruit from the tree, although I commanded you not to. Through hard work, you will eat the food that comes from it every day of your life. The ground will grow thorns and thistles for you …" Gen. 3:17-19 (NIV)

"Hey, let me read that," Adam said reaching for her Bible. "That sounds exactly like what happened."

"It explains the confusion about priorities and why our relationship was unfulfilled," his wife agreed.

Pulling her shell collection from under the bed, Holly picked up a favorite—the triton, a turreted shell with a colorful, twisted spire. It reminded her of building the castle with Adam at the Amore Resort, one of the highlights in their fragile relationship that represented hope.

When the tide came in and washed it away, dreams of rebuilding their marriage crumbled.

She tenderly touched the other fragile treasures. The scallop was fan shaped with a delicate, fluted pattern around the edge. The starfish was more solid. The color inside the conch was brighter than on the outside. Seashells intrigued her but she never understood why until now.

A living animal sheltered inside, braved the harsh realities of weather. Its demise meant another trinket in her box.

"I wondered what smelled under there," Adam said walking into the room.

"You should have noticed years ago—and taken action to make our home smell better," she said.

"I wasn't much of a leader for our family then; I was too involved with my job."

"Well you're here now. Hey, can we talk outside over lunch," Holly asked.

With lunch on a tray, they dined in the backyard. Birds flitted overhead, eager to share the tasty morsels.

"I met a wonderful woman named Libby Thomas at the hospital. She's the calmest person I know. When I was stressed over your accident, she showed me a verse about God feeding the birds—and how we're much more valuable to Him!"

"Does that have something to do with the change in you?" Adam asked.

"Maybe. Realizing there really is a God who loves me—definitely has changed my perspective," Holly said.

"Do you honestly believe that?" he asked.

"Just a minute—I'll get my Bible."

She showed him Romans 1:20, "Since the creation of the world, His invisible attributes are clearly seen, being understood by things that are ... so men are without excuse ... Professing to be wise, they became fools..."

"Remember when I wondered about the stars being so precise?" she asked. "It didn't make sense to have something like the constellations, which men can document in charts with specific times, seasons, and patterns of movement—to just appear in the universe with a big poof, by accident." Holly moved her arms up in animation; and accidentally spilled her iced tea.

"Oops! Yeah, just like that," she said bursting into laughter. "Accidents destroy instead of creating incredible masterpieces."

"That's the truth. Early sailors used sextants to decide accurate headings in the middle of nowhere and sail boats to specific targets," Adam said more seriously. "Military aircraft used the same charts to navigate the night skies across oceans. Some planes had observation bubbles to gather data—I believe they call it celestial navigation."

"Under a cloud cover, none of that works," Holly added. "The stars need to be shining. Isn't that amazing?" Her eyes sparkled.

"It's still a very accurate tool but nobody knows how to use it anymore ... almost a lost art." Adam continued to explain about the accuracy of slide rulers and using E6-B flight computers for dead reckoning—eager to share more information.

"You're losing me, here," Holly said, taking a deep breath. "Anyway, I want to tell you more."

"Are you happy to know my brain still functions?" Adam asked.

"Absolutely! I'm thankful you survived."

She moved her chair closer, reaching for his hand. Butterflies, birds, and a squirrel caught their attention for a while. "Can we get back to nature?" Holly asked.

"Can't get much closer than this, can we?" he asked jokingly.

"Look at the complexity of the planets—each one is unique yet they all have a specific order and revolve in a precise pattern that we can depend on. If you take a group of children and give them directions—like in a marching band—they can try as hard as they want, but you will always see someone out of place, out of step, or out of costume."

"Is this where man's foolishness comes into play?"

"I guess it would fit here."

"What's the solution to a bloke's foolish predicament then?" Adam asked Holly. "Do you know the answer?"

"Yes—it's all about Jesus coming to earth as a tiny baby."

"Seems almost too simple," Adam said, standing up from his chair. "My leg's getting sore and I need to exercise. Can we talk about this later?"

Walks around the neighborhood became possible with Adam growing stronger. Sometimes kids joined him. When she could, Holly tagged along. "Don't go running off—'cause I can't catch you anymore," he teased.

She held his hand and said, "Being with you is more important."

They chatted about creation, people in the neighborhood, and priorities. Holly was at peace with herself and the world. It intrigued Adam. "You've always possessed great charm but it was hard watching you slide off the cliff," he said, "Something went haywire. I wanted to hold you and protect you but you wouldn't let me near."

"Robert Browning said it best. What I aspired to be, and was not, comforts me."

"I like that man. But seriously, you're morphed into a more beautiful creature than before," he said. "And I don't ever want to go back to the hell we were enduring."

"Good. I finally know the answer."

"Well, I'm finally listening," Adam said.

"Our journey on earth is like taking a trip by train. Neglecting the track, ignoring warning signals, and rushing ahead in dangerous terrain results in calamity—but if you have no engineer, the passenger's in even bigger trouble and won't make it to his chosen destination."

"Duh!"

"Who is your engineer?" she asked.

"I've never thought about that. Myself, I guess."

"Are you willing to crash again?"

"Now you're scaring me, Holly. Is it time for lunch?"

"Can I tell you how a baby fits into this first?" she asked. She could no longer keep the wonderful information to herself.

"Sure, go ahead."

"It all goes back to what you believe about a Jewish carpenter who died on a cross," she said. "Libby Thomas gave me some clues in the ICU waiting room. Jesus was more than a man who walked on the earth doing good things. He was the long-awaited Messiah who came to earth for one reason—to pay the price for our sinfulness. Some reject him as savior, wishing to control their own destiny. The choice is theirs to make; but our time on earth will end with one final breath. Nothing can change our destination after that. We chose heaven or hell. There's no second chance. I'm going to heaven. Where are you headed, Adam?"

With a desire for mercy and grace—greater than he could verbalize in words— Adam accepted the gift Jesus offered. Holly hugged him as he talked to God.

"What if I had died not knowing?" he asked when he finished.

"We would have spent eternity in different places," she said.

Before dawn, they anticipated seeing the glorious sunrise together. Adam poured coffee while Holly grabbed jackets and they waited in the backyard. Drinking coffee in the dark—while holding hands—was a romantic experience.

"Do you remember looking in my eyes at our wedding?" Adam asked.

"Your baby blue eyes looked totally different from the steely blue eyes I saw many times over the years," his wife said.

"Do you remember me tracing a heart over my chest?"

"I almost cried when I saw that."

As the sky gradually lightened, they stopped talking and looked up. Pale pink light replaced the gray mist. It seemed as if time stood still. Adam winked at Holly. Layers of coral, tangerine, and bronze filtered through the cerulean blue. A mound of crimson formed in the eastern quadrant, accented with a halo of orange—and then a gold ball appeared—almost too dazzling to look at. There she sat full of glory! Watching the magnificent colors float across the horizon, in contrast to the dark infinity preceding it, they were speechless.

He leaned over for a kiss.

"I used to love a solid azure sky with only the sun shining," she said quietly. "When clouds moved in, I was disturbed. Did you know clouds and wind are necessary for sunrises and sunsets? It's interesting how the things we like least—sometimes are the most beneficial."

"I'm glad you cared enough about me to stay, Holly. And even more than that, I'm thankful you had courage to share the truth about my sinfulness."

"We need to keep our eyes on the destination," she said. "Our excitement begins when we discover what the almighty Creator offers."

"Are you ready to learn more?" he asked.

"If I had known what I was getting into when you proposed the first time, I would have shouted a louder, YES!"

He kissed her again before getting up to find a Bible.

"Look at this." he said, reading Joshua 24:15, "Choose for yourselves this day who you will serve ... as for me and my house, we will serve the Lord."

"That's going to be out motto," Adam said.

"Can I have another wish?" she asked over breakfast.

"If it includes me."

Holly had long admired the church with exquisite stained glass windows near the Art Center. Brilliant scenes enhanced the entrance; a second group of vibrant designs rose higher on the right side of the building. The works of art were breathtaking, gleaming in the sunshine.

"I really want to go this Sunday," she said.

"And listen to that scary minister tell theories of an afterlife?" Adam said.

Holly laughed, remembering back. Congregation members raved about the minister, Reverend Jeffrey David, but she feared he might try forcing meaningless opinions on her. Avoiding his lecture was imperative; but seeing the beautiful windows from inside piqued her interest—perhaps how paradise might look to dreamers who make up theories of an afterlife. Something within her spirit always urged her to slow down. Would the door be open?

Excited to attend, she called for information.

At 10 o'clock on Sunday morning, hundreds of parishioners entered through the lobby of Grace Fellowship, inspired by glimpses of heaven through exquisite stained glass windows. It took her breath away! She grasped Adam's arm as a stranger reached out his hand. His friendly smile and cordial greeting surprised her. Others warmly welcomed them.

Holly noticed a "Welcome Friends" tapestry on the wall.

Centered in front of the looming sanctuary—a modern day Noah's Ark with embellishments, minus the animals—flickers of sunlight hinted of eternal beauty longing to be seen through stained glass. They entered and found seats near the back.

Responding to the time of worship brought mutual joy. Holly sang animated but Adam's voice joined in with depth. "All creatures of our God and King ..."

She wished they had come sooner!

"Let all the world rejoice ... How great is our God ... everyone sing ..." Beautiful stained glass windows joined in with their glorious radiance. No doubt, the Almighty smiled.

Rev Jeffrey David's sermon began with exactly what they needed to hear. "Don't listen to this lunatic," Adam whispered in her ear, jokingly. She gave him a smirk, getting out a pen.

Holly took notes as fast as she could write.

"Trusting Jesus as your personal Savior changes attitudes, thinking, and desires. Life takes on meaning and purpose. We may begin sincere—but before long are confronted with reality, living in a sinful world. Perhaps no one explained the process of staying on track. Belief in the Almighty and including Him in your life does not mean we escape problems and suffering. Will we always understand reasons for difficult circumstances? No, but blessings result when we obey God and leave the consequences to Him."

"Schedule some time every day to study scripture; Read Proverbs 3:1-6, Psalm 1:1-3, and Joshua 1:7-9. Write them on your hearts. Post them on your walls. Teach them to your children. Meditate on them day and night. If you want your life to really count, walk on a path that allows consistent connection with godly principles. Will you like everything scripture tells you to do? It's not always easy to do what is right."

"Allow the Spirit of God to infuse your mind with truth and energize you with his power. It's like having electricity functioning in a home versus encountering a power failure. Doing things in your own strength is futile and pride will get you in trouble."

"Keep your eyes on your destination."

Sunshine burst through the beautiful stained glass as they sang a final hymn. Spreading light through each brilliantly colored piece, the entire wall was illuminated. Together, the colors filled the sanctuary with an awesome display of majesty. "Oh Lord, my God ... When I in awesome wonder ... consider all thy hands have made ... then sings my soul ... how great thou art ..."

"We're coming here again next week," Adam said as they left.

"It was better than I imagined."

Holly couldn't wait to read the scripture Rev. David mentioned and opened her Bible on the drive home. She read it to her husband ...

He read it again, after lunch.

"Those verses in Joshua about being courageous are powerful," he said. "I'm going to make spending private time with the Almighty my priority. Even Jesus talked to His father. Must be essential while we're on earth—especially if situations become frustrating and difficult."

"I enjoy the reference in Psalm about being like a tree firmly planted," Holly said. "Studying scripture energizes me. It seems I can't learn fast enough. Being firmly planted, that's the key to inspiring others."

"These verses need to be an anchor in our lives," Adam agreed.

"Isn't our life amazing now!" Holly said.

Back from California—Jake and Abby noticed the transformation immediately. They whispered in the back of the Pacifica, riding home from the airport.

"We want to hear about your trip," Adam said.

"Something's up and it's not Jake's hormones," Abby said laughing.

They shared a few incidents, guarding their thoughts, and answered questions briefly.

Holly shrugged her shoulders.

Hearing their father's deep voice talking to God late that evening, Jake, and Abby came to the kitchen doorway puzzled. They had heard shouting and seen animosity for years. Shocked—they stood frozen and gawked at their parents kneeling side-by-side on the floor. They tiptoed back to their rooms.

"Did aliens come while we were gone?" Jake whispered. "I think they took our parents."

"We're gonna figure this out soon," Abby said.

"Before the paint fumes get to us," Jake joked.

Curious about the dramatic changes taking place, they watched and listened. "From one viewpoint it looks entirely positive," Jake said to his sister.

"But cults brainwash even the smartest people," Abby answered. "Because of Dad's weak body and current job situation, it's possible he's gone completely overboard out of fear."

"Another official letter arrived today," Adam said, when Holly returned from work.

"Why didn't you tell me on the phone? How bad is the review?"

"It's on the table."

She picked the document up and read,

> *For your information:*
>
> *News organizations have recently been informed of Thermal Energy Enterprises stock activity. You may see news reports indicating shares are now @ .10 and expected to go higher. Please be advised, your shares purchased twenty years ago remain restricted and are not eligible for trading. We will keep you advised regarding any change in status lifting these restrictions.*
>
> *The Securities Exchange Commission*

"What is this? Holly asked, bewildered by the information.

"Joe Wallace and I invested in penny-a-share stock in a start-up company during our senior year in college. The stock was worth little at the time but we hoped our $1,000 investment would be worthwhile someday. I almost forgot about the investment," he said grinning.

"So what does that mean? I'm confused."

"The Legend on the Certificate restricts trading the stock—so it's worth more money, but only on paper. Perhaps we can take a second honeymoon someday though. Time will tell."

They had much to be thankful for over Thanksgiving.

Holly roasted a turkey and made traditional side dishes. She showed Abby how to fold napkins creatively to resemble their honored fowl. A cornucopia with fresh fruit was the table centerpiece. "I forgot you knew how to entertain," Adam said.

His prayer beginning the meal was heartfelt. Jake and Abby laughed when he said, *"You're our unseen guest."*

"I haven't spent much time talking to God out loud but he knows my intent," Adam said when he finished.

They took turns poking each other's arm—and giggling—as the meal continued.

"Let's share what we're most thankful for," Adam said.

Abby began, "I was afraid Dad would die. I'm sure glad he didn't."

"I'm happy Abby and I went to California for two months and I learned how to surf," Jake said.

"I am thankful there really is a God and most of all—that He forgives," Holly said.

"And I'm thankful God knows the future and we don't need to worry about what tomorrow might bring," Adam said.

Wanting Jake and Abby to know options for the future, he discussed the situation at the bank. Challenging each other not to get discouraged as they faced an uncertain future, Adam said, "We're all in this together, no matter what."

"Who wants some pumpkin pie?" Holly asked.

As holiday lights flickered around the community, the Clarks celebrated with candy canes and hot chocolate while playing games together. Having Adam home added extra joy to the festivities.

Butterscotch chased ribbon on the floor.

Putting up a tree, they talked about the past. With twinkling bulbs in place, Holly brought out boxes of decorations. Jake and Abby carefully placed each one in just the right spot. "Move that over one inch," he joked.

"It's fine," Abby assured him. "She's not yelling anymore!"

"Not yet, but that will change." Jake said. "Mom can't pretend forever. She's going to resort to her old tactics sooner or later."

Holly gave him a look of disgust.

Before his mother could respond, they heard carolers on their front porch. Opening the door, friends from the new church sang, "Away in a manger, no crib for a bed … the little Lord Jesus laid down his sweet head … The stars in the bright sky looked down where he lay; the little Lord Jesus asleep on the hay."

Thanking the carolers with candy canes, Adam closed the door and sat down—tears welling in his eyes.

Jake and Abby stopped laughing and looked at their father.

"That's the first time I've heard that song and understood its meaning," he said, his voice quavering. He wiped his eyes. "I appreciate hearing those words."

"I felt the same emotions—and would have bent down and kissed that little baby, if he had been here," Holly said.

"He is," Adam said, looking into her eyes smiling.

Jake and Abby looked at each other and shrugged their shoulders.

Wrapping presents while listening to Christmas music, Abby asked her mother, "What will happen when Grandpa and Grandma Armstrong arrive?"

"Why do you ask?" Holly said.

"Will they notice the change? How will they respond?"

"Don't be silly, Abby. They'll love it!" Jake replied.

Ted and Susan Armstrong were warmly greeted at the door when they arrived. Holly seemed happier than usual. Adam appeared robust with a healthy glow to his checks. Abby couldn't help but whisper, "My parents have a big surprise!" when she hugged them.

Noticing a difference in Holly, her parents wondered about the circumstances. They were surprised to discover significant warmth between the couple. "Do you suppose she's pregnant?" Susan asked her husband.

"I doubt it but who knows. We'll find out soon," her father said in private.

Sensing changes in Adam, as well—following the past year's traumatic events—Ted Armstrong inquired how he was doing when Holly went to get groceries.

"Your recovery is remarkable," Dr. Armstrong began. "But how are you doing internally?"

Hesitant at first, and then with a decisive tone in his voice, Adam decided to share the good news. "I prefer waiting until Holly's with me but I'll start at the beginning—and let her fill in when she returns."

"I was a passive husband at one point but God is changing my heart ..."

The Christmas Eve Service began with a drama of shepherds in a field watching their sheep under a brilliant star. The young 'sheep' were eating grass, occasionally bleating. Most were resting on the platform while late arrivals found their seats—a couple waved to parents; and one needed to use the restroom.

When angels began singing, an 'aaahh' could be heard throughout the congregation. The children looked innocent in halos as they raised sweet voices in praise to an almighty God.

The three kings looked wise beyond their brief years on earth. They eagerly tried to find the newborn baby so they could worship him properly. One needed his big brother to help carry his gift to the manager because it was heavy. When his brother hesitated he yelled, "It's for Jesus—hurry!"

Rev. Jeffrey David encouraged the children to sit around his knees—like Jesus would have wanted—as he shared the meaning of Christmas.

It was beautiful and touching. Holly saw her mother wipe a tear.

Adam followed with a solo. "O little town of Bethlehem ..." The words penetrated Holly's mind as he sang. What joy they gave her—as she finally understood the meaning. She prayed for her children and parents to grasp the truth somehow. The Armstrongs, sitting next to Jake and Abby, listened intently.

The program ended with the entire congregation singing *Silent Night* as candles glowed—one at a time. The sanctuary filled with a golden light illuminating the stained glass windows—this time from the inside, for people passing on the street.

"The delicate, mellow colors remind me of letting *our* light be seen," Holly whispered to Adam.

With people crowding around to thank Adam, and shake his hand, Jake and Abby stood close to their father. Holly chatted with her parents who were, "fascinated by the presence of a baby who entertained us this evening," Susan Armstrong said.

Unwrapping gifts at home was pale in comparison.

Adam and Holly knew of a gift that was better than any other they received that year. "I wish we could tell—with more persuasive words—about the peace the manger offers," Holly said, as she got ready for bed.

"We can tell with our lives until someone asks specifically," Adam said.

Looking out at the sparkling stars Holly thought she heard angels singing.

Chapter 14
Hope

"OH, WHAT A BEAUTIFUL morning! Oh, what a beautiful day!" Holly woke with a smile on her face. She loved dreaming that particular dream. The song penetrated her mind while she slept and stayed in her head for hours.

A sense of peace surrounded her as she got out of bed and went into the kitchen.

Adam and the kids could continue sleeping but Holly had something important to do. Putting her sweater on and grabbing a cup of coffee, she slipped out the back door. Reading her Bible in the garden was a treat. These minutes alone with God were priceless before responsibilities distracted or anything could disrupt her plans.

He offered hope when everything was a disaster. She couldn't find words to adequately express her gratitude—nor could she thank him often enough!

Her prayers were answered with a love for scripture.

"Tweeeet, tweet, tweet." The birds sang their own praises as she opened the pages of her very favorite book.

Adam walked out as the sun crept higher in the sky. "Good morning, my love." He kissed his wife before sitting down to join her. "You look beautiful meditating—with the flowers and greenery surrounding you.

I'm a privileged man!" He knew Holly was exceptional the first time he saw her but never guessed she would become *better* than he expected.

At one point, I considered discarding her. I would have been a fool.

Not that he was exempt from doing foolish things. He attempted a significant amount of them—and Adam was a man keenly aware of numbers. God had somehow protected him in spite of his foolishness.

The minister's sermon the week before was on God's Empowering Presence.

"God gives us evidence of His presence and speaks clearly through His Word," Rev. David said. "Sometimes He wakes us up, giving insight and understanding about problems; or He provides a new idea during the day. He works through complicated circumstances, so that deep down we will know God has been there and intervened."

Adam knew in his heart that was true.

After breakfast, a mail truck pulled in the driveway and he answered the door. The mail carrier greeted him with another certified letter.

"The writing is on the wall," Adam said. He opened it, preparing for the inevitable. His wife leaned over to see the words.

"Oh! It's not about the bank," he exclaimed—handing it to Holly.

Notice—

The restrictions have been lifted for your 100,000 shares of stock purchased twenty years ago when Thermal Energy Enterprises was formed. The current rate is $7.50 share. No longer restricted, you can do what you want with these shares at this time.

Glancing up from the letter, she looked at her husband. "Does this mean what I think it does?"

He nodded his head, jumping in the air, and shouting, "Thank you God!"

Adam hugged her and they both reread the words.

"I was preparing for the worst," Holly said. "What a surprise!"

Jake and Abby appeared in the doorway wondering why the commotion. Both waited in eager anticipation for what would come next.

"What's happening?" Jake asked, knowing joyful exuberance—especially when his team was winning a game.

Adam finally spoke. "God provides when everything we work for isn't enough. At our lowest point, this is a pot of gold at the end of the rainbow."

They got on their knees to thank Him as a family.

The next day was even better.

Adam received a phone call from the insurance company, wanting to settle for the loss of his car in the accident. The payoff was much more than the car was worth but Adam accepted their generous offer. Depositing money in the bank, he knew the creator of the universe was in control of his life.

"I'm asking God to show us how to spend it wisely," he told Holly.

Fantasizing about moving to the country for years, Adam found an advertisement for a rustic ranch with moderate accommodations—just north of the city. "Are you interested in checking it out with me?"

"We won't need to work in the city anymore?" Holly asked.

"If we sell our home, we can start over debt free," Adam said.

Looking at the property was better than going on vacation. The blue sky was surreal with fluffy clouds looking like little lost sheep that needed a shepherd. The house had a big front porch shaded by large trees—and the red barn begged for a horse, perhaps the same one Abby daydreamed about.

"We loved it from the minute we set our feet on the soil," Adam told his father.

Noticing Lisa Stewart by the fence, Holly told her about their plans to move.

"It sounds exciting! I'll miss you," she said glancing over at Jake. He shifted nervously on the patio, aware of her eyes.

"I'm getting a horse," Abby announced.

"You're lucky—invite me out to ride," Lisa said.

Finalizing the purchase, the Clarks signed papers and arranged to move. The process went smoother than expected with a quick sale of their home. Nostalgically, they sat under an apple tree the last night on Brookshire Lane.

"The journey God has taken us on since our wedding has been extraordinary," Holly said reflecting.

"We were so idealistic, proud, and driven to succeed—and almost lost everything on our path to self-destruction," her husband said.

"Adam, do you remember Fontaines with its crooked, cobblestone streets and half-timbered houses—dotted with the tiny fountains? It was one of the most picturesque villages we visited. In contrast, towers and gates fortified the castles in France keeping their enemies from penetrating the walls."

"Do you still think of me as an enemy?" he asked, jokingly.

She shook her head.

"And then there was Heidelberg's old town in its half-ruined state sitting on the tranquil riverside—opposite from the inspiration bustling Paris offered."

"Do you remember what I told you under the apple tree in the Nowatny's back yard?" Adam asked.

"Somehow that slipped from my mind when we returned home."

"Only God knows where He's taking us from here," Adam said. "Difficult periods of our lives last long enough for God to accomplish His purpose—Rev. David said."

Hope surged through their souls as they watched the stars twinkle.

Replacing his smashed Lexus with a tractor was the first item of business for Adam. Visiting the local implement dealer was a thought-provoking venture, discussing best deals with sales representatives. Shopping at a tractor supply store was equally challenging.

"I felt like a teenager buying my first car," he said at dinner. "How was your day?"

"I rearranged furniture trying different combinations," Holly said. "Once I was concerned about our home looking fashionable but my focus is now on comfort. The boxes can be unpacked as we settle in"

"Getting to know neighbors is more important," she continued.

"So who did you meet?" Adam asked.

"Tim and Karen Janssen live on the east side of our property. They have kids in college—I don't know the names or ages—but they have a friendly Collie."

"Can we get a dog?" Jake asked.

"Maybe. We'll talk about that later," Adam said.

"John and Kelly Sorenson live on the west side and have a 7 year old daughter Kristin, and 5 year old son Daniel. They have the cutest black puppy named Milo."

"And what did both of you do today?" Adam asked, looking at Jake and Abby.

"I found a tree to use for building a deer blind." Jake said.

"Eww, no way!!!" Abby said.

"Jake and Abby ran all over the property with the energy of young children," their mother said. "They came in for lunch hours late—not realizing how fast time had gone."

With rosy checks and soaring spirits, they ate dinner together. "When I get my horse, I'll beat you to the end of the pasture," Abby said.

"We should have ostrich contests like the Swiss Family Robinsons," Jake said laughing.

"Are you going to tell Mom about the creek?" Abby asked.

"I think you just did," he answered.

Holly smiled as she listened to them talk. They loved the place almost as much as she did.

Sitting on the porch, the Clark family shared interesting stories.

Abby came up with a rotation plan. "Dad's always the storyteller on Mondays. His sagas are the most gripping," she said. "Mom's turn is on Tuesdays. She's more imaginative and will give us something to figure out."

"I'll entertain you with tales from the Wild West on Wednesdays," Jake said.

"And on Thursdays I'll tell exciting stories like Gigi used to make up," Abby said.

Everyone looked forward to hearing the stories each week. Some were real life—others were make-believe. Finding interesting tidbits of information to add to their creative narratives kept each family member observant of other people and events. True journalists, they asked questions and took notes.

"How long will it last—since Jake and Abby are getting older?" Holly asked Adam in bed. "Teenage activities will soon compete for our time."

"We'll enjoy the stories as long as we can," Adam said.

Little did they know, Jake and Abby would *still* sit on that porch telling stories years later.

To receive an agricultural tax exemption Adam decided to purchase sheep. He talked to neighbors and inquired at the local feed store about which ones to buy. Tim Janssen gave him valuable insight and helped find some Barbados.

"We're the proud owners of three ewes and a ram," Adam announced.

The new shepherd observed his flock as the sheep grazed. They appeared content and at peace. Most wouldn't eat out of his hand—but one trusted him, brushing against his leg. Rebecca loved corn and munched as much as she wanted. When the others saw her eat, they nudged closer and closer, trying to muster courage to nibble themselves.

"Who wants to feed the sheep?" Adam asked. He always had helpers.

"Take a little corn and hold your hand straight out, Abby. She'll come in a minute if you're quiet."

"It tickles, Dad," Abby said giggling.

As a shepherd, Adam did nothing to make them afraid but sheep are fearful animals—often jumping from their shadows. Trying to reunite with the others, a ewe charged into the side of the barn.

"Why are they so stupid?" Jake asked.

"Sometimes they foolishly hurt themselves because of fear," Adam explained to his son. "They need someone to watch out for them."

"Maybe I should learn how to take better care of myself," Jake said. "The girls are all in love with me at school and won't stop chasing me."

"Sounds like we need to talk about this some more," his father said.

On his tractor mowing grass, Adam had hours to think about Holly's birthday in a few days. He contemplated how to surprise her—considering funny ideas and some serious possibilities.

Holly had accumulated all of the possessions she needed. Her desires no longer included receiving expensive gifts or glittery jewelry.

"Being with friends and family means a great deal," she said—but moments spent with Adam seemed to bring the most joy. *The perfect gift for Holly would be a day away from home, alone with him.* He considered her favorite places and decided to accentuate the celebration with something unique.

Adam got up while his wife slept on September 14 and made breakfast. Placing the garden omlete on a plate, adding strawberries on vanilla ice cream, and a blueberry muffin from the bakery—with a candle in the center of the silver tray—he delivered it to her in bed, with a kiss. "Happy Birthday my little chickadee … Do you know what you mean to me?" he sang.

"Did you make all of this?" she asked. "I'm impressed!"

Holly laughed as she ate—amused at the menu.

Adam smiled as he sat on the bed. "Dress in casual clothes and come outside for another surprise when you're finished."

When Holly peeked through the doorway, she giggled. Adam was standing with a big red bow around his chest and a key in his hand. "My gift is myself and I'm taking you on a treasure hunt. Here is your first clue," he said, handing her a piece of yellow paper. "I have a key to the treasure chest when you find where the last clue is hidden," he said.

She read the note. "Lions, monkeys, and elephants make their home in my wings."

With hints he wrote on various slips of yellow paper, the birthday girl had to figure out where to go for the next clue. They started at the zoo, walked in the sand at the lake, sat by the waterfall at Water Works Park, and Adam pushed Holly on a swing. For dinner, they ate lobster at a gourmet seafood restaurant and then had cappuccino at her favorite coffee shop.

"You'll treasure the words that I hold," was the most difficult clue. She assumed it meant Treasure Island, her favorite bookstore.

Holly was unaware the last clue would take them to Oasis Christian Bookstore—so Adam helped. Finally, at the right place, she turned the key in a wooden chest and found a gift certificate for a new Bible.

Deciding which one was the best was the hardest part.

"It is my best birthday ever!" Holly said. "Thanks for such a wonderful day."

As they lay in bed snuggling, Adam sang again.

"Happy birthday, happy birthday … just for you. Happy birthday and may all your dreams come true …" He looked forward to growing older together and promised her next birthday would be even better.

The last thing Holly remembered was Adam gently stroking her hair.

On the first day of winter, Adam ran to the house announcing, "Snowball is having a baby!" They ran to the barn to watch as the little lamb was born.

The mother was protective, licking her offspring and nuzzling the adorable critter. After eating some hay, she called to her lamb with a soft "baa" and Snowflake ran to her mother and took a gulp of milk. Her tiny tail swished in the air.

"Seeing God's gift of life right in front of us—brings tears to my eyes," Holly said.

"This really is awesome," Adam said, hugging her while they continued to watch. "It's an experience I hope we see often."

After observing the lamb's birth—Adam sat between Jake and Abby. "I've made a lot of mistakes in the past but I love you," he said hugging them. "I want to be a better father in the future."

Not accustomed to quality time with their dad during childhood— or privileged to much emotional and verbal support—they listened quietly.

Abby smiled at Jake.

Happy whenever lambs were born, Adam had extra sheep to count. Frightened, they often sprinted past—jumping in the air.

Occasionally he searched for a missing lamb.

The sad bleating of a tiny creature caught in a fence caused Adam almost as much pain as its mother endured. He tenderly balanced one trembling lamb with his hand while stretching wire with his other. Gianni squirmed and jerked trying to get loose, not able to free himself. He was dehydrated and limp.

The ewe rejected her injured lamb when he tried to drink milk. With his survival in question, Adam held a pan of water to his mouth and the animal took a sip. Hesitant to leave but with nothing left to do but pray, the tired shepherd went to bed.

The next morning Gianni was up and running around, nursing from his mother.

Compassion for Adam's own children increased—as his love and concern for the lambs developed. Connecting with Jake was difficult emotionally, but Abby was becoming more of a joy.

Dreaming about owning a horse since childhood, Abby found an 8-year-old white Arabian. Adam was impressed with the health and temperament—and agreed to purchase the mare for his daughter. "You're the best dad in the world!" she said, after they unloaded the horse.

"Don't fall off and break your neck," he said.

Abby could think of nothing else. She loved caring for Princess and went to the barn with grain and fresh water. Occasionally, she brought an apple.

Princess loved apples!

Grooming the mare with a brush and picking out hooves, she hummed. "Sounds like one of those lullabies I sang to calm you as an infant, Abby," her mother said. Princess stood patiently while her mane and tail were braided.

Abby spent as much time as she could with her prized Arabian, riding Princess around the delightful ranch. When finished, the mare was turned out to graze—while her stall was mucked.

"Mom, I discovered a fantastic view from a hill," Abby said. "Princess and I go there to talk about our dreams." She babbled on. "Princess gazes in my eyes and listens. That's what I like best about having a horse."

"Abby used to be a fussy child who didn't like to get dirty. Shoveling manure now brings her great joy," Holly told Adam, intrigued by the twist in events.

"We should have given her a pet sooner," he said.

Jake burst into the house accompanied by a new friend, Peter Johnson. "We're going to swim across Lake Hiawatha," he announced. "Pete's an excellent swimmer and we want a challenge."

Holly gulped.

"Few people have attempted swimming across—but it's been successfully accomplished I've heard," his father said. "You won't be the first!"

"It's that or climb Mt Everest," Jake joked when he saw his mother's shocked look. He knew she was capable of canceling his plans.

"I'm excited to hear the news," Adam said. Because of his own athletic prowess and water skills, he assumed that would be exhilarating. After he thought about it, he wasn't sure. This was his only son.

Talking it over, Adam and Holly recognized his need to make decisions—under their watchful guidance. "Whether or not he might fail is no reason to abandon worthy endeavors," his father said. "He needs to consider all the options and learn to make wise choices."

"Jake needs to discover it's necessary to continue trying even if he fails," his mother said. "Fear of failure paralyzed us. We over-achieved with no regard for consequences, in order to ensure success for our fragile egos."

"In the end, our immature actions were almost catastrophic ... and without God's mercy and grace, we could have sunk to the bottom of a lake much bigger than Lake Hiawatha," Adam said.

They discussed teaching their kids how to set beneficial long-term goals.

"We made mistakes not being realistic in what we attempted. Let's practice learning how to do that together as a family," Adam said.

Foolish in their parenting for years, they would do the right thing now with God's help.

"Can we make cookies the right way?" Holly asked her daughter. The stress filled cookie-making day crossed her mind on occasion.

"I remember the first time," Abby said.

Getting out ingredients and mixing batter became more fun when Holly patted flour on her face. "I want to look beautiful like my daughter!" she teased.

"And I wanna look like my mother," Abby said, doing the same thing.

Almost the same height, though slightly heavier, this daughter looked more like a sister. Her platinum hair was deepening into the honey blonde tresses Holly proudly brushed—with Abby's baby blue eyes the only difference.

Laughing, they used their imaginations while shaping cookies, adding some creative designs with a knife. They chatted and giggled while the cookies baked. The kitchen smelled heavenly with vanilla, almond, and cinnamon swirling in their nostrils.

Abby became more serious. "You act different than you used to, Mom."

"What was I like?" her mother asked.

"You rushed here and there trying to accomplish tasks while appearing like a good mother." Climbing on a chair, Abby continued in a mocking voice. "Attractive capable Holly could leap from buildings and do amazing feats but would berate herself all day long. Then she would complain about Abby who never seemed to do anything good enough."

"Did I really?" Holly asked, with a quizzical look on her face.

"Why did you push me away?" Abby said quieter.

Crushed to hear what damage her good intentions caused, Holly apologized. "I'm really sorry. Will you forgive me? You'll never fully know how much I love you until you hold your own child in your arms someday."

"What caused you to change?" Abby asked.

"While I was in the ICU waiting room, I met a woman who answered some questions about my existence. My life was a mess! Back in our house on Brookshire—sitting at this table—I cried out to God for being such a terrible mother and wife ..."

Abby had known that her parents were miserable—in fact hated each other in their old house. She sat down as Holly shared her story.

"No matter how much love you receive from earthly parents, God loves you more," her mother said. "He wants a special relationship with you, Abby."

"And I do, too!"

Sitting at the kitchen table, just like her mother one year before, Abby became personally acquainted with the one true God.

"Will you teach me to paint, Mom?"

"Of course—I didn't know you were interested." Getting out her art supplies was a special privilege for Holly.

With easels set up and palettes loaded with brilliant colors, they painted the sky, the barn, and Princess running in the pasture.

"Do you know why the sky is blue?" Abby asked.

"The earth's atmosphere absorbs color and the sun's rays scatter it. Blue spreads out the easiest. And rainbows are made when drops of water in the air act like prisms and separate into colors—instead of just blue."

"Is red on the outside or inside of a rainbow?"

"Red's on the outside and violet on the inside of a rainbow. If a second rainbow forms above the first, the colors are reversed," Holly explained.

"I love doing stuff with you."

"Me too, sweetie! It's time to clean up—but we can paint Butterscotch, wildflowers, and a sunset another day."

For Abby's 13th birthday, she received a pine box—with little hearts carved on the front—filled with art supplies. She also received a Bible with *Abigail Susan Clark* inscribed in gold on the cover. Inside was a note. "Delight yourself in the Lord and He will give you the desires of your heart." Psalm 37:4 (NIV)

When Abby went to Kings Crossing Camp with church friends, Holly wrote a letter and mailed it—on the day her daughter left. Receiving it the next day, Abby sat on a bench and read,

> *Dear Precious Abby,*
>
> *I miss you already! The house is lonely with you gone and I can't wait for you to return. I have a special place saved just for you. As I pass your picture on the wall, I think of the treasure God gave me when my sweet baby Abby was born. You give me great joy—even if I don't express it. No matter how far away you are, I'll keep memories of you close to my heart! I love you more than you will ever know.*
>
> ♥
>
> *Mom*

Abby had an enjoyable time at camp knowing she was deeply loved. When Holly returned to pick her up on the last day, they hugged tightly. "This is my mom," Abby said to her friends proudly.

"I wish I could have been here having fun with you," her mother said.

While driving home, Holly listened to each detail of the week—including about the cute boy who kissed Abby down by the lake.

"I learned about the stars," Abby said. "Maybe, I know even more than you."

"Will you show me tonight?"

When the sky darkened, Abby said, "Look over there, Mom. Do you see that hunter holding a bow? That is Orion. Do you see his right hand up above his heart? That is Betelgeuse—it's easy to spot because it is red."

"Wow! You're a real astronomer!" her mother said smiling.

Adam was still working in the barn so Holly turned the porch light on before going to bed. She couldn't wait until he climbed in next to her to snuggle. Maybe he would touch her hair in the moonlight.

In the stillness of the night, she poured her heart out to the one who cares the most. There was much to discuss about her children—they each had specific needs and tender areas requiring wise parenting. She needed His help to be an effective mother. Bungling it badly before, she never intended to rely on her own strength again.

Holly thanked God for giving life to Abby *twice* and for the privilege of being there to observe both times.

She longed for Jake to have a personal relationship with Jesus. "I know you hear my prayers and will answer my request someday," she said. "In the meantime, make him envious of the glorious transformation taking place in his family."

Holly fell asleep knowing the Awesome Creator cared more about a relationship with Jake than about the majestic stars in the night sky.

Chapter 15

Satisfaction

HOLLY INCHED ALONG A fallen tree trunk to cross the rushing stream—holding her arms out for balance—eyes focused straight ahead. *I'm sure it stood proudly on the hillside before meeting its demise*, she thought. Adam shouted encouragement from the other side.

"You look like a tightrope walker at the circus," he said.

"I feel like a blind woman ready to fall off a cliff."

"That reminds me; you never finished telling the story about climbing Blind Man's Bluff. Did you do that with your eyes closed too?" Adam teased about Holly's former hiking adventure with her father.

She remembered vividly. It was the scariest thing she had done. Tales were told that a blind man was lost and ended up at the bluff, trying to find his dog. Because it was such a treacherous climb, he never made it back alive. They found his remains in the valley below.

"I'll tell you the rest when we stop to eat," Holly said.

"We've hiked two hours already. I'm hungry and need to rest."

Holly retrieved turkey sandwiches and corn chips from her backpack and they sat on a big rock. Squirrels under a nearby tree watched playfully, waiting for a morsel. A Blue Jay chortled a friendly tune.

"Tell me about the bluff," Adam said, eager to hear the end.

Holly proceeded to tell him about the beautiful wildflower field she trekked through before coming to the rocky rise. Her foot had slipped twice as they navigated over the stones, scraping her knee. Holly's father wrapped gauze around it before they continued.

"Going around a group of trees, we followed a rustic path that curved and twisted as the incline got steeper. Initially, the trail consisted of a couple feet of earth on the left side, gradually becoming a narrow pathway—right on the edge of the mountain."

She paused to take a few bites.

"The hike required maneuvering over a series of rugged ledges. Nearing the top, we came to a place where we had to walk sideways—holding on to roots sticking out of cracks in the boulder—to make it the last ten feet. Climbing onto a fifteen-inch step made of granite, we looked out over the most incredible view in Colorado. Tradition requires that whoever makes it to the top alive, carves their name in one of the rocks before starting down."

Not realizing her canteen had fallen over, Holly reached for a drink of water. Picking it up, she was aghast there was no water left. "We have at least another hour to hike before returning to our car," she groaned.

"Like the woman at the well, I was thirsting for things that could not satisfy," she said as they started back. She meant it sincerely. For years, she craved everything money could buy but none of it satisfied.

"Is your name carved at the top?" Adam asked when they got back to the car.

Holly grinned, holding her hands out—to show how big the letters were. "With blisters covering my hands, my dad helped me finish. You can see it from an airplane if you fly close enough," she said.

"Someday I'll accept that challenge," he said.

Fascinated by nature, Holly discovered a fresh sense of joy being outdoors. Deriving pleasure from country living, she sewed, painted, and read under the azure sky—waiting for her next sun-drenched kiss in the Garden of Eden. She brought outdoor living to innovative heights with picnics, barbeques, and campfires in the evening—providing opportunities to chat around a fire or sing under the stars.

Even when Jake and Abby were gone didn't matter.

She grew to love her home much more than the *fairy-tale castle*—their nickname for the house on Brookshire. "A mansion versus a cottage with a heart," Adam said. "We now desire contentment more than perfection or affluent living—a wise trade."

"The ranch provided stability when everything crashed in the city," Holly said. Formerly trying to impress neighbors and friends, their current focus was establishing positive family relationships.

"I reserved a seat for you," he said.

She lit a candle before sitting on his lap with a twinkle in her eye.

Healthy exercise and fresh air allowed Adam to recuperate from his injuries. His body healed rapidly. Holly watched him tinker with tools, maintain a garden, and care for the flock of sheep—joining in with enthusiasm. "Need a hand with that?" she asked.

"How did you guess?"

"I brought a snack for you and decided to stay," Holly said.

"Did you see the tiny lamb?" he said pointing. Counting sheep brought Adam *much more* joy than counting money used to provide—unless one of the sheep happened to be missing.

"Can you remember any other life than this?" she asked.

"Steering a tractor around the fields is considerably more relaxing than driving any Lexis we've owned," he said.

Adam climbed out of bed early to take care of chores. He hurriedly ate breakfast. The tractor tire was flat, needing air before he could mow. Pulling an air compressor from the corner of the shed, he noticed a pile of baby kittens in the hay. They meowed and wanted their mother.

Butterscotch was nowhere in sight.

He jumped on the tractor eager to mow with tires inflated, but the engine refused to start. Entering the shed again to get his battery charger, Butterscotch rushed past—eager get inside to take care of her babies.

"I accidentally shut the door and the kittens might have died if I drove off on a daylong mowing job," he said at lunch. "It's like the minister's story of the Old Man and the White Horse. No one can tell whether our circumstances are bad or good. Only God knows!"

Rain started falling later in the afternoon and he reluctantly stopped mowing, going inside the house to wait. Water began pouring from the back of the washing machine as he walked in. Adam shut off the valves, stopped the flow, and spun the water out of the machine.

Holly helped clean up the mess when she returned from grocery shopping. "What a relief! You were here just in time," she said hugging and kissing him.

They both knew who was responsible.

Holly made hot tea and they talked on the porch—until the rain ended. Before long, the most beautiful double rainbow appeared across the sky. "What did you expect?" Holly said.

Singing a solo in the sanctuary as sunlight streamed through the stained glass windows, Adam sang, *"I'm satisfied with just a cottage below, a little silver and a little gold ..."*

Adam and Holly actively courted in front of their children.

He pulled his wife to his chest as she tried to put food on the table. She ran to the door showering him with kisses and hugs when he came inside after finishing chores. They whispered things in each other's ears and then laughed. Adam winked as the kids came into the room and held his finger to his lips.

"What are you planning to do together?" Jake asked.

"Can't tell you."

Sitting on his lap watching a football game, Adam tickled Holly and she fell on the floor. Extending his arm to help, Holly pulled him down instead. They wrestled for several minutes, giggling.

"Not again!" Abby said, getting up to find a snack.

"I'm glad she's busy," Abby heard her father say from the kitchen. "I have a surprise for you at halftime."

As he promised, Adam pulled out a new game—*An Enchanting evening*. "Take the top card," he said. Her card read, "What romantic spot would you like to be at right now?"

"Hawaii," Holly answered. "Your turn."

"What qualities do you admire about your partner?" he read.

Listening to Adam's answer was the best part of the evening for his wife. "Do I get to hear love songs when we're done?" she asked.

He never turned the football game back on.

For Valentine's Day, Holly made heart shaped sandwiches, pink applesauce, and cinnamon cookies for a picnic lunch at the lake.

Enjoying sunshine and shimmering water as they ate, they reminisced about their vacation to the Amore Resort.

"I didn't like that lifeguard who you were infatuated with—in spite of my attempts to charm you," Adam said.

"Who was infatuated with me," Holly said correcting him.

"Glancing around at the other females, I realized no one would ever compare with you and resigned myself to a lonely life." Pulling out a little red box, Adam got on his knees. "Holly Elizabeth Clark—Will you be my lover for the rest of your life?"

She just laughed. So he held the box tightly. When she answered, "Yes!" she found a gold locket engraved with their initials, and a picture from their wedding day inside.

Holly gave Adam a pair of silky boxers with little red hearts later that night.

Back on Brookshire, Jake and Abby struggled with what might happen to their family unit, unable to change the negative atmosphere. Abby responded to the positive changes with open arms. Warmly accepted at a friendly school and eager to spend time around their property, she thrived.

Chirping birds greeted her in the morning and robins sang cheerful songs as she helped with chores. Exuberant while seeing buttercups appear, or a tulip push its head through the dirt, she tried hard not to pick them.

Abby experienced inspiring moments of baby lambs being birthed and whinnying coming from the barn. Spending time with Princess was her favorite activity.

Everything was especially tranquil when the stars emerged. The brightness of a full moon lit the ranch like a streetlight. Tantalized by the glow of planets in the sky, she gravitated to the wonderful exhibits of nature her mother relished years before in Colorado.

"You were lucky to grow up there Mom," Abby said.

"I know, Sweetie. Seeing the cascading waterfalls send misty spray over lush foliage below is awesome; but the most spectacular for me is watching the spellbinding northern lights. These particles of charged electricity create one of the most remarkable natural phenomenon.

Shifting rays of green and yellow stream in vertical lines upward from the horizon; or they can look like flaming torches hurling through space radiating light. Other red, blue, and purple lights look like moving draperies with the colors passionately mixing at random. Sometimes great arches of shimmering light crash into each other, or glow like ocean foam beating on the shore. Arches of green are most common lower in the sky—around forty to sixty miles high. Draperies of red are higher, around seventy miles up."

"I remember seeing them once when we visited Gigi; and I can't wait to see them again!" Abby said. "Now a lunar halo will be boring."

"I don't think so—Psalm 19:1 says, *The heavens declare the glory of God; and the firmament shows His handiwork.* Every masterpiece of creation we see, will leave us in awe of God's glory."

Abby put Princess in her stall and ran to the house. She had an hour to shower and change clothes before a *date* with her father. They enjoyed weekly father/daughter dates since she turned thirteen. Choosing a sapphire dress—appropriate for the fancy restaurant—she looked at her muddy shoes. "These might have been alright while wearing jeans and a cowboy hat to the steakhouse last weekend, but NOT tonight."

"You look beautiful!" Adam said. "Please let me continue being the lucky male in your life—not some other jerky teenager."

Using polite courtesies, he opened and closed his daughter's car door, held restaurant doors open as she went through, and pulled her chair back. Abby felt special.

"Tell me about school this week," her father said.

He wanted to know about classes, her teachers and friends, and after school activities. Adam asked his daughter questions; and sometimes Abby asked her own. Discussing her parents—except as a casual reference—was forbidden this evening, allowing them to focus only on each other.

"This candle on the table reminds me of the night the electricity went out," Abby said. "I was surprised when you came to my room."

"I didn't spend much time with you before that did I?" he asked. "I was busy with work and preoccupied with sports."

"When we laughed playing games, downstairs in the candlelight, I hoped you would continue acting like that. In my bed, I thought my prayer would be answered—but nothing changed."

"Well miracles do happen," Adam said.

"I know Dad," Abby answered.

Adam planned a camping trip with Jake after months of talk. "This week-long campout is a coming-of-age-affair now that Jake is turning sixteen," he announced at dinner.

"Before you drive my car, I want to make sure you're responsible," he told Jake.

"More importantly, I want to teach my son some things that might be helpful in life." Adam said to Holly.

"Next time I see you, Jake, you'll be a man," Abby said teasing.

Sleeping bags, camping gear, cans of food, fishing poles and tackle, hiking clothes, bad weather paraphernalia, and a first aid kit were loaded into the truck. Jake and his dad drove off smiling.

"This looks like a good place to camp," Adam said, spotting a clearing near the river. "It's the right distance from the water and has trees for protection. When we get our stuff unloaded, we can take a swim."

"How do you know what to do?" Jake asked, helping set up the tent.

"I taught my brothers years ago. We roughed it a couple of times."

"I'll grab the sleeping bags," Jake said when the tent was secure.

They swam, fished, cut firewood, and started a fire … before grilling four little fish that tasted delicious.

Talking by the fire, father and son discussed becoming a man and responsibilities people acquire as adults. Jake had questions and Adam answered honestly and openly—sharing painful choices from his past.

"Having a relationship with another person requires time together and a desire to learn. How do they think? Why do they act that way? What do they enjoy? It's the same with God," Adam said.

Rubbing his eyes, they called it a night.

A faint glow near the horizon greeted them in the morning. "Sometimes, just before sunrise, a brilliant pillar of colored light rises above the sun," Adam said. "We should see some great sunrises and sunsets out here."

Adam made lumpy black pancakes and heated water for coffee. "I'm still starving," Jake said.

"Don't laugh. You're cooking alone on the last day," his father promised.

They ate hearty beef stew for lunch. Dinner included more fresh fish and potatoes out of a can. A raccoon rattled their trashcan looking for leftovers while they slept.

Remnants were scattered on the ground when they woke up. Tracks showed Rocky retreated toward the trees.

"Here's rope to practice making knots," Adam said on the third day. He taught Jake bowline and slipknots, clove hitches, sheepshank, and a fisherman's knot. "You don't start out as an Olympic champion but learn new skills one step at a time."

"Good job, son."

"Okay, let's make a fire," Adam said, getting hungry again. "Do you want to gather kindling or get the grub out?"

They enjoyed a typical cowboy campfire with tasty beans and beef jerky.

As they talked under the stars, Adam felt God's presence stronger than before. "They say a true sailor can chart his course by the stars," he said. "I wonder if that's true."

"Do you know the constellations?" Jake asked.

"No, but your mother does," Adam said. "Actually I'm learning. Long ago, we watched stars in the backyard and Mom made it seem interesting. Then she started asking questions I couldn't answer."

"I know the Big Dipper and North Star—Mom taught me those," Jake said. "I'm glad you decided to teach me ranch chores before I leave home."

"A father is responsible for what happens to his children spiritually," Adam said quieter. "I'm sorry for failing to care about that when you were young."

"No problem, Dad. The past is over," Jake said.

They looked up into the darkening sky and watched an eclipse of the moon. Neither of them said any words as the sky turned a reddish hue. Adam wished Jake would be interested in spiritual things.

Smothering the embers with dirt, they said goodnight and got into sleeping bags.

Hiking the next day, they came across a little cabin in the woods. Although it appeared deserted, Adam knocked on the half-opened door. "No one's here," he said. Curious, they walked in. It was dusty and the floor squeaked.

Some books were on a back corner of the table—Adam spotted an old Bible. He pulled it toward himself and gulped. Opening the pages, words spilled out of his mouth. "This treasure chest will change your life, Son." To his surprise, Jake was receptive.

After telling his story of despair and redemption for several minutes, Adam paused. His son was actually listening.

"Thanks for taking me on this camping trip, Dad," Jake said. Sun flickered through a broken window. With a creaking voice he continued. "Will you help me talk to God?"

Getting on their knees in a little cabin in the woods, Adam and Jake became brothers. Their heavenly father was not an ordinary man; He was a king.

With a deepening bond between them, Adam and Jake returned home to tell Holly and Abby the wonderful events. After taking care of chores, they shared the thrilling story. Dinner that night was a glorious occasion—with talk continuing until the wee hours of the morning.

In a hand-painted frame on the kitchen wall, Holly displayed a favorite saying:

Oh Lord, Let my words be sweet and tender;
For tomorrow, I may have to eat them!

"Holly loved vocabulary from her first word 'ya' at eight months," Susan Armstrong boasted. In school, words fascinated her as she put them together—first in sentences and then in stories. As a child, Holly read the dictionary looking for interesting meanings.

As she grew, Holly learned the power of words. Ted and Susan Armstrong spent a considerable amount of time communicating with their daughter. Guests coming to the home provided conversation meant to stimulate. Her grandmother discussed the beauty of creation using descriptive language—growing up in the Rockies was a great place for that.

Adam used loving words when he courted Holly convincing her to become his wife. "Your desire for validation—my approval—makes me feel important," he said.

"What do you like best about me?" she asked.

"I love that brilliant mind stored inside your gorgeous head. You have an answer for every topic." His words changed to expressions of resentment as *wrong values* affected their union.

With the crisis looming over them, silence followed.

Holly fully understood the power of negative words, as she looked inward at her life. She and friends gossiped and criticized. Instead of wisely building their homes, they allowed disrespect and insults to become termites. She nearly destroyed herself, her husband, and her precious children with an unkind and destructive vocabulary. *Thank God for second chances to use positive words to guide my teenagers, as they become adults.*

Life-giving words in the Bible after Granny's funeral started her dramatic turn from disaster. Holly loved Grandma Armstrong dearly and was inspired by her good character. Granny cheered her whenever she was discouraged. If Holly had a problem or decision to make her grandma said, "I'll pray for you. Granny's example was influential, although Holly was unaware of the significance as a child.

"Oh, my goodness," Holly said, remembering the last time she saw her grandma.

Granny said, "One of these days I'm going to take a wonderful vacation." Everyone laughed and thought she was teasing but Granny smiled and replied, "My best friend wants to spend more time with me." *She knew Him personally!*

Holly was overjoyed. Granny's voice echoed in her ear.

"Always leave the porch light on!" Granny used to say.

"Twill light the path if one goes by ... and welcome those who stay."

"Halleluiah!" Holy said clapping her hands. "I finally know what the saying means." She determined to live like Granny—full of life but with an emphasis on spiritual truths.

A lover of poems, Holly believed they lifted her beyond the ordinary. "You can almost see and feel the action in the rhyme," she said. *Poets paint pictures with words just as she painted with colors.* With a desire to share her soul but unable to fully express herself verbally, she got out paper and pen. For future generations to understand the complexity of her transformation, she composed a record of her quest—as a family keepsake.

Holly's Quest
Searching but never finding
Meaning for my soul;
Striving to somehow satisfy
A yearning to be whole.
Looking for the illusive
Ingredient of joy;
Trying to gain happiness
From what money can buy.
Longing for inspiration,
Seeking with all my might,
Finding the perfect answer
In the awesome sky at night.
Observing God's precision,
Viewing all He's done;
Doesn't faze me near as much
As discovering His Son.

Reading in the garden, Holly turned to Isaiah 58:11 and read, "The Lord will guide you always; he will satisfy your needs in a sun-scorched land and will strengthen your frame. You will be like a well-watered garden, like a spring whose waters never fail."

"I know one thing," she whispered. "You alone truly satisfy."

Chapter 16
New Perspective

WAKING ABRUPTLY FROM A deep sleep, Adam reached for his wife.

"Mmmm ..." Holly sighed, turning to hug him. "Few mornings were this enjoyable not long ago."

"I'm glad you're here," Adam said.

They lay in bed talking about their life together—reminiscing about Adams's ski trip, their exciting courtship, and the dream vacation to Europe when Adam sang love songs while riding around Salzburg in the carriage.

"I remember wishing the whole house would burn down that night the garage caught fire," Adam said. "I planned to use insurance money to buy two houses, one on each side of town, so we could live apart."

"That's much nicer than me daydreaming about you having an affair and running off with someone else—leaving my dream home for me alone to enjoy!" she said.

Neither could forget the night Holly had been angry about the leak in the bathroom ceiling when the electricity went out. "That was a terrible storm—both inside and out," Holly said. "But you looked so strong coming down the stairs with Abby in the candlelight, my anger melted."

"You looked pretty sexy with the candlelight flickering on your hair while we played games," Adam said. "I hoped to keep you warm in a sleeping bag that night; unfortunately, the electricity came back on."

"That reminds me—I longed to touch your body in bed *many* times," Holly said. "Occasionally, I would feel the skin on your arm, or touch your back while you slept."

Adam's growling stomach brought them back to reality.

Regardless of the weather, or the circumstances, having someone to enjoy breakfast with was just the beginning.

"Thanks, sweetheart … It was delicious!" he said, finishing the bacon, eggs, and berries.

Holly glanced at a tea towel with two entwined hearts as she sipped her coffee. "Tell me Adam … was I really so obsessed with my image that I didn't notice the mirror was broken?"

"My own ambitious goals blocked me from seeing my darling wife's needs," he answered. "It was my fault for not providing leadership in our home. I made terrible decisions but wanted you to trust me anyway. I'm learning how to make better choices—but not by myself."

"Thanks for being honest. I'm still learning how to do that."

"I can't wait until lunch! … but I have chores to take care of right now," Adam said, bumping into Jake coming through the kitchen doorway.

"Good morning, Dad. I'll help you after I eat breakfast."

"Great! I could use an extra hand and do appreciate your help. You might want to put on old clothes, though."

Adam cared about others but his primary concern was to love and encourage his wife. He bungled that responsibility earlier—advancing his career in lieu of providing emotional closeness and developing a fulfilling marriage. Brief telephone calls when he was away from the ranch, "Just to say I love you," reminded her of his devotion.

An occasional bouquet of flowers appeared on the kitchen counter with an endearing note. Romantic stickers mysteriously appeared inside books she was reading, or on bookmarks.

When he finished farm chores, he would stand outside under a window and sing love songs. "When I fall in love, it will be forever, or I'll never fall in love…"

Hearing his voice, she paused what she was doing and listened to Adam sing. The love of her life was expressing himself—and the whole world could hear. *How she adored that man!*

She determined to celebrate their anniversary on the sixteenth of every month. No matter what the circumstances of their lives, everything paused for a reflection on their commitment many years before. Ruby goblets and plates waited for candles to be lighted and dinner to be served—as eager participants arrived with hearts beating for the touch of one who still excited.

"Couldn't wait to get done with my chores," Adam whispered over dinner.

"I now measure wealth by the things I have ... those things I would never exchange for money," Holly said.

Tim Janssen had mentored his new neighbors when the Clarks purchased their ranch, giving valuable advice in multiple areas. Generously pitching in with time and energy, he humbly accepted their thanks and refused to be compensated. On several occasions, his wife Karen made extra biscuits and desert for him to bring over. So far, the scale tipped heavily in Tim's favor.

Adam surprised his friend with a hot air balloon ride for his birthday. "I've got sights you don't want to miss," he said. "Meet me at the airfield by 7:00AM on Saturday for our launch."

"What a spectacular day!" Adam said when he arrived.

"This weather's ideal for ballooning," the pilot answered. "Those clouds are quite a ways off and add to the beauty of the sky."

"Wow!" Tim said, while ascending.

Sailing through the sky offered panoramic views for miles. The smooth sapphire lake mirrored reflections of the blue, red, and yellow gondola as it glided over. Ridges of spruce popcorn dotted the hillside— camouflaging the colorful homes and other structures interspersed with ribbons of asphalt. They went over Tim's home, Adam's ranch, and a nature preserve nearby.

While seeing the world from a different point of view, the guys talked nonstop.

"My house and shiny sports car look like tiny little specks," Tim said. Other things he previously thought were significant, apparently lost their appeal. Instead, the brilliant blue sky and gorgeous colors in the distance were focal points.

A plume of fire, heating the balloon, suddenly became all-important. It sputtered and flickered—and the conversation stopped temporarily while a burner was re-lit.

Luckily, they continued moving forward. Adam and Tim watched the pilot exhibit exceptional landing skills as the basket gracefully brushed the grass.

Safely on the ground, the friends continued discussing life and the frailty of man, especially as he strives to be strong. Tim had questions.

Sharing his soul, Adam told his neighbor about the best decision he had made.

With his voice choking up, Tim made the same choice that day.

A few days later, Tim brought his wife over to visit the Clarks—hoping to talk about spiritual issues. "Come in Tim. This must be your lovely wife Karen … I feel we already know you," Adam said. "Thanks for all the delicious food."

Karen greeted him with a hug.

"Hi neighbors," Holly said, walking into the front room, encouraging them to sit down. "We appreciate Tim's insight and his assistance has been priceless. He bailed Adam out of numerous pinches—and probably kept him from getting into more." Holly's eyes glistened as she offered a tray of treats.

"Karen has questions about spiritual issues that I can't answer," Tim said.

"Jump right in," Adam said. "We don't know everything but we'll do the best we can."

"I used to be an agnostic and cherished creation but denied there was a creator," Holly said. "I was foolish just like the Bible describes in Romans." Karen leaned forward as her neighbor began sharing personal thoughts.

"Every wife longs for her husband to know her intimately," Holly explained. "So does God. He made an exquisite world for us to live in, created interesting people to surround us, and desires for us to choose a personal relationship with him. Are you interested?"

"You make it sound so appealing."

"Do you have a Bible, Karen? Reading Psalm 139 will warm your heart."

"Both of you need to study the Bible. That's the best advice I can give," Adam added.

"We have an old family Bible from my grandmother," Karen said.

"Are you willing to believe God, trust him, and watch him become real in your lives? He has more wonderful things planned than you can imagine," Holly said.

Karen called not long after leaving to tell them good news. Their answers had been icing on the cake.

"Be a friend to people and watch God open doors to reveal himself," Rev. David said.

"Let's visit the Grand Canyon before Jake graduates; we haven't been there for 25 years. We'll watch a sunset from the rim," Adam said enthusiastically. With Holly's exuberant agreement, reservations at a lodge were booked, suitcases were packed, and the Clark family left for the Grand Canyon National Park.

Jake entertained himself with a new Extreme Sports game on his Nintendo; Abby listened to her iPod, stopping to chat when assorted ideas popped into her head. Holly read from a travel guide as they headed toward the awe-inspiring natural wonder.

"The size and magnificence of this spectacular gorge consists of waterfalls, a complex of caverns, and intricate ledges," she read. "The main canyon is 227 miles long and one mile deep—with no bridge to span the eighteen-mile distance across. Lush flowers and plants flourish in the middle of the desert. Nobody forgets his or her first view of the Grand Canyon, unmatched throughout the world for the vistas it offers. It offers something new, no matter how often you visit."

A hush filled the car as they rounded a bend.

The intricate and colorful landscape was almost too much to absorb. The panorama, stretching as far as the eye could see, continually changed with the shifting sun and moving clouds—altering hues on the rocks below.

"Sometimes the Grand Canyon seems intense; but we'll hike down the Bright Angel Trail early tomorrow and get a more intimate and manageable perspective," Adam said. "In spite of all the tourists, there are still spots for solitude."

True to his word, they were ready to descend by sunrise.

This was the easiest and most popular trail, following Garden Creek. Singing as they hiked, the Clarks stopped to let a convoy of mules pass. "Phew!" Jake said turning—before stepping on a smelly pile of droppings.

"Oh, yuck! Too bad we didn't walk faster and stay ahead of them." Abby said.

Gazing out from one of the vantage points, Holly sighed. "It's hard to imagine the tiny stream of water meandering along down there is responsible for cutting through this Colorado Plateau."

Jake snickered. "The Colorado River is actually swift and powerful close up—providing dangerous rapids for adventurous travelers. Who wants to go whitewater rafting with me?"

Holly pulled bottles of water and sandwiches from a backpack. Her body ached but the beauty of creation was invigorating. Knowing the Creator personally made it seem even better. "It's as though we're completely alone on the earth—under the watchful eye of a loving father," she said.

"Oh Lord, my God ... when I in awesome wonder ... consider all the worlds thy hands have made ...," Adam sang, as they rested.

"Are we going to turn around at the second rest station?" Holly asked, looking at the map.

"Probably not. The second rest station is near a tree-lined spring at Indian Garden where the path divides—one branch goes almost flat for two miles to Plateau Point which has great views of the Colorado along the inner canyon gorge," Adam explained.

"We should have ridden the horses," Abby said.

"Amen," Holly agreed.

Exhausted and sunburned, the whole family appreciated pillows and a comfortable bed more than they could imagine. Holly snuggled close to Adam and whispered, "You do make good decisions. I'm glad we came here."

They fell asleep with dreams of more spectacular views to come.

After driving down a 14-mile dirt road, the glass-bottomed Grand Canyon Skywalk came into sight. Adam cleared his throat. "I understand why this has mixed reviews," he said.

"Come on, Dad … don't be a chicken now!" Jake laughed. "You already paid for the tour package. Let's get out there and see what we can see."

"Do you want to wait with me in the gift shop?" Holly asked her daughter.

Jake would allow none of that.

Reluctantly they put on booties and gingerly stepped on the horseshoe-shaped glass walkway, higher than most of the world's largest skyscrapers. Holly withheld her knowledge that about 600 deaths have occurred in the Grand Canyon since the 1870's. Some were the result of overly zealous photographic endeavors; some were injuries to hikers or visitors drowning in the Colorado River. Most were the results of flying mishaps over the canyon, and a few were freak accidents like lightning strikes.

I belong to you, God … do what you want with me. She peered out over the edge in disbelief that He could have created something so beautiful.

"The earth must have cried in pain as water rushed over it, carving deep wounds in an already useful piece of ground," Adam said soberly. "Imagine the sensation of being destroyed—when in reality the Creator was making an exquisite treasure for mankind to enjoy."

"That was really awesome!" Jake said when they finished.

Holly and Abby breathed a sigh of relief.

"I'll get some coffee for you," Adam promised, as he ran off. He made it to the café a few minutes before closing.

Lingering at a bookstore, Holly found an interesting bookmark. It read, *Life is Like a Book … We keep writing chapters.* She bought an extra for Abby.

"I found a souvenir for you."

"How did you know I want to write a book?" Abby asked.

"You're already writing it, Sweetie. When you were little, I screwed up but God loved you too much to let me continue abusing my privilege as your mother. So he changed both of us, inside and out …

Abby smiled as she remembered her childhood.

Some things that happened since—her mother had no idea. I hope that with God's help, the worst part will be forgotten. If not, the future would be entirely different from normal teenage expectations.

"There's more to life than living long; it's living well—pleasing God to your last breath," Holly said. "When God asks you to do something, just do it. Don't worry about the outcome. Only pigs have the right to eat and then go lay down."

"I don't want to leave home; you're turning into such a fun person," Abby said pensively.

"You'll change your mind someday when you're more ready to spread your wings," her mother assured her. "Right now, God wants you to learn how to use the talents He's given you. Discover how to start godly conversations with friends; and care about people around you—if we're not careful, we can lose our perspective. Spend time with Him and you'll get insight into His mind."

When friends returned from the Gulf of Mexico where they learned to Scuba Dive, Adam and Holly listened with interest. It sounded like a different world—filled with enchantment and adventure.

"The dive shop downtown is offering a *Welcome-to-Scuba* orientation next week. You need to try it out," Fred Paschal said.

Adam relished water sports and though Holly was not a strong swimmer, she enjoyed water—so they reserved a spot. Immediately they caught the bug and signed up for classes.

Successful with initial training, they prepared to certify in the Florida Keys. Wetsuits, masks, goggles, and fins were purchased; additional gear could be rented onsite. With dive logs and tables ready for use, Adam and Holly studied sunken treasure maps.

The first dive—a skin dive-check out—took place by a sunken civil war boat just fifteen feet below the surface of the water. The second dive involved checking equipment and clearing masks at twenty feet. A third dive offered buoyancy practice. Neither had any trouble with ears.

Adam was ready to plunge deeper.

"I can see how a diver might experience rapture of the deep, if they aren't careful!" he said.

"It's exhilarating being under the water and exercising your body in a strange new way," Holly said, eager to practice more buoyancy control.

Sitting on the sand watching the ocean during a break, Adam started singing. "Pearly shells from the ocean ... shining in the sun, covering the shore ... When I see them; my heart tells me that I love you—more than all the little pearly shells. For every grain of sand upon the beach, I've got a kiss for you ... and I've got more left over for each star that twinkles in the blue ..." Holly was delighted.

Certification dives four and five followed the next day.

The incredible visibility made each descent enjoyable as they experimented with viewing treasures under the sea. Adam motioned for Holly to turn around—and she found hundreds of colorful fish right behind her.

"Oooohh," she mouthed and continued to watch.

Angelfish were the most curious on the reef. Their gaudy colors blended in as they fluttered among sea fans and nibbled on bright-hued sponges. The parrotfish and some grouper flashed brilliant color as they swam past the variegated masses of coral.

Holly's favorite was a Fairy basslet, a shy but flamboyant-colored three inch fish that often swims upside down under ledges. She tapped Adam's arm and pointed to it smiling.

As Adam and Holly dove around coral reefs, colorful fish, and barracudas, they realized that as significant as this venture was—an even bigger change had taken place in their lives, that their friends were unaware.

Sitting on the shore eating lunch, divers discussed the awesome underwater habitat. It was the perfect time for Adam and Holly to talk about a heavenly dimension they recently added to their lives.

"Have you ever seen the Northern Lights?" Holly asked.

The group shrugged.

"I've seen pictures of them and they're beautiful!" Linda Paschal said.

"Watching the aurora borealis is a spellbinding experience. Great arches of shimmering rays—from violet through yellow, and green to the orange-reds—dance as curtains of colored lights across the sky," Holly said. "The aura of mystery surrounding these most spectacular natural phenomena eludes even the wisest men. What impresses me most is the Bible describes it perfectly."

Adam nodded and interjected, "Psalm 19:1 says, *The heavens are telling the glory of God; they are a marvelous display of his craftsmanship.* Another verse in Romans says, *Since earliest times men have seen the earth and sky ... and have known of his existence and great power ...*"

"But they became utter fools, instead of worshiping the glorious living God," Holly exclaimed. "That would describe me perfectly!"

Glancing at his watch to check *sit-time*, when they could dive again, Adam shared how creatures of the deep know nothing about life above. They face predators, weather, and survival with no hope for eternity. "I struggled to find personal meaning in life; sought with all my strength to achieve fame, happiness, and satisfaction but couldn't—on my own. Desperation brought us to our knees, where the one who made us and loves us more than any other heard our cry."

"Discovering that Jesus was more than just a pretty baby on Christmas cards has been my best present ever," Holly said. "And watching him change my life is the most spectacular thing I've seen—better than the Northern Lights!"

"The breathtaking undersea world pales by comparison when you consider what heaven will be like someday," Adam said.

Adam and Holly looked up and silently thanked God.

Their friends had listened eagerly—actually seeing the glow on their faces and hearing power in their words. Fred Paschal grasped Adam's arm before leaving, "I need to talk to you."

They chatted over dinner.

A night dive at Molasses Reef brought a different group of nocturnal fish. The Glasseye snapper changed rapidly from deep red to a striped silvery pattern and the tiny Peppermint bass emerged after hiding all day.

"A unique paradise lies under the surface of the ocean," Holly said, when she returned home. "Movies have been made using mermaids to simulate the enchanting effect."

Adam compared it to skydiving—"Only you have more control."

For Holly's birthday, Adam invited scuba diving friends over for a cookout. It was a casual get-together—"no gifts please!"—he asked.

The important thing was to share joyful moments, building on their testimony of God's goodness.

"Things will never again overshadow people," Holly said the night before.

Adam couldn't wait to see her response to his present.

He welcomed guests and made a presentation—handing his wife a fragile 3-D glass frame wrapped in shimmering ocean-blue paper, tied with silvery ribbon.

"Oooohh!" she said, opening it.

The Seashell

The Seashell is the likeness of our life in many ways,
An image of our spirit, a diary of our days:
In our thirst for life's true meaning, we seek God, the only One
Who can lead us to the living water offered by His Son ...
We find new life in the Savior, who designs our destiny,
As He forms the seashell's pattern in such perfect symmetry:
Once reborn in Christ we leave the old shell lying on the sand,
As we follow new horizons, walking with Him hand in hand ...

Anonymous

Conversations followed about seashells and God's grandeur. Holly showed her collection and explained her discovery that a living animal was once sheltered inside each seashell—braving the harsh realities of weather. "Its demise meant another trinket in my box."

It was another birthday to remember!

Adam stepped out of the shower just in time to grab a ringing phone. He dropped the slippery receiver as his father began talking. "Sorry, Dad. I missed what you were saying."

Scott Clark's voice was shaking as he explained the situation to Adam on the telephone. "Of all the tremors I've experienced this was the worst at 5.9, but we were pretty lucky. No one was killed by the devastating jolt; however, millions of dollars in damage occurred. The aftershocks are also taking a toll on our community."

"Are there injuries?" Adam asked.

"Yes, some by falling debris during the earthquake but mostly by people trying to clean up yards and businesses."

"How are you and Mom?"

"We're doing okay except for some damage to the back of the house. As soon as things settle down, I'll take care of that."

"Thank God. Let us know the outcome. Hope things improve soon, Dad."

Two nights later, his father called back. "We came home and found the house in shambles."

"More aftershocks?"

"Somebody tried to use our misfortune from nature to make a quick buck. We were robbed of most everything of value," Scott Clark said.

"Can I come help you?" Adam asked. "Holly and I planned to visit California this fall anyway."

"At this point, it would probably be better if we visited you. Your mother's pretty shaken up. We could leave in the morning after I talk to my insurance company. There's nothing else to do here until the area calms down. We have nothing more to lose."

Adam and Holly prayed for wisdom and courage to address spiritual truths when his parents arrived. "You never know why God allows things—maybe so significant life changes might occur naturally," he said.

Chapter 17
Hospitality

GLANCING INTO THE KITCHEN, a dramatic change was obvious in the Clark home. Smiling, with eyes that twinkled, Holly listened as Adam talked.

"Listen with your eyes," Granny used to say. Holly didn't understand what that meant as a child but enjoyed seeing her grandmother's face light up. The warmth she portrayed was obvious from her glow.

"The eye is the window to the soul," Granny explained on her last visit. A sense of strength pervaded her character and feeling of joy exuded from her spirit.

Holly wanted to be just like her.

Enjoying another beautiful day, she sipped coffee while looking at her favorite saying proudly displayed on the wall:

Oh Lord, Let my words be sweet and tender;
For tomorrow, I may have to eat them!

"I'm sorry for being unreasonable last night. Will you forgive me?" Holly asked her husband. She regretted having shared opinions about his farm chores—that led to an intense argument. "I had no business giving advice for subjects I'm not directly involved in, and that you know more about."

He cleared his throat before responding. "Those words on the wall apply to me as well."

"Glad to see we're applying the wise things we learn," she said, reaching under the counter for a pan to scramble eggs. "Just to check this further, watch my actions and see if you can figure out what I'm saying."

He started laughing. "Sure you want to know?"

"Of course."

They chatted over breakfast about their personalities. Adam and Holly studied non-verbal communication after learning to scuba dive—*to better understand* each other under water. There are certain classic behaviors that give telltale signs, they discovered.

"Peering into a mirror every day, we don't observe ourselves realistically. We either see nothing ... or are overly critical," she said. "But others can tell if you're self-centered—consumed with yourself."

"Thankfully that's no longer true about you, Holly."

"Fortunately," she said. "As our selfishness diminishes, our interest in others and concern for humanity emerges."

A visit to a restaurant for lunch offered much more than good food.

After being seated by a friendly young man, a server's smile penetrated the crowd as she walked up to pour coffee. "Good morning! It's only my third day here," she said, rearranging her nametag. She calmly listened to the order, repeating it perfectly—"concealing a trembling heart," she said later when complimented. "I want to do a good job. Let me know if I can get anything else for you."

Sipping coffee and glancing around, Holly noticed other employees smiling. She watched more intently.

"Hmmm ... There's something going on here," she finally said to Adam. "All this interaction between customers and servers is highly unusual and must have something to do with the manager."

Delicious food accompanied by a pleasant atmosphere and caring employees compelled Holly to make a comment before leaving.

"I remember when you chewed servers out," Adam said as they left.

"Out of the overflow of the heart, our mouths speak," she said. "Our words can be much wiser when we control our tongues and ask Him to fill our hearts with love."

"Hitler and Caesar were strong and powerful; Jesus was meek and gentle—but who had the most powerful words in history?" Adam asked.

"You know who I want to be like. Right?"

The Clarks contemplated how to reach out warmly to anyone coming into their home—puzzled how to explain their faith in words; yet hoping to show it by their actions. *Treasured moments with recent guests would hopefully never be forgotten.*

"Our relatives, friends, and acquaintances are seeking a thrilling new flavor in their lives. How can we be salt and light for them?" Adam asked.

"Guests will be delighted to find something better than good food."

After watching a beautiful sunset, Holly talked about her love for entertaining. "In spite of my selfish motives in the past, welcoming guests into our home and creating an enjoyable ambiance for their benefit truly is my passion. Surely, there will be more opportunities to offer pleasant words, refreshment, and kindness."

Adam listened while she babbled. "You tried hard to have superficial interactions with people in the past and did an extremely good job of achieving your elaborate goals. Now, though, your zeal is to reach out with something more rewarding ... and of eternal significance. I completely understood what you're trying to say," he said.

At church, Rev. David talked about how each of us has a lonely part inside, a vacuum only God can fill.

"We long to connect meaningfully so He often uses people with skin on to take care of our basic needs. The world uses people and loves things; we need to be the opposite. Are you aware that hospitality is essential in godly homes? Our faith is seen in our love for people—so get beyond yourself, and care about others!"

"God met your personal need for a deep relationship. Offer something to those who are yearning around you," he said.

Adam squeezed Holly's hand as the minister closed with a prayer. "Our passion for bringing people into our homes should be growing stronger than ever. Help us make a difference!" Rev. David said in closing.

Driving home, Adam suggested a plan. "Let's invite our neighbors over for dinner. We hardly know John and Kelly Sorenson."

"I was about to say the same thing."

"Looks like we need to share our food," Jake said to Abby.

Holly's creativity actually doubled. No longer obsessed to *impress others with her entertaining skills*, she served with a flourish now—out of love. Starting with her immediate family, she gave it her utmost attention and effort.

Breakfast became an event. Lunch and dinner became extravaganzas. Snacks took on a new twist. She practiced showing hospitality to Adam and the kids on a daily basis. They were her first priority.

"Wow! This is great," Jake said.

"And you thought we were going to share food?" Abby asked.

Holly found ways to meet needs as meaningfully as possible. Paying careful attention to each person, she wrote down little things she observed and ideas that worked. Her reward was a big smile, several times a day, and a feeling of satisfaction deep in her soul.

Thoughts of Carissa kept coming back as Holly scrubbed and polished—ready to meet the world in a new role. "What do you think?" she asked Adam.

"Go for it! Nothing like the present to start a task; and who better than your best friend to practice your skills on?"

Carissa was overjoyed to receive Holly's invitation. "I've wanted to see you again for eons. Give me an hour to pack my bag. I just happen to be free this weekend," she said.

Holly was out cutting fresh flowers when her best friend drove up. Carissa honked as she parked. "I'm really excited to be here." They jumped in circles while hugging.

"We have so much to talk about," she said.

"Come on in … Here, I'll take your bag," Holly said.

Showing Carissa to the guest room and giving her a few minutes to freshen up, Holly made sandwiches and waited on the porch.

They munched and chatted, barely stopping to breath.

"Seems like an eternity ago when we stayed up half the night talking about dreams and laughing about good things to come," Carissa said.

"Back then my life was like going to a candy store and making choices—feeling great joy with the purchases," Holly said. "When I unwrapped and ate them, they tasted better than I imagined. Soon my tummy started getting queasy, so I ate more—thinking it would help me feel different. It wasn't healthy consuming all that sugar but I didn't want to give up my treats."

"You always did have a fondness for acquiring the biggest and best that could be purchased," Carissa answered. "That's why it was fun being around you. My life became more interesting, latching on to your thrills."

"Greed and selfishness indicate we're off track."

Holly stopped to get her dictionary. "Look at this, Carissa." She pointed to the word *materialism*—"the theory or doctrine that physical well-being and worldly possessions constitute the greatest good and highest value in life; undue regard for worldly concerns."

"Sounds pretty foolish, doesn't it?" Carissa said. "But I'd give anything for love."

"Well then, I have good news for you. After Adam's accident when life looked hopeless for both of us, I discovered there is someone who loves me so much that he literally died for me. He's passionate about having a relationship with you too."

"Is there a catch?" Carissa asked.

"No, God waits patiently for us to tire of our loneliness and decide to get to know Him." The two best friends got on the floor and Holly spent a few minutes introducing Carissa to the most wonderful friend she had hoped to meet for a long, long time.

"You're always welcome here," Holly said as Carissa was leaving to return home.

Aware of the intense needs of friends, neighbors, former co-workers, and extended family, Holly gave hospitality her heart and soul.

"I've appreciated your acts of kindness over the years. Now it's my turn to repay you," she said to Theresa Marshall. "This isn't a real Bed and Breakfast but I'll provide the same services for your anniversary weekend."

For check in, Holly designed a welcome note and map of the property adorned with ribbon lying on the bed—with fresh flowers in the guest bathroom. "Would you prefer breakfast at 8 or 9 o'clock?" she asked.

The Marshalls chose to wander around the property before sitting on the porch. Instrumental music played in the background as they talked privately. Holly left a tray of refreshments in the guest room and turned back the sheets while they were out.

Before going to bed, Theresa returned the silver tray to the kitchen and saw Holly, coming in the back door. They chatted for a few minutes—mostly small talk about the Art Center.

"Your candy dish fascinates me," Theresa said looking down at the note.

Taste and see that the LORD is good; blessed is
the man who takes refuge in him. Psalm 34:8

Holly was excited to share the best thing she ever tasted.

"Do you remember when Adam had his terrible accident and they didn't know if he would live?" she asked Theresa. "Well, I had a bigger problem—my hope was gone and nothing was working out; I was the one who was dying. Then I discovered there is a sovereign God who longed to make my life new."

Holly reached for her Bible and opened it to Psalm 40:2-3. *He lifted me out of the pit of despair ... and set my feet on a hard, firm path ... and He has given me a new song to sing.*

Theresa asked question after question before finally saying, "Do you mind if I use your Bible to show my husband some of these verses?"

Ready to leave following their refreshing weekend, Theresa wrote in Holly's journal of guest reflections. "Your words were once bitter, cutting, and mean. Out of the overflow of your heart, we have now experienced words so sweet they are compelling us to consider the claims of Jesus further. Thanks for a memorable anniversary."

The Clark home became a refuge for those searching for something that would finally satisfy their hunger and thirst, and give hope. Food no longer just filled hungry stomachs but soothed aching souls.

I need to find more ways to enrich people's lives and refresh their tired bodies.

Holly carefully printed, "How sweet are your words to my taste, sweeter than honey to my mouth ... Psalm 119:103" on note cards, to place on future trays of refreshments.

She prayed for those God would send to her door and the ability to meet their needs, whatever that might involve. While friends were at her home, she prayed. "Help Adam and me be sensitive to the needs of these guests. Let them know someone understands their difficulties." After guests left, Holly prayed as she cleaned—for specific needs they divulged and that God would touch their lives with godly people.

"Hey, beautiful ... save some of that energy for me," Adam said after dinner.

Holly laughed. "It's ironic how self-reliance used to be my middle name. Even now, I usually resort to doing things on my own but need to remind myself to ask for His help."

"... and mine." Adam distracted her from finishing the last of the chores—by kissing and hugging the woman of his dreams. "I assure you that in the morning I'll help do anything still undone."

And he kept his word.

Things sparkled from the extra touches Holly took—that really didn't take much time. Fluffy pillows cradled tired, confused, and lonely heads. Cozy comforters warmed chilly bodies, aching from stress or pain in complex lives. Strong, comfortable furniture provided support for friends to sit on while they chatted about the issues going on in their lives. Vivid pictures Holly painted of God's gorgeous creation radiated from the walls.

You've surpassed all previous acclaim about your outstanding entertaining abilities," her husband said beaming.

"Oh, Adam ..."

He hugged his wife tenderly.

Their big oak table became the center of activity and not just because it was usually adorned with delicious food. "Fellowship and acceptance occur at tables. People eat around the world—not all experience the benefits of peaceful, social interactions while eating. This table is different," Adam said.

"There's no room for complaining, cynicism, or disrespect. A sense of optimism and attentive listening is essential," his wife added.

Adam and Holly put on a pot of soup, or a casserole, at a moment's notice. Conversations on a variety of topics followed, with one theme cementing them all together. "You are a special gift from God to us—and we would love to know you better." Guests felt valued, even honored, thought all felt it was undeserved.

Perhaps it was a glimpse into how much God loves us.

Salad luncheons became opportunities for Holly to spend time with friends and neighbors. Individual candles at each place, or a thoughtful note, conveyed the feeling of individuality and uniqueness. "Tell me how you're doing …" was always met with eager concern and positive encouragement.

Grilling burgers or chicken became routine on weekends, with Adam using his talents. Holly whipped up accompaniments and deserts. "There's more joy in impromptu gatherings with leftovers than in elaborately planned extravaganzas," she explained while preparing food for neighbors.

"You have a knack for making people feel comfortable," Karen Janssen said.

If friends weren't invited—people with needs sometimes called. No matter what the intrusion, Adam and Holly took time to befriend anyone God brought to their door.

Abby and Jake's friends came over, too.

Teenagers felt the warmth and caring Adam and Holly provided in their quest for hospitality. Putting their own beliefs in action, Jake and Abby helped offer the hungry teens more than pizza and cola.

Sometimes Adam made campfires and the group roasted hot dogs. Singing songs around a blazing fire always followed—with marshmallows for roasting over the embers.

Jake's girlfriend Angie Hahn giggled sitting on a log, waiting for Jake to toast one to the perfect golden color.

"Not quite!" she said.

He never could get it right and usually the puff went up in smoke.

As stars came out, Adam talked about how God intricately plotted the fabulous constellations and the enormous galaxy we live in. "Yet more important, the almighty Creator wants to know each of us intimately and can satisfy the deepest longings in our souls."

"Mr. Clark, my cousin is coming next week. Can I bring him over here?" Jake's friend asked.

"Sure, Tyler. You can bring anyone you want," Adam answered.

Feeling personal pain growing up in a house filled with conflict—and seeing consequences that caused sadness—Jake and Abby could sympathize with friends. They offered compassion, affirmation, and love as they listened.

Receiving money from grandparents for her birthday, Abby investigated clothing stores at a shopping mall. Now that she was sixteen, her wardrobe needed to be updated into a more mature image. "I'm tired of my bright stripes and polka dots," she said.

Holly was happy to oblige her. "We haven't been out together for a long time. You're not trying to catch Peter's eye, are you?"

Abby grinned but her mother knew the truth.

They laughed and chatted as they wandered down the long corridors—glancing in windows and going into places that fascinated them. "Hey Abby ... Let's check this out," Holly said, finding a boutique going out of business. She bought an assortment of quality towels and linens at a fraction of the usual cost.

Leaving with their purchases, Abby's mouth opened wide.

"Mom, I've got the best idea! Can we make some tiny soap for company to use when they stay at our home? I think you can buy the stuff we need—or do we melt old soap?"

"Great suggestion," Holly agreed. We have just enough time to buy the necessary ingredients at Michaels." They ended up choosing multiple fragrances, several colors, molded templates for various shapes, and a bunch of glycerin.

"I promise this is my last request," Abby said when they got to the car. "Can I use your keys?" Reluctantly Holly let Abby drive back home.

Eventually, she would be driving alone.

Jake's graduation from high school was exhilarating but poignant as his parents realized their years of training were ending. Holly arranged a special open house celebration to commemorate his childhood years and encourage him for what lay ahead.

Pictures from infancy through his teen years were displayed—with special reminders of memorable experiences that highlighted his brief 18 years. His tattered bunny *Happy* and favorite book "Corduroy" sat in the corner.

Holly wiped a tear when she remembered moments with *"the apple of her eye"*— especially entertaining his little sister. His antics amused everyone who knew him as he joyfully interacted with people. His enthusiasm for life was contagious and his friendly spirit energized numerous friends.

"We have until fall before we send him off to college and an independent future," Adam said. "I'm going to spend as much time as possible with my only son until then."

Becoming widely known for her culinary talents, friends encouraged Holly to enter her applesauce and other creations in a contest at the state fair. Challenged to do something she had never done before, she called for information.

"The fair is held every September, so farmers can have plump pigs and ripe vegetables for judging," Holly said exuberantly when Carissa called to see how things were going. "Youngsters are involved with 4H projects during the year and summer provides opportunities for perfecting their cooking and sewing talents. There are sections for adult participants, also. I just have to try another challenge."

"You'll do great! I know you will," Carissa answered.

Intrigued, Holly decided to improve the recipe for her famous apple pie. Trying a bit of this, a dab of that, and a pinch of extra flavor, she experimented. After trying variations, her friends and neighbors decided on the one they liked best. She copied the recipe down in her red notebook ...

"Hey, I heard they're having a barbequed rib contest for men," Adam said.

Not wanting his wife to get all the attention, he baked, grilled, and smoked ribs with a variety of sauce combinations and served them to guests. Carefully listening to their 'oohs' and 'aahhs', he came up with the best tasting recipe anyone tasted.

When the judging was announced, Holly won a 'Blue Ribbon' for her *Awesome Applesauce*. A short time later, *Holly's Delicious Apple Pie* (with its carefully woven lattice crust topping) won the 'Grand Prize Ribbon' at the state fair. Her hand-smocked dress and counted cross-stitch sampler also won ribbons in the textile division.

Adam stood proudly when he won the 'Best-of-the-Best' for *Adam's Barbequed Ribs*. Holly cheered from the sidelines. "Who would have guessed?" she said.

"I have a surprise for my favorite winner," Adam said afterwards. They walked to the south end of the food court to enjoy a European Circus with nouveau theatrical flair—performing stunning music, dance, and acrobatic routines.

Holly was dazzled as the *Cirque du Soleil* guaranteed she would be. "Just like God when we give him a chance."

Holly planned a Christmas Coffee inviting neighbors from around the area. Decorating the porch with greenery and red bows, music filled the air. Adam strung mini-white lights around the fence that could be seen a mile down the road.

The celebration for neighbors turned into a more elaborate plan than the Clarks imagined when Jake arrived home for the holidays, from the University in Phoenix. "Is it all right if my friends come over for a Christmas get-together," he said to his father.

"Okay. Will you be the one arranging this?" Adam asked.

"Yeah, I'll handle all the details."

Abby was even more excited to be a part of the plans. "We've got to have a living nativity for people passing by on Christmas Eve," she said. Princess neighed from her stall in agreement.

Jake and Abby figured out details and invited younger friends to the Christmas Open House—convincing Adam to drive his tractor around the ranch, pulling a hayrack while caroling friends sang Christmas songs as lights twinkled in the distance across the hills. Hot cider and cocoa were waiting in the barn when they returned—thanks to Holly's assistance. The cookies Abby made were arranged on trays nearby.

Teenagers huddled together while Jake talked about the significance of Jesus' birth. Abby passed out candy canes and told the story of how it originated. Sheep were *baaing* and peace filled the barnyard.

It was a most spectacular night, not unlike one two thousand years ago.

Holly found a thank you note in the mailbox.

"Thanks for creating a warm, friendly atmosphere in your home. Your story of how we need to focus on an unseen Creator and not on what is visible, encouraged me. I have been going through discouraging circumstances and struggle to keep going. I'm sure God has great plans for all of us in the future."

Layers of pink, mauve, violet, and sapphire danced in the sky spreading across the horizon, illuminating the clouds. Mixed in were streaks of the lingering sun, glittering like gold in the sky. Adam and Holly could hardly look at the brilliant canvas. A glorious sunset, hearts full of love, and memories to last a lifetime filled their beings.

"You're a living mystery, Holly."

"If that means my life *wouldn't* make sense if God didn't exist—then I agree."

Granny's voice echoed in her ear. "Always leave the porch light on!" Granny used to say. Twill light the path if one goes by … and welcome those who stay."

Adam winked at Holly as he reached for her hand. They had the rest of their lives to enjoy each other.

Chapter 18
Reunion

THE CRISP MORNING CHILL gave way to warm sunshine and for unknown reasons a twinge of excitement filled the air. After meaningful minutes with God on the porch, Holly hung her jacket on a hook, put her cup in the sink, and ventured down their path to the mailbox. Humming, she noticed violets poking through the ground.

"Wow! What beauty!"

Breathless, she stopped in the barn on the way back. "Hans and Halle Kirchner are really coming!" she told Adam excitedly.

Receiving a letter from treasured friends in Germany, Adam and Holly prepared for their long awaited visit. The Kirchners had endeared themselves years before and brief communications by mail simply were not enough.

"I've never met these people," Abby said at dinner. "The way both of you talk, they could be the King and Queen of Germany."

Adam pushed his chair back from the table. "Wait until they get here. You'll see what we mean."

"Too bad Jake's at college. He's a ball of fire—and would enjoy interacting with such distinguished guests," Abby said.

"And no doubt, they would enjoy him," Holly said.

Weeks passed before the guest room was ready—with fragrant flowers from the garden and a Longaberger basket of appetizing fruit. A welcome note and two bottles of water rested on the bedside table.

Holly brushed her hair back before answering the door. *I wonder if they will notice anything different about us.*

After exchanging enthusiastic hugs and double kisses, Hans and Halle brought their bags into the house.

Adam heard the commotion from the barn and joined them. "Welcome friends … it's good to have you visit us here," he said. "Make yourselves at home and feel free to wander around the property. What we have is a gift from God and we're eager to share it with you. Later we'll explain some other things He's doing in our lives."

Hans broke into a wide grin and whispered something to Halle in German.

Before eating dinner, he reached for her hand. "I vud like to tank Gott. Yes?" His prayer was a conversation between two persons who love each other—beginning in English and lapsing into German. "I'm sorry," he said when he finished.

"God doesn't care what language we use," Adam answered. "He just likes to hear us talk to him."

Holly turned toward their guests.

"Halle, do you remember in Germany when I asked what was important to you? You answered that you love the outdoors and God talks to you in your garden."

Adam translated in German hoping that partially hearing it in two languages, the Kirchners might understand what she was trying to say. She continued to explain and he continued to interpret—before Holly stopped to reach for her Bible.

Hans and Halle struggled with English, as Adam stumbled with his German, but with an open Bible, the words became clear. "Since earliest times men have seen the earth and sky and all God made and have known of his existence and great power … but became utter fools … instead of worshiping the glorious, ever-living God." Romans 1:20-23 The Kirchners fully understood—nodding their heads in agreement.

Hans turned to Psalm 19:1-2, "The heavens are telling the glory of God; they are a marvelous display of his craftsmanship …"

Adam pointed to Psalm 96:3-4, "Publish his glorious acts throughout the earth. Tell everyone about the amazing things he does. For the Lord is great beyond description, and greatly to be praised."

"Eet izz truff," Halle said.

The Kirchner's stay was refreshing and the friendship became sweeter when they realized they shared a spiritual heritage. The visit provided opportunities to experience life on a ranch, reminisce about past memories, and share conversations about God.

Abby listened intently—snuggled under Halle's gift of a rainbow hand-crocheted afghan.

With more than their names in common, Holly and Halle bonded in a new way.

Joy welled in Holly's heart when she learned to connect despite language barriers. Out in the garden, with luscious scents filtering from the flowers, the friends laughed and talked together. "For us who believe, he is precious," Halle said.

"Imagine what I might have missed."

Hans shook Adam's hand before departing. "Live as you vish you had, ven you stand before God."

"I look forward to our next meeting, perhaps in a new place," Adam answered.

Preparing for Abby's graduation was bittersweet. "What are we going to do for my celebration?" she asked her mother.

"Why don't you plan it?" Holly said holding back tears.

"Seriously?"

"Well, you understand complex issues—and have this uncanny ability to detect problems when people deny they exist—so surely you're aware this will be a difficult time for me."

Holly had attempted developing a closer relationship with her daughter since Granny's funeral but following their significant heart-changes, an increasingly meaningful connection resulted between the two. Now it was time to let her daughter fly off alone.

"I'll miss you so much, Sweet Baby."

Abby hugged her mother. "We can make cookies together one last time and have them on a plate, in case anyone stops by." That started a torrential flow of tears—that Abby mopped up. She also made dinner.

After eating, Holly came to her senses. "Where are Benji Bear and *The Country Bunny* book?" she asked. "We'll need to set those out. Do you want to go through old pictures with me?"

Laughter, joy, and more tears followed and the night ended long after midnight when Adam came out for a snack.

Holly created a unique gift for her daughter, hoping it would generate awesome conversations over Abby's lifetime. A small piece of wood was wrapped in exquisite foil—and tied with a gorgeous silver bow—never to be unwrapped but set aside in a visible spot.

"The beauty of this *permanent present* should spark the interest of your friends," Holly explained. "Out of curiosity, they will want to know who it's for and ask questions. You can talk about God's gift to us; or your gift to God; or you can come up with a million other significant things to talk about."

"I love it!" Abby said. "Looking at the present will remind me how we ought to be the most joyful people on earth, celebrating every day." After graduation, she secured a job working at a horse camp for the summer. Her experience taking care of Princess was invaluable and her faith in a sovereign God spilled over into concern for youngsters. Abby energetically jumped at the chance to help.

"Do you remember your first horse camp?" Holly asked. "This one is much better."

"Don't forget our date on Saturday," her father said. "I have a special place picked out. Someday, a guy is going to *try* to replace me—I need to make that next to impossible with your expectations elevated a notch."

Holly shopped with Abby for necessities, helped pack her belongings, and talked about the future before their daughter left to attend a Bible College in California. She decorated a card for her daughter to keep as a reminder—with Joshua 1:9 printed on it.

"It's not really so far away," Abby said. "Think how far the moon is—and the stars! Then you won't miss me so much."

"Don't forget who loves you the most!" Holly said when she left.

"Who's going to sit with me in my empty nest?" Adam asked as Holly walked out on the porch. The house had echoed for days. Both were lonely for their children; taking care of sheep was an inadequate substitute.

"The key to a vibrant marriage is thinking like a teenager," she said, sitting down on his lap. "Do you have plans tonight?"

He pulled her closer, kissing, and hugging a few minutes before she remembered the chicken cooking on the stove. "Oops! Gotta run," she said dashing to turn it off. "I'll be right back."

Adam followed her in with his stomach growling.

E-mail and phone calls filled lonely days with bright moments.

Soon they were arranging for a college break—with a visit back to the ranch for their offspring. Having Jake and Abby back home at the same time was a highlight for everyone. Strong individuals, with fervent desires to be what they were created to be, the Clarks encouraged their children to even deeper faith.

"Don't let anyone think little of you because you are young. Be their ideal … be a pattern for them in your love, your faith, and your clean thoughts." Adam read from I Timothy 4:12.

"And your daily lives shouldn't embarrass God but bring joy to Him," Holly said, quoting I Thessalonians 2:12.

Watching Jake paint the barn with his father, Abby expressed concerns about her roommate Marsha.

"She's caught up in herself. She doesn't have a clue who God is, yet she chose to attend a Christian college. I want to talk to her—but I'm afraid I'll make her angry."

Holly listened attentively.

"We're all looking for meaning—something that will satisfy the longing in our hearts—and somebody needs to share the answers. Libby Thomas told me about God in the hospital waiting room. Who told you, Abby?"

"How could you forget?"

"I didn't, darling … you know what I mean."

Abby giggled, nodded her head, and continued with questions about knowing God's ways and understanding spiritual issues.

"Learn as you go along what pleases the Lord. Scripture is powerful," Holly said. "Make an appointment with Rev. David before you go back to college and he'll give more insight than I can."

"Thanks, Mom. I will."

The meeting was so informative, Abby signed up for a Mission's Trip to Costa Rico the following spring. A brochure caught her eye; and her heart compelled her to respond long before her mind processed the details. Checking further, she discovered the trip was during an important week of finals at college.

When Jake's friend Peter Johnson came over, Abby peeked in the room and smiled. "You can join us," Pete said. The afternoon was hilarious and the fun continued into the evening.

"You like him, don't you?" Jake teased Abby, after his friend left.

"Oh, by the way, Jake ... Tina Parker called and says she misses you dreadfully," Abby said. "It's a good thing I answered the phone. Does Mom know about her?"

He just smirked.

A birthday celebration at the *Melting Pot* provided an evening of pleasure for Adam. Each course was superb. "I thought we might need to order a second round of meat but with all those vegetables, I'm stuffed," he said.

"The deserts were delicious—tasty treats, fit for a king!" Holly said. "Now I'm going home to sleep with him." A gentleman sitting at the next table grinned.

Adam and Holly lived with such playfulness toward each other; observers were intrigued by their relationship. If they had only known the difference a few years before and seen the miraculous transformation.

Adam reached across and stroked Holly's neck. He motioned toward the door with his head and they stood up.

They came up with ways to rekindle early memories of love by revisiting places enjoyed during courtship. Going through picture albums and souvenirs, multiple ideas popped into their minds. Lazy conversations while doing chores brought up more.

"We're *not* going to get into situations that included conflict—are we?" Holly asked.

"Maybe we should," Adam said. "There is much to be learned from fighting fair. Every relationship has conflict and couples need to understand the difference between attacking versus addressing issues in a healthy way."

"What about the Amore Resort and the Cozy Cove?" Holly asked.

"Absolutely!" Adam answered. "I'm not afraid of the little puny lifeguard anymore."

His thoughts drifted to the summer Karen dumped him for the Argentine swimmer. His heart was broken, crushed that she could lead him on for so long. *God was there all along protecting him from a conniving female who knew no love from her fractured past.*

"Thank you for bringing Holly into my life."

Their intentions turned into double-edged blessings in disguise. Wonderful new memories—filled with joy—replaced pain.

The salty air pierced his nostrils as Adam waded in the California surf. His thoughts were far away and he begged God for words to say. Josh was receptive to hearing about spiritual things but David closed up tight with any mention of God.

A smelly fish floated in on the sand and he stepped over it.

What better way to love people than to effectively listen to their plight. He spotted his brothers getting out of the car and ran over with arms open wide. Wiping his wet face, he greeted them. "What took you so long? I always knew you were slower than me but you're almost ten minutes late."

"It was David's fault," Josh said. "He forgot to take the garbage out and his girlfriend stubbornly insisted he do that before leaving."

Adam sat on the beach reuniting with his brothers. They filled him in with the latest happenings in their lives, updating him on current personal relationships and jobs. Unfortunately, Josh's bitter divorce resulted in chaos arranging visits with his children, so hadn't seen them recently.

"That's not the worst of my woes," Josh said. "My job is eating me alive! How I get up and go in every morning is a miracle. You'd think the fires would burn themselves out but they just keep smoldering and relight into bigger bonfires."

"Sounds like the women I know," David said, joining in. "They look so sweet in the beginning—then play us for fools. I'm ready to dump Sally if she doesn't change her ways. She's starting to annoy me."

"So what I'm hearing is you're both miserable with people in your lives. Is that right?" Adam asked.

"Bingo," Josh said.

His brothers continued articulating their struggles and contempt for difficult circumstances in life. "They sure didn't teach us how to relate to disgusting people back in school. I have no idea how to deal with these losers." Josh shook his head and stood up before sitting back down. "So how did you figure it out Adam? I know you were miserable for a while."

"You can learn more about human nature by reading the Bible than by living in New York City," he answered. The tone of the conversation changed as Josh leaned closer, listening to his words.

Adam told about his frustrations, his brush with death, and answers that are so obvious most people miss them. "God not only desires for us to know him but to believe him," he said quoting Isaiah 43:10.

Jake called his parents out of breath. "I have an internship at KMOL in Albuquerque this summer. The station manager just confirmed I start on June 1st."

"Will we see you on television?" his mother asked.

"Not unless I make a big mistake! This is an opportunity to gain valuable insight into becoming a great anchor after I graduate next year."

"Congratulations," Adam said. "I'm proud of you, son."

His first day on the set was chaotic with adrenalin bursting from his scalp to his toes. He tapped his foot waiting for station manager, Mike Hintz, to finish a phone call and show him around. Watching the action at KMOL increased his desire to be involved in this business of reporting news. "Sorry for the interruption," Mike said. "I want you to meet Joe Garcia before I introduce you to the anchors. He's a producer you'll see often."

Brianna Smyth flashed a big smile and welcomed Jake before running off to follow a story. Most of the morning was spent with anchor Paul Esse who explained his usual tasks, did research, and showed Jake the news desk. Reading over newssheets—while Paul prepared to go on camera—he couldn't help but envision himself doing the job better. Jake watched people come and go between segments but most of the action was the few seconds before *on-air* time.

"What a difference a few lights make," he thought.

Enlightened with tips of the trade, he went on a shoot with Paul and cameraman Hector Lopez. The van was abuzz with the breaking news of a solar-powered aircraft attempting to set a record for the longest unmanned flight. Jake listened with interest.

By Friday, he had a handle on news reporting. Thinking there was no more to learn, Jake casually locked his car and strolled across the parking lot—deep in thought about going out with Brianna to do a story on a hot new movie being shot in the area. He smiled at a female getting out of her car.

Then he glanced again.

"Lisa? … Lisa Stewart? What in the world are you doing here?"

"Hello Jake, I almost didn't recognize you. It's been years since I last saw you; I can't believe you're all grown up. I work at KMOL. Why are you here?"

"Are you teasing? I haven't seen you around this week."

"The technical people are locked in their offices. We seldom see the reporters and anchors," she answered.

"That's wonderful! I'm interning for the summer and hope to see more of you." Jake held the door open as Lisa walked through. His mind was on reporting news but his heart was beating wildly. He had a crush on quiet little Lisa when he was young—never imagining she would grow up to be so beautiful.

"You always did look at me with that seductive smile, like you knew something I didn't," he said when she passed him later in the day. "Hey, my 21st birthday is on Sunday. I'd love to spend it with you—and reconnect—if you're available."

"You know where I live. What time should I be ready?"

Driving up Brookshire Lane, Jake's thoughts raced. *So much has happened since we moved. I don't feel like the same person.* He glanced at a squirrel racing across the front lawn of his former home. Lisa looked ravishing when she opened the door. He hugged her energetically, without thinking. It was a sweet reunion.

"Tell me more about what you do?" he asked after ordering dinner.

"I'm the promotion coordinator for our creative services department. My job involves processing multi-station logs, handling department bookkeeping, coordinating various projects, and performing administrative functions. I guess you could say I'm an extremely organized, efficient, and hardworking individual—who works well under pressure."

Jake stared in her eyes as she talked.

None of his old girlfriends had been anything like Lisa. Her personality was unique—soft-spoken but firm in her convictions. Something special sizzled under that veneer of stability and dependability. *If only she was interested in a flamboyant younger man who was capable of much productivity as he aged. If only she would give him a chance to prove his worth to her.*

"You'll never guess who I met," Jake said to his mother. He didn't pause to hear an answer. "Lisa Stewart works at KMOL!"

"I've been thinking about her," Holly answered, excited to hear the news. "I wonder how her family is doing. We lost contact after moving and I've meant to reconnect with our old neighbors for several years."

After their fourth date, Jake asked if Lisa wanted to get together with Adam and Holly. She agreed wholeheartedly. A day was chosen, and Holly planned a barbeque dinner.

Jake brought lovely 25-year-old Lisa Stewart to his parents' home after work. Fresh mown grass and *baaing* sheep greeted them. Driving onto the property, she took a deep breath.

"Are you okay?" he asked.

"Yes, just a little nervous. I remember being intimidated by your family when you lived next door—you all seemed so together and a step above the rest of us normal humans. In spite of that, I was fascinated and wanted to know you better."

Jake reached over and took her hand, pressing it to his chest. He would do everything he could to make this creature feel more at ease—without question. She was the one who possessed the depth of character his family had been so sadly missing for all those years.

Now he just needed to find out her spiritual aspirations.

Following a meteor shower display, Adam and Holly reflected on being married for twenty-five years. They meshed from the beginning with both being idealistic and driven to achieve selfish dreams. Neither would back down from their tenacious views on how to accomplish things and focused on tasks with determination.

"Unfortunately, that included trying to destroy each other in the process," Holly said wincing. "I'm ashamed to even say it. Thank God for second chances."

"Character, conversations, and conduct reveal the truth; no sense denying the facts," Adam said. "I'm grateful you're my wife—and that God protected our relationship despite selfish and foolish choices. Moreover, I still want you by my side when I'm 100." They kissed passionately for several minutes in view of the Creator.

"On our anniversary, let's invite family members and friends over to give God glory for the things he has done for us," Holly suggested.

Adam winked.

Prone to making big deals out of little ideas, she set out to show the world how much love they now had for each other.

Twinkling white lights were scattered in the trees and torchlights made a path to the front of the chairs. She wore a white sundress and Adam looked stunning in his rainbow flowered Hawaiian shirt. Preceded by smiling Jake and Abby, they exited the back door of their house arm-in-arm and made their way to the vine-covered Gazebo.

"We're glad you're here to watch us renew our vows today—July 16th—our 25th Anniversary," Adam said.

Making promises under a canopy in the moonlight, the world stood still as God listened. The sheep sounded like a heavenly choir from across the field.

Rev. Jeffrey David added some personal thoughts. "God didn't plop us on earth and expect us to take the journey all by ourselves—but desires to have an intimate relationship with us, laughing, and crying as we walk together. We see breathtaking views of skies and mountains; go through deserts, valleys, storms, and periods of sickness; and he refreshes and rebuilds when necessary. This evening is a tribute to the transformation that has taken place in Adam and Holly Clark's lives. Thanks for sharing it with them."

Adam sang a song in appreciation.

"How can we say thanks for the things that you have done for us ... things so undeserved, yet you gave to prove your love for us ... the voices of a thousand angels could not convey our gratitude ... all that we have and ever hope to be, we owe it all to you. To God be the glory ..."

Platters of yummy croissant sandwiches, trays with assorted relishes, and tiers of pink peppermint frosted brownies were arranged on the linen-covered tables outside. Clusters of candles with fresh flowers tucked around were lighted centerpieces.

Lisa and Abby giggled when Adam got pink frosting on his lip.

The happy couple greeted spectators with baskets of foil wrapped chocolate hearts. Following the festivities, they went on a cruise to Belize—hoping to rekindle romantic feelings and celebrate a new period in their lives—as Mr. and Mrs. Adam Clark, children of royalty.

"This time let's make him proud!" Adam said as he carried his wife through the entrance of the ship.

Chapter 19
Excitement

CHASING BREAKING NEWS STORIES—WITH thrilling jaunts and action galore in front of cameras—was right up Jake's alley. The only thing better was seeing a certain lovely female walk past the set when he was at the station.

"Hi, there." Lisa smiled demurely and continued to her ivory tower.

Fortunately, Jake knew her phone number and practiced dialing it. Interesting dates filled their evenings and weekends. Wearing the latest fashions gave him an air of sophistication. Lisa dressed more conservatively but nothing could keep excitement from her face.

Passing his former home reminded Jake of childhood days when frivolity was just around the corner. It also brought up memories of life before the coming-of-age camping trip with his father. He determined to include God in his adult life—it was the only way to ensure success.

"Are you aware how much hostility that house once held?" Jake asked Lisa as they walked hand-in-hand around the block. "My parents talked about enjoying life but never figured it out until we moved away. Emotional conflict, constant bickering, and intense resentment were inhabitants that wouldn't leave. To keep myself from exploding, I disappeared as often as I could."

"I saw you laugh and chase your sister," Lisa said. "The fun appeared to start in your yard."

"Our family was just pretending," he said. "Abby cried herself to sleep most nights while my parents yelled at each other. On weekends, people came over for our fancy parties that caused even more chaos after guests left."

Lisa listened. "It seemed so perfect!"

Jake shared what he knew about his father's terrible accident, and his mother's faith that began major changes in their home. Looking at the beautiful sky filled with stars, he explained that God cares more about satisfying the deepest longings of our hearts than providing a show for us to enjoy.

Thoughtfully, Lisa considered what he said.

"I'm beginning to understand what you mean," she said the next day.

Paddling down the Tappahannock River, their canoe capsized dumping both of them into the water. Jake acted as if he was drowning, thrusting his arms in the air, and gurgling. He had no idea how serious it appeared to his distraught girlfriend. She struggled to reach the rocks while he floated on his back.

Sitting on the bank later—drenched—Lisa's quivering lips calmed enough to ask a question.

"Can a person really make sure you go to heaven … when you die?"

"Of course," Jake explained.

Together on the grassy slope, she accepted Jesus' gift of eternal life. Streaks of heavenly sunshine flickered on the water spreading warmth through their souls. Jake kissed the top of her head.

The final weeks of summer passed with a happy duo enjoying good things in life. Conversation flowed and Jake amused with his wit. Lisa provided dependability and stability to the relationship.

"Do you remember trying to kiss me through the fence?" she asked.

"No! I was too little." He beamed knowing it was probably true. *She wasn't the first.*

"Abby told me you set out to win all the girls hearts."

"Well, there's only one female that matters now." He proceeded to kiss the top of her head, her forehead, and her nose. Lisa giggled.

Eventually, he would try again.

Eager to reconnect with Lisa's parents, the Clarks invited their former neighbors to the ranch. "It seems a hundred years since we moved," Holly said. "We would love to catch up on what's happening in your lives." A barbeque was planned—near the garden.

The weather cooperated with a sunny sky, pleasant temperature, and a gorgeous sunset. Along with their son Jason, his wife Brenda, and granddaughters Christie (5) and Chelsea (2), Pete and Mary Stewart casually chatted during the meal.

"Pete's job has evolved from computer programming to being an IT. I'm still just a librarian," Mary said. "We've grown to appreciate Jake in the last few weeks. It's hard to imagine him turning into such a fine young man after all those pranks."

Jake squeezed Lisa's hand, smiling bigger than usual.

"Well, your daughter's been transformed from a cute little dolly into one of the most beautiful creatures on earth. You're fortunate the wolves didn't eat her before I found her down at the station. Looks like God protected her." She giggled and shook her head.

Everyone laughed.

"There's something different about your whole family," Mary said. "Must be the fresh air out here." The former neighbors bonded closer than ever sharing theories about life and communicating beyond their usual superficial level of conversation.

"Did you hear about the Anderson's son Zach breaking into all those homes around us?" Pete asked.

"What are you talking about?" Holly asked.

"It was all over the news last month. Guess his ex-girlfriend got into her own legal troubles, so she ratted on him about a bunch of past robberies," Mary said.

Holly reached for Adam's hand, deep in thought.

"Have you talked to the Andersons about this?" Adam asked.

"No, they moved a year ago. Don't know where they headed—but their son is going to end up in the slammer," Pete said.

"All we know is that Zach was apparently into drugs. No wonder that kid seemed so spooky," Mary added.

"Whoa ... good thing we got out of there when we did," Jake said.

Seeing the colorful flowers and vegetables begging to be picked soothed Holly's racing heart but invigorated the Stewarts. "Nice garden," Pete said, winking at Holly. "You'll have to come see our place again and catch a glimpse of your old apple trees."

Watching baby sheep jump in the field—playing with friends—was a highlight of the evening. Christie and Chelsea chased them until they were out of breath. "Would you like to hold one?" Adam asked.

Munching corn from tiny hands was a great reward for the lambs.

After the Stewart family left, Holly sat with Adam on the porch reflecting about the evening. "I think Zach was most likely the one who stole my jewelry," she said pensively. "I'm so ashamed for making such a bad judgment about Ranelda. She was probably innocent. What can we do now?"

"I agree but it was so long ago, probably nothing."

"Can we at least drive over to her house tomorrow so I can talk to her," Holly asked.

"First thing in the morning," he said.

And when they talked to Ranelda's neighbors, Holly discovered her former worker had been deported from the country years earlier based on accusations of stealing.

"I knew she was innocent," the small statured woman said in broken English. "So did everyone around here. She was the most honest and hardworking woman we knew. No one believes poor foreigners, though."

"I'm so sorry," Holly said to the woman. "Do you have any contact information where I can reach her?"

"No."

Adam and Holly got in their car reluctantly, feeling great remorse.

"My next step is to visit Zach if he goes to prison," Holly said quietly.

Holly stopped at the Oasis Christian Bookstore to select a present, before meeting Lisa for a special birthday lunch at *Grounds for Celebration*. A creatively wrapped surprise inside rainbow foil with wisps of glittery ribbon waited on the table.

Dashing into the restaurant with a big smile, Lisa scooted into the booth.

"Hi! I'm sorry I didn't invite Adam to join us. He would have enjoyed celebrating your special day," Holly said.

Engaged in conversation, they barely noticed the server who seemed eager to please. "This is a rare opportunity to enjoy my special friend," Holly said after the food arrived. "Just refill our tea and bring the *birthday delight* in a few minutes, okay? Our time is limited today."

Munching cranberry chicken salad, the two females re-established their friendship with delightful conversation. Following tantalizing snickers cheesecake slices, Holly handed the present to her soon-to-be-daughter.

Lisa beamed while unwrapping the delicate ribbons and rainbow foil—and discovered a leather Bible tucked inside. "Oooohh! Thank you so much, Mrs. Clark."

"Did you know this is a love letter written to you, by God himself? It's fresh and new every morning. I hope you enjoy reading it."

"You've made my birthday happy," Lisa answered. "Jake's lucky to have you for a mother." She glanced at her watch and clutched the gift. "I need to get back to the station. Thank you, again."

They hugged before parting company.

Only God knew what the future would hold but both said private prayers.

A phone call from Arizona interrupted Lisa's afternoon.

"Hi beautiful! What could make your birthday more special?" Jake paused—just long enough for a knock on her door. "Sounds like you're kind of busy. I'll call back later." He redialed almost immediately. When Lisa answered, singing voices could be heard doing exactly what he instructed.

A loud pop indicated her bouquet was one balloon short.

"Are you there? Can anybody hear me?" he asked.

Lisa laughed—but before she could respond, a clown grabbed the phone. "We've got a party going on here. Do you mind calling back after we eat the cake?" The singing of "Happy Birthday" began … as the receiver clicked.

Jake heard more details from his surprised girlfriend when she retold the story later. Lisa couldn't stop laughing long enough to hear his response.

"Joe Garcia was hilarious dressed as a clown. Paul Esse cut luscious chocolate cake with flair, while photographers documented his finesse. By the way—Brianna sends her greetings and Mike Hintz says you owe him for arranging the party."

Unfortunately, no one took a picture of Lisa for Jake to see.

Distracted from studying, he plodded through a final year in college. His major required perfecting communication skills—in hands-on ways—so he pursued it with gusto during class, and at night. Friends intrigued him with innovative ways to have fun while stress about the future preoccupied their minds.

"Brenda thinks you're sweet on her," his roommate Stan informed him after a party in their room. "She kept leaning on your shoulder. It made Hilary angry so she left with Ryan."

"I don't see a future with either of them," Jake answered.

Talking to Lisa killed two birds with one stone. Her voice calmed his soul and gave him a sense of direction. Her insight into the business world was a valuable resource. He considered returning home most weekends.

"Did you ask your boss for time off? I have places I want to show you," he said on one surprise visit.

"You come up with the most unexpected ideas, at inopportune times. This is a busy time at the station."

"Come on. Try harder," he said kissing her neck.

In front of college friends, Jake bent on one knee and handed her a little box. "You can't be serious," she said blushing. She whispered in his ear, "Why are you doing this—with them here? Is this why you wanted me to come to Arizona?"

Ignoring his girlfriend's uncomfortable predicament and cry for privacy, he insisted she open it. Her breath quickened and hands shook as she finally peeked in the gold container. A scream pierced the air—when a fat bug popped out and slid down her blouse. "Jake!"

He fell on the ground, laughing so hard his face turned red. "Just wanna have a little fun with you," he said, pulling her down on top of him.

Embarrassed, Lisa smiled at the crowd watching his antics—then laughed when he tickled her. "If you weren't so much fun I'd have nothing to do with you," she said under her breath.

Waiting for her parents to return home on Christmas Eve, Jake pulled a gift from under Lisa's tree. "Do you think it would matter if you opened this now?"

"Not until everyone gets here."

"Why not? You prefer private moments with me. You might even want to wear this tonight. It's your favorite color."

Convinced Jake was sincere; Lisa pushed red and green tissue paper aside and pulled a journal from the bottom of the bag. "You prankster!!!" She shrugged and then opened it. The inside was cut out and a diamond ring sparkled from the middle.

Jake held his hands together like he was begging. "Please, Lisa. Will you marry me?" His eyes looked deep into hers and waited for a reply.

He winked.

"You stole my heart years ago. If you promise to take care of it forever—yes, I'll marry you," she finally said.

He hugged her affectionately and they were still kissing when the Stewart family arrived home. "Look what Jake gave me to wear tonight," Lisa said beaming as she flashed a dazzling ring on her finger. Sparkling diamonds covered the band, with a brilliant mount surrounded by smaller jewels on top. "Even though he's still up to his old tricks, I decided to marry him."

After their sincere congratulation died down and presents were open, he pulled her aside and reached for his phone. "We need to make arrangements with the *all-time-best-party-planner* to welcome you into our family over the holidays."

Hearing the wonderful news delighted his parents.

"I think you've made a good choice," Adam said. "Lisa is charming and dependable. She'll make a great wife."

Holly was interested in figuring out the perfect engagement party. When a day and time were decided, she phoned family and friends. Abby energetically joined in with the preparations. Creativity soared to new heights.

The "fireworks" cake was a hit, with sparklers singeing Jake's hand when he sliced a piece, popping the balloon hidden inside. Laughter from friends muffled his response but he seemed to enjoy the excitement. "Life is starting off with a bang for you two lovebirds," Peter Johnson said.

Friends and relatives recounted shared experiences with the couple. He provided gusto with his fun loving ways, usually offering warmth and encouragement. She could be counted on to provide insight and stability. Together they were like a huge stadium with enough electricity to light it.

"We want to make a difference in this world," Jake said before they left.

"If a miracle will convince people, why not be one?" Adam challenged them.

An unexpected call from Tina Parker surprised Jake later that week. "I think about you night and day. Are you positive Lisa's the right girl for you?" He was at a loss for words. When he didn't answer, she continued. "How often do you think about me?"

He rubbed his chin and cleared his throat. "Tina, you dumped me for a South American soccer player. What happened to him?"

"He doesn't compare to you, Jake … I miss you, Sweetie Pie."

After hanging up, the sick feeling in his gut lingered but he decided to let her go for good. However, the stickers on his car window the next morning convinced him it wasn't her final attempt to win him back.

After cancelling an earlier mission trip to Costa Rico, Abby found another her schedule could accommodate. While close friends planned a vacation to Cancun over spring break, she volunteered to assist at an orphanage, help local missionaries, and build a small church in Haiti.

Raising funds was easy—with grandparents donating a generous share. "God wants to use you to influence others," her mother said. "Don't waste the most precious thing you've been made to do."

Adam read I Peter 4:10, *Go above what is expected when God asks you to do something.*

Joy filled Abby's heart as enthusiastic team members prepared and packed extra gifts for the children they would nurture and locals they could encourage. With a desire to make a difference and a burst of adrenalin, she paced at the airport.

Stifling heat tried unsuccessfully to diminish the functioning of young laborers. Lugging buckets of cement taxed their youthful bodies. Overused muscles ached climbing ladders, but nothing stopped the momentum. Their spirits soared with each new task. Food aversions were minimal, with water becoming more valuable than gold. Thin mattresses on the floor—repulsive back home—beckoned as evening activities ended.

Smelly children, timid and shy early in the week, became adoring friends eager to connect. Stories, songs, and games began when chores were completed. A small inflatable swimming pool was presented— and filled with water. Groups of five were given time to splash in the afternoon. Pungent odors were replaced with fresh air and love.

"Stay with me Abby," one brown-eyed girl begged, clutching her hand tighter. Kisses and hugs from desperately lonely little ones made parting harder each day.

"Until you meet these children personally, you won't know what a blessing they are," she told her parents on the phone. "We cleaned their rooms, painted the living areas, and built a play yard outside. My friends back at school have no idea what they missed but I'm going to inform them."

Broken down in an overheated van, tired Americans leaned on each other to catch extra winks. A tropical breeze cooled them briefly. One female glancing out the window got a bright idea.

When it was time to fly home, Abby put on her oldest clothes and emptied her suitcase into a box. "Who wants to join me?" she asked. Several girls quickly agreed. The articles were given to host missionaries to distribute to needy natives—Haitians who carefully watched them all week—who probably wondered if team members sincerely cared or just wanted an interesting vacation. Now they would know.

"Anybody willing to give up these memories for a lounge chair at your favorite beach?" the leader asked on the trip to the airport. Not a sound could be heard.

However, Abby intended to bring ten more friends on her next visit.

🍎

The air was muggy after a brief shower; Adam was eager to finish chores. Car tires screeched in the driveway and Holly peered out. "Wonder what's up," she said with a quizzical look.

"I'm a reporter for KMOL," Jake shouted, rushing through the back door.

"Congratulations! Can you join us for lunch and share the details?" his father asked.

"Sure can," he said sitting down. In between bites of food, he talked about his responsibilities reporting the news, the fresh wardrobe he needed to procure for visibility in front of cameras, and the pay. He beamed.

"Wealth will grow wings and fly from you," Adam said. "Don't fix your eyes on it or cater to it. Be rich on the inside. Nobody can take that away from you."

Abby heard the commotion and walked into the kitchen. "So you got a job at the television station? That's a great graduation present—I'm sure your fiancée is delighted." Almost finished eating, he jumped up.

"I forgot all about telling Lisa." He wiped his mouth and dialed her number.

Anchor Paul Esse stared into the camera when the newest reporter arrived on set and sat to watch his news report—not even flinching when a paper clip grazed his ear. His aloofness continued after the segment. "How are things going?" Jake asked, with no acknowledgement from Paul.

"Have we met?" Jake asked mockingly, as they passed in the hall before Brianna Smyth rushed up for a hug almost knocking Jake over. She held him tight to stabilize the situation. "Darling, I'm glad you're back so we can enjoy more intimate moments." She kissed him on both cheeks before running off.

Jake turned around embarrassed. Luckily, no one was watching. *Was she in the dark about Lisa?*

"Hello," Paul said at lunch when Jake greeted him again. He appeared deep in thought. I wonder what his problem is.

Fine-tuning his responsibilities as a reporter required meeting with Mike Hintz, station manager, and going over policy with Joe Garcia. Jake had no intention of doing anything but fantastic at this job. As soon as possible, he hoped to become the station's top anchor. For the moment, as many shoots as he could manage with camera operator Hector Lopez were priorities. Nothing else mattered. A few seconds before *on-air* time he puffed his chest, lifted his chin, and thought about dazzling the viewers.

"What a difference a few lights make," he thought.

The scheduled physical was routine and Holly cheerfully babbled about events going on in her family. Adam had fully recovered from his injuries and the ranch provided a healthy alternative to city life. With multiple occasions to celebrate, there was no reason to complain about anything.

Comfortable in most doctors' offices, she couldn't help noticing a look of concern on Dr. Baldwin's face. "How long have you had this?" he asked.

"What?"

"That suspicious growth under your arm," he said, touching the nodule.

"I didn't realize anything was there."

"We'll need to do a biopsy and check this out." He peered at his sheet, scribbling additional notations quickly. "Can you make it over to the outpatient clinic before you head home?"

"Yes; I hope this is nothing serious."

"We can hope for the best—but we need answers as soon as possible so we can come up with a plan, in the event tests come back positive."

Holly was shaking from her health scare; and eagerly waited to hear results. "The more difficult our circumstances, the more strength he'll provide," Adam reminded her.

She poured a cup of coffee and sat down in the sunny kitchen.

"If anything ever happens to me, I hope you reach out with joy to those around and don't allow depression to turn into negativity. Promise me you'll continue sharing the glorious truth about our awesome Creator."

"After what we've been through, what else can discourage us?" he asked.

"In Pilgrim's Progress, the Bypath Meadow looks enticing—just don't take a detour when everything gets comfortable, or when life crashes around you."

"You're preparing for a worst case scenario," he said.

"It doesn't hurt to consider all of the possibilities. I was in shock when I heard about your accident, Adam." He frowned, thinking about options, grateful to have Holly by his side.

Negative test results were reason to celebrate.

Holly bought a fancy gold gilded mirror with filigreed ribbon wrapped around the edges and a bow in the corner—simulating a present—for the guest room. "Every time we look at our own image, we should see how God looks at us—a delightful gift."

The future appeared bright with Jake's graduation from college and beginning a career perfectly suited for him. Voted most popular in school, he would continue providing joy for others with his endless supply of enthusiasm. The performer would surely leave viewers spellbound as he perfected his talents as a journalist on television.

His plans to marry former neighbor Lisa Stewart excited the whole Clark family as Jake and Lisa's big day approached. Jake would make a charming though somewhat unpredictable mate—providing his wife with immense pleasure, mixed with tension that results from living on the edge. Her dependability and intelligence would enable their home to be the inspirational lighthouse everyone believed possible.

Trusting God for what would unfold was essential.

Holly placed treasured photos in the embossed silver album, lingering over each pose. The past filled with memories, provided her soul with delight. The present—too glorious to describe in words—was a gift from God. The future offered unknown adventures under the watchful eye of an Almighty Creator.

We ought to be the most joyful people on earth, celebrating every day.

She turned the page.

READING GROUP GUIDE
Discussion questions

1. What is your heart's desire? What are you willing to do, to achieve that craving?

2. Why do we continue doing the same things over and over, when they have obviously been unsuccessful in the past? Practice does not make perfect—but permanent.

3. How can pursuing our goals prevent us from accomplishing meaningful interactions with those we care about most? Can both be done simultaneously?

4. What makes you feel loved? How do you demonstrate love for another person? What happens when they turn against us? Was it really love in the first place?

5. Why did Jesus come to earth as a baby? What did growing up as a human include for this carpenter's son? What would be the benefits of knowing Him now ~ versus knowing Him personally while He was on earth?

6. For what reason would anyone want to be like Him?

7. How does the dictionary define redemption?

8. Is there any merit to the saying, "The apple doesn't fall too far from the tree?"

9. "Always leave the porch light on!" Granny used to say. "Twill light the path if one goes by and welcome those who stay." What does this quote mean? What does the porch light symbolize? Who might pass by? Who might stay?

10. When you're fifty years old, what will have mattered most in your life? When you're eighty-five, what will matter the most?

"A year from now, you may wish you had started today."
–Dr. Robert Schuller

About the Author

A Taylor University graduate, Cindy Jean Wilson married sweetheart Doug and birthed four children—who she writes occasional *Sugar Cookies* for—and has nine precious grandchildren. An enthusiastic storyteller, oil painter, and scuba diver, she enjoys watching majestic sunrises and sunsets as the heavens display the glory of an awesome Creator. However, seeing His masterpieces in a darkened robe of space can never compare to Jesus satisfying the deepest longings of her heart. Experiences include owning and managing a 60 acre Bed & Breakfast with Barbados sheep, wedding coordinator, teacher for Gifted & Talented (IA) and Soaring High at Harvest Academy (TX), and a contributing devotional writer @ saworship.com. She lives with her husband in the Washington DC area. Another novel, *A Time to Celebrate*, will be available in the summer of 2012.

"Once in a while I sneak away to a secluded cottage in the woods, where serenity in nature soothes my spirit, as stories crowd my head and burst on paper when I type. Singing birds, frisky squirrel, curious fox, leaping deer, and moments with my charming husband ~ enable extrovert tendencies to flourish. My current passion is painting pictures with words."

A Time To Celebrate ~ sequel to *Here's An Apple Sweet Adam* ~ This inspirational novel begins with a glorious wedding between charming Jake, and his dependable bride, Lisa, who desire to inspire the world in unique ways. In a shocking twist, they lose precious Angela and experience unimaginable heartbreak before being dramatically molded into examples of great faith. Lisa struggles to survive life's trials in a turbulent ocean; while Jake loses his prestigious career as TV news anchor—plunging into a self-centered search for dignity on a houseboat. Creation displays the Almighty's majestic handiwork; with godly parents providing a legacy of unconditional love. The sovereign circumstances prove to be exactly what is necessary for Jake and Lisa Clark to become a brilliant lighthouse of hope and encouragement beyond their wildest expectations. Could their secrets provide the key to unlocking a poignant story?

CPSIA information can be obtained at www.ICGtesting.com
Printed in the USA
LVOW041354310512

284093LV00002B/5/P